Slanted

and

Disenchanted

SLANTED & DISENCHANTED

A NOVEL

LISA CZARINA MICHAUD

BARRE
CHORD
PRESS

BARRE CHORD PRESS

Barre Chord Press
P.O. Box 150
Albertson, New York 11507

www.barrechordpress.com

Library in Congress Control Number 2021938517

Cataloging-in-Publication data
Names: Michaud, Lisa Czarina, author.
Title: Slanted and disenchanted: a novel / Lisa Czarina Michaud.
Series: The Disenchanted
Description: First edition. | Albertson, NY: Barre Chord Press, 2021.
Identifiers: LCCN: 2021938517 | ISBN: 978-1-7369445-0-9 (hardcover) | 978-1-7369445-1-6 (paperback) | 978-1-7369445-2-3 (ebook) | 978-1-7369445-3-0 (audio)
Subjects: LCSH Musicians--Fiction. | Bands (Music)--Fiction. | Eating disorders--Fiction. | Sexual orientation--Fiction. | Bisexuality--Fiction. | Friendship--Fiction. | Family--Fiction. | Bildungsroman. | BISAC YOUNG ADULT FICTION / General | YOUNG ADULT FICTION / Social Themes / Emotions & Feelings
Classification: LCC PS3613.I34482 S53 2021 | DDC 813.6--dc23

Printed and published in the United States of America

Slanted and Disenchanted is a work of fiction. All characters, names, places, and events presented in this novel are products of the author's imagination and are used fictitiously. Any resemblance to events, places, or persons, living or dead, is purely coincidental.

First Edition 2021

Jacket design by Hayley O. Illustration

This is for my parents.

To my mom for the prosciutto and my dad, George, for the pataflafla.

I was made for another planet altogether. I mistook the way.

— Simone de Beauvoir, The Woman Destroyed

1

Carla

Was I supposed to desperately want a boyfriend? I wondered that to myself as I watched a couple making out at Yogurt and Such on a random Monday night. With my wallet clutched in my hand, the kid who looked twelve but was probably my age filled the Styrofoam cup with fat-free peanut-butter frozen yogurt. Peanut butter because they ran out of my lemon chiffon. I would have been disappointed, but I was just happy it wasn't the regular guy who always made me say the whole thing when I tried to simply order lemon. He liked to pretend he had *no idea* what I meant. And I kind of hated him. So maybe there wasn't my favorite flavor, but there also wasn't *that* guy, which relieved me of having to say chiffon for the day. Progress.

My eyes then slid over to the other guy scooping out the day's scabby-looking egg and tuna salads; the advertised "such." I then glanced back at the couple slithering their tongues in and around each other's mouths, which made the idea of peanut-butter anything kind of gross.

The thought of having a boyfriend didn't consume me or anything, but every so often, I wondered if it was something I should have wanted. It also made me wonder if I was the only person my age not having sex, even if I didn't get what the big deal was all about. I mean, I'd had it before. Three times with my best friend's cousin who also just wanted to get it out of the way . . . three times. It ended up being more science fiction than hot and sexy because there was *this other human being inside my body*. Anyway, I kept my shirt on. He kept his bottom retainer in. And sometimes we kept in touch on AOL.

At twenty, I thought I'd have a little more going on than hanging out by myself in an about-to-close yogurt shop on Long Island. But as static as it all felt, this rated as thrilling because it was either this or Nair the hair off my Italian-girl arms.

That week, I decided I was finally going to teach myself the guitar, something I had been putting off, well, my whole life. I had been in a million bands in my head, good ones too, and decided to finally go for it. Why not? At Sam Ash, I bought myself two books: one to learn the blues and a heavy metal one that made me laugh. The cover had this model wearing nothing but a leather vest, holding a pointy guitar, standing in front of a cloud of rising steam. This guy—my inspiration—had been sitting on my bedroom floor, staring at me in all his leather-vest glory, daring me to open the book.

I scraped the spoon across the bottom of my cup and took the last bite of my yogurt. Too settled in the comfort of discouragement, I thought about what I could have accomplished if I hadn't gotten in the way of myself. I'm not talking big things here, but maybe better SAT scores or more friends signing my yearbook. Or maybe I'd have a skill, like playing the guitar, that would garner me some respect.

Unable to go back in time for the SATs, my options were to make friends or make music. Not being much of a people person, I chose music.

Pete

The sun cutting through the skylights across my slanted ceiling told me all I needed to know when I woke up. Like a rock n' roll sundial, if it covered half of Herbie's analog African mask on the *Headhunters* poster, it meant mid-morning; once it crept over to the New York tenement buildings in Zeppelin's *Physical Graffiti*, it meant lunchtime, and when it continued on to the psychedelic rendering of death and fertility on *Aoxomoxoa*, it was afternoon. However, when it reached a 1950s Gretsch ad with Art Blakey, it meant, holy shit, I overslept!

I slid the thick rims up the bridge of my nose where the red blurs of my digital clock came into focus, letting me know I only had forty-five minutes to dress, eat, and smoke up before work at three. Nights had me on the phone with my girlfriend Allison, who was away at school in Boston. I felt guilty sleeping in when she had class as early as nine. The night before, we talked about everything and nothing. I taught her the French expression *refaire le monde*, which translates to "changing the world" — she practically purred into the phone. She loved that I spoke the apparent language of love. But I told her, like I tell most people, to not be impressed and that I only speak it because of my dad.

My mom, a flight attendant from Astoria who is of Eastern European descent, identifies mostly as a New Yorker. I spoke English with my mom, French specked with a regional dialect with my dad, and an odd mix of it all when we were together. Using a calling card bought at the gas station, I spoke to mamema, my grandma in France, once a week, who complained about my accent.

3

Carla

I should've been a junior in college, but instead, I worked at 24-Hour Photo near my house in Albertson. Each town on Long Island reminded me of the next with the cookie-cutter post-war houses; strip malls with pizza parlors and tanning salons that smelled like rusty coconuts; and streets with misleading names like Old Country Road, where a Panera Bread and a Boston Market were as "country" as it got.

I felt as predictable as the vacation photos I developed at work. When pressed by a nosy parent about my wasting time at a day job, I feigned a professional interest in photography — not that my job entailed any actual photography outside of the passport photo I took every few weeks. I worked alongside my boss, Abel, a slim man from Senegal who wore round glasses and didn't say much. He kept to himself during my first few weeks, as we worked in complete silence, with only the sounds of the blue *Beatles Greatest Hits* cassette crackling through the dusty player under the desk. For my birthday, though, he surprised me when he came back from lunch with two scoops of rainbow sherbet he had picked up at the Baskin-Robbins next door.

Fall meant all the kids I went to high school with had settled back in school. I found comfort in not having to bump into any of them wearing their college hoodies and looking at me like a charity case. After two semesters at Stony Brook, I took a year off to figure things out. That was two years ago. I didn't go back to school because I didn't know what I wanted to do with my life and didn't think my indecisiveness was worth the tuition. Coming from a working-class Italian family, though, no one went to college, so there was no pressure to continue. My mom liked to

4

tell people I was in "transition." Transition to what? I never knew. But it was the nicest thing she had ever said about me. But then again, she was always nicer to me with strangers.

2

Pete

I didn't get what the big deal about college was or why people looked at me like I was total white trash when I told them that after a year at Nassau, I didn't go back. Then they would look at me like I should be committed for blowing off acceptance to Juilliard for Community College. So I just got used to telling people nothing about me since everyone had such a strong opinion about what I should be doing. My parents were okay with it, though. It was mostly Allison, who I think only loved the idea of having a boyfriend at Juilliard. Mortified by the whole thing, she wanted to murder me for deferring and threatened I'd be a barista for the rest of my life if I didn't finish college. I called her threat out-of-touch and totally elitist before accusing her of planning to vote for Dubya in November.

To pass time when not playing my drums, I carnivorously read whatever I could get my hands on. I leaned toward rock and jazz biographies because life really is stranger than fiction. Also, novels with complicated and misunderstood protagonists trying to make sense of their lives in America. I also knit, which was something I kept to myself. A scheme cooked up by my grandmother, she thought it would get me to smoke less and give my fidgety hands something to do during the summers I spent in France without my drum kit.

Before work, I liked to go to Clark Gardens to think before getting bitched at about coffee. Sitting in the wooded area under the hemlocks, I discreetly smoked a joint while feeling an indifference that started to worry me. Hating my job would have given me the motivation to change something. But work was okay, and only a few customers were annoying. You know, the ones who didn't quite grasp that a long line of *other customers* meant it would take a little longer to get their coffee. Or the ones who asked for dumb shit like coffee, extra hot, and then came back to complain they burned their tongue. When I bitched about work, my girlfriend would give me a sharp "I told you so" look as if having a college degree would relieve me of entitled fucks like that.

Carla

I couldn't figure out if I took myself too seriously or maybe not seriously at all. As a teenager, I felt irrelevant, underestimated, and, well, plain stupid by my fellow classmates. I slid by as a below-average student, and my teachers often complained that I daydreamed too much. But I didn't hate high school or anything. I just think high school sort of hated me. Thank God, though, for my best friend, Alex, who called me Lala and was the only person in the world who got me.

I spent every Saturday night at her house and even had my own drawer for clothes. With Snapple sugar highs, we would imitate the dance moves in the Janet Jackson music video for "If." After, we would pearl-clutch in preteen shock over Alex's older sister's explanation of what Janet meant when she sang about something smooth and shiny feeling good against her lips.

7

Sensing our intrigue, she then gave us Liz Phair's *Exile in Guyville* to expand our *oral* education.

We would stay up late in her pink canopy bed, where she knew we could talk about anything but my family. In the dark, we'd giggle sketch comedy references from *The State* to each other or talk about our place in culture. Technically, we were Gen X, as in we were old enough to remember the first time we saw the "Teen Spirit" video but not old enough to do anything about it because, well, we were eleven, and we'd have to hold out another year or so for the famed teen angst.

When we read her sister's *Sassy* back issues and listened to records of bands who had already broken up, started glossier new bands, or were dead, we felt like we missed out on all the cool shit and just had to appreciate the watered-down second wave handed off to us. The feminist riot grrrl movement got butchered and then repackaged by the mainstream as Girl Power; the post-grunge bands sounded more like soft rock with the radio replacing bands like Soundgarden with Matchbox 20; and fashion looked plastic and cheap, which made us feel like sort of a Gen X afterthought.

Alex was always trying to get me to start a zine or a band she wanted to call The Saturn Peaches. A big F-You, she would say, to our ignorant classmates who would scream "Hole!" at us when we walked down the hall. With her dad's old Telecaster he handed down to her, she'd try to play chords, and they sounded plain awful. Eventually, she gave it to me, citing that the color washed out her completion. I think we liked talking about the band more than playing in it. Alex would even go so far as to strategize our *Rolling Stone* cover that *had* to be shot by Mark Seliger. We'd then look at each other and laugh that we'd probably end up as accountants and then put on our favorite albums in resignation that the best music was already out there.

I once dragged her to a Battle of the Bands at school, where we watched the real musicians in our class—all guys, of course—effortlessly crank out complicated Phish and Led Zeppelin songs while these girls from other schools in patchwork tops danced on the side like it was Woodstock. Not that I was into any of that stuff, but as I watched the effect they had on the crowd, I wished I could do the same.

Pete

To make Mondays less lame, I held jazz ensemble in my basement, a generous term for getting together with some guys from high school to mostly talk shit, smoke up, and watch TV. I played drums; a guy Tony plucked the bass; and Mark, a taper at Phish shows, played trumpet when he wasn't on tour. Nothing close to the bands we played in high school, but with both our rhythm and lead guitarists and our pianist away at school, we had no choice but to turn our prog-slash-classic-rock-slash-blues-band into a jazz ensemble.

Mark usually canceled, so practice became me and Tony, a two-hundred-pound aspiring firefighter who listened to metal and dance music he called "Guido-core." We looked like complete assholes and usually stopped after fifteen minutes to watch taped episodes of *Mr. Show*. I didn't need much in life, since I had my girlfriend, a job, and a place to live, but sometimes I wished I had someone to play music with . . . as in really play music with. It didn't need to be some big emotional connection. After all, it was just music, and I didn't think I was asking for too much.

3

Carla

I always wondered how I managed to become the person I was, having been raised in a family of total Guidos. Coming home from work on a rainy autumn night, I walked into my house through the garage just as my brother Claudio was pulling into the driveway, his headlights shining on the slabs of hanging meat we dried in the garage. Through his rain-beaten windows, I could hear the dance station "The Beat of New York" playing music known to us in the tri-state area, affectionately as "freestyle." The post-disco dance music featured basic synth laid over electro drumbeats with bleeding heart lyrics more desperate than your first crush. I waited for my brother as he turned off the car in the middle of "Louder than Love" by TKA—yes, I knew the titles *and* the artists. I smirked at him.

"You mean you're not going to finish the song?" I said as he shut the door to his grey Altima.

"Nah," he said, knowing I was being snide. "I got the tape. Wanna borrow it?"

"Tape? Please. I have it on vinyl." I paused. "Limited edition."

"Smart ass." He put his arm out to give me a hug.

As we got older, our parents were around a lot more than when we were kids. I remember being as young as eight and letting myself in the house after the bus had dropped me off up the street. Even if my brothers weren't home. It made me feel sort of unloved, and when I expressed this, my brothers called me dramatic. I couldn't be mad, they explained, because our parents worked and not every girl on Long Island had a live-in nanny. My dad owned the local shoe repair shop. Everyone thought because he cleaned crap off rich people's shoes that we were poor, not realizing a shoemaker in a high-end shopping center on Long Island made a decent living. Since he didn't have any employees, he spent most of his time there. My mom worked part-time as a bookkeeper at an Italian deli, which got my family involved in curing meat in our garage, the smell permeating my clothes and hair. I didn't know it, though, and it wasn't until my math teacher drew attention to it one day. Sniffing around me like a pig in a truffle forest, she announced to the class she smelled *soppressata*. Realizing it was me, I sunk into my seat, hoping she'd drop it, but all too satisfied with her discovery, she announced it was me who smelled like salted and dried-out pork product. The cool girls in class eyed each other in horror, thus marking my birth of the uncool.

That night, my brother and I walked into the kitchen where our other brother Lorenzo had my parents' full attention with some story, talking so loudly the windows clattered. People always thought my family was fighting, but really, they were just talking. To counter this, I turned inward, making myself as small as possible with my nose in a book or my ears wrapped in headphones. Noticing us walk in, Lorenzo put his arm out to hug Claudio and then me. My dad was at the stove making a Stracciatella soup with sausage. I gave him a squeeze as I inhaled his comforting scent of cologne mixed with pungent shoe polish.

11

While my mom, sitting at the table, gave me a pat on my back, anxious to hear the rest of my brother's story.

"I was just telling Ma and Pop" —Lorenzo stopped himself to turn around to make sure they were still there, his captive audience— "about these assholes that came into work."

I wanted to remind him he worked at a restaurant on Long Island, and of course, there was an asshole at work. But instead, I leaned my back against the kitchen counter and half-listened. My mom sat at the table, sipping wine in an orange juice glass, which assuaged her shame of day drinking since it wasn't in a real wine glass. Since I graduated high school, her cocktail hour got closer and closer to noon as she justified her day drinking with our European roots. "They drink wine at lunch in Italy," she'd say at the disapproving face I knew not to make anymore. But something told me that on the coasts of Amalfi, they weren't serving foamy glasses of Franzia "White Zin" that sounded like piss when it poured out of the box.

"I can't even believe it," my mom said, snacking on each detail of my brother's story. "So then what happened?"

"Well, I'm just gettin' to the good part," he said, sneaking a glance at his reflection in the large kitchen window behind her.

"Then get to it already!" My dad waved his hand in impatience at my brother's theatrics when telling a story.

Ignoring my dad's response, my mom's glassy eyes focused back on my brother. My mom, the middle sister of three, tried to stand out by getting good grades in school and being the best behaved. With efforts unrewarded to her satisfaction, she fell into an endless state of irritation with the women in our family, which made me wonder if she was a misogynist.

As a kid, I found safety in my aunts. But after my grandmother passed away, they stopped pretending to want to be part of their sister's life and left me to brave the jagged edges of my mom's moods alone. I tried to only recall earlier memories of my mom when we'd spend summers out east at the beach at Zia Jo's house in Rocky Point. In her Spiegel Catalog cropped sweaters, I could still see her at the kitchen table husking summer corn we had picked up at a roadside farm stand with a look of quiet content on her face. On the table was her glass of Pinot Grigio on ice and a crowded ashtray of smoked Kents. When I'd rush in from the beach to go to the bathroom, she would sometimes reach out and hug me for no reason and tell me what a great kid I was. I'd sometimes push her away, not knowing this would be the extent of her maternal love for me. Had I known, I would have stayed in her arms forever. Things changed when Zia Jo died, and they sold her house, where I don't think my mom ever recovered. Soon after, I committed the deadly sin of developing breasts that stood at attention against my small build — a curse from my dad's side of the family — making me a target for my mom.

"Those make you look cheap," she'd say after a few vodkas.

I tried to keep my weight down to make them smaller, but the ratio never evened out. As I got older, though, I could see her perfectionism deteriorating as her need for control got the best of her as she self-medicated with cheap booze. Dwindling down to nothing, she starved herself to balance out the drinking because weight gain to her was a sign of weakness.

Being the youngest and the only girl, I never felt like my voice counted. My words remained muffled over the baritones of the rest of the family. I suppose this was why I turned to rock music and classic fantasy fiction, where I could tune them out and imagine a world I wanted to live in.

Pete

I lived with my folks in a small brick house in Albertson, on a side street off the busy I.U. Willets Road. I woke up that morning groggy from the fire whistle blowing two times in the night. For emergencies, a nearby horn—or as the locals inaccurately called it a whistle—blared out a high-pitched alarm for about twenty seconds. To the joy of all light sleepers, this happens six times. You hope it's the last one until another one starts up again, and then go the fire trucks barreling down the main road. I've always wondered what these overnight local emergencies were because we almost never heard about it the next day.

With a heavy head, I leaned over the bed to collect my old track sweatshirt I had peeled off in my sleep and pounced heavily down the two flights of stairs to the kitchen. As I leaned against the counter eating plain yogurt with a sugar cube in it that I crushed with a spoon, my dad walked in. Through the back door, he let out a grunt and a sigh to express the long day he'd had.

"*Hopla,*" he said, sliding the door behind him. "*Les Américains, je te jure.*"

Whenever he walked into the house grumbling about *The Americans,* it usually came with an anecdote about something he didn't understand. My dad wasn't just from France; he was from Alsace, a complex region in Eastern France. Because my ancestral home shares its border with Germany, it has been a territorial war trophy for the competing countries, where its occupation has fluctuated four times. Today, it's technically France, but as far as my family is concerned, it's Alsace. Possessing a strong regional identity, my dad spoke a Germanic dialect with my mamema that made him sound like a medieval knight.

"*Geht's?*" I walked over to greet him with a kiss on both cheeks in anticipation of his anecdote because Long Island was as far from Alsace as you could possibly get. "*Café?*" I then offered.

"*Ja, je veux bien, mon grand.*"

I walked over to the machine as if I wasn't about to spend the next six hours doing this very thing.

"Getting in some practice?" He smiled, his light eyes teasing me a little.

"*Ouais, c'est ça.*"

Taking his tool belt off, he settled into his seat at the table and audibly unloaded his day with more sighs and grunts. I looked up at him, waiting to hear about it as the espresso pulled through the machine into our small red and white ceramic mugs. My dad then went into a story I had heard a few times before. It was the one about the shutters. His company, Beau des Bois, once again got contracted to build shutters to mimic the French country look. And what happened every time was he got frustrated trying to understand why Americans didn't want the shutters to be functional.

"They're too small!" he complained. "They won't even cover half the window when closed!" I would then explain that no one was intending on closing them because people don't do that in the States; they were there to simply frame the windows for aesthetic consumption. They were show shutters, not like in France, where they opened and closed at the beginning and end of each day.

"*C'est incomprehensible,*" he said as he shook his head like I was taking "their" side.

"*Pfff.*" I would shrug as if to say, "It is what it is."

In France, my Dad liked to recount these cultural *amuse-bouches* to mamema, who would shake her head at lavish Americans who wasted money on things like fake shutters. "Show shutters!" I'd intervene, trying to rationalize it to the French side of my family, who thought their way, the French way, was the only right way. They'd then look at my mom like I was being indoctrinated by grandeur. My mom would retaliate by setting out forks for dessert instead of the *mandatory* spoons.

"*Service.*" I grinned at my dad as I set down the tray of espresso and joined him in my third, but certainly not the last coffee of the day. While I didn't have a whole lot to recount, it was nice having this quiet moment with him.

With my parents, we talked about everything...everything except my relationship with Allison because without having to say it, I knew they didn't approve. They did this annoying eye thing when they felt presented with steaming hot evidence of our incompatibility, dumb things like not agreeing on a movie. They really cracked the case when they discovered the time Allison and I went to Hollywood Video and I wanted to rent *American Beauty* while she wanted *American Pie*. We should have broken up. Immediately.

My mom once said she felt I was building my life around hers, which I would argue only made sense since her life was more interesting than mine.

Carla

My fingertips screamed for the first few weeks of learning the guitar. They went from stinging to burning to throbbing before the preferred state of losing all feeling entirely. I had achy wrists and joints, and my fingertips felt coated in wax, which then crusted over in hard skin. No one could accuse me of having beautiful hands now. The scabs made picking up the photo envelopes at work difficult. I didn't realize how much I relied on the friction of my fingertips to grab things. Wrapping the tips in Band-Aids only got in the way.

I had been staying up until two in the morning practicing in my cold, unfinished basement, stretching my hands, and working my fingers in ways they had never moved before. I gave up on the metal book and focused all my attention on the blues because I liked the way it sounded with my guitar. I had down the 12-Bar Blues Chord Progression, simplified versions of Muddy Waters songs that made me feel like a real guitarist, and my first scales. I clocked in about three hours a day with the taut strings feeling like shards of metal slicing through the pads of my fingertips.

I already had my rock guitar idols lined up with Gina from the Lunachicks, whose shredding could rival any arena-rock guitarist, to Babes in Toyland's Kat Bjelland, whose Rickenbacker—a guitar that usually fosters a brighter, more pop sound—was haunted and spindly like cobwebs. Seeking to expand my education, I went to Mr. Cheapo's and told the clerk with the curly bangs that I wanted to learn how to play guitar like a rock god. "Where do I go?" I asked. Thinking he'd send me where the Jimmy Pages, Brian Mays, and Stevie Rays were, I was surprised when he walked past them on display. "This is what you need to listen to if you want to play like those guys. And I say this to everyone who comes in with more or less the same request."

I looked down and in my hands was *Give it Up* with a super-young Bonnie Raitt on the front and Heart's *Dreamboat Annie*. "No Zeppelin? Or Satri—" I stumbled over the name.

"Satriani?" he said. "All amazing guitarists but big fat showoffs if you ask me. Bonnie and Nancy over here have more talent and the attitude to back it up." When he saw my surprise at dismissing these "celebrated" guitarists rock magazines treated like royalty, he said, "But don't listen to me. I'm just a dude who works in a record store."

I did end up listening to him *and* both albums in the car while sipping on a vanilla coffee I had picked up at the drive-thru at Dunkin next door. Looking down at my raw fingertips begging for a break, I listened to see if any of their fingers were screaming in pain. But they all sounded like pretty happy fingers, dancing up and down the frets. I also heard the confidence in their playing. Like, you knew *they knew* they were good. Not like when I played, and my insecurities reverberated through the strings. It was then I knew what I wanted to sound like…like someone who knew she was good.

4

Pete

I started taking piano lessons at six, which taught me the architecture of melody, and at twelve, I got to pick a new instrument. My parents thought I'd go for something I'd get bored with, like the violin or the glockenspiel. Ha! I'll never forget the looks on their faces when I picked the drums, something they only agreed to after my dad soundproofed the basement. I owed my education to my teacher Dale, who taught me drums and threw in some acoustic guitar when he saw I needed a break. My dad found him, so when I arrived at my first practice at eleven years old, I wasn't surprised he spoke French Creole. My dad had this way of finding French speakers, like a sixth sense. "French face," he would say. "I look at someone and just know."

Dale introduced me to the legends and taught me the rudiments of jazz drumming with their funny names like paradiddles, flam paradiddle-diddle, pataflafla, and the flamacue, which got a chuckle out of us every time because, with our accents, it translated to "ass in flames." He had me doing one-handed 16th note exercises where I thought my arm was going to fall off. He made sure I understood the art form from the ground up before guiding me through famous solos like Joe Morello's "Take Five" with that gorgeous five/four-time signature. Eventually, I worked up to an insane 1958 performance of The

Jazz Messengers doing Gillespie's "A Night in Tunisia," where Dale was a total prick making me start over when I missed a tiny single beat. That was when I learned there's no such thing as a tiny single beat. They all matter, and I had the blisters I popped with a sewing needle on my hands to prove it.

I played along to a click to keep my time consistent and tight until Dale said I was ready to go off on my own. That was the day I felt like a real drummer. I liked hammering through the Chili Peppers' *Blood, Sugar, Sex, Magik* and disciplining myself with negative space and snare-driven minimalism pioneered by the Velvet Underground's Mo Tucker. From the rim-shot hard-hitting sound of Grohl to the unusual syncopations of Bruford to the symmetrical rhythmic patterns of Liebezeit, I consumed it all. When playing Battle of the Bands with the guys at school, I wanted to fuck around with these different genres of rock from Devo to Nirvana, but they only wanted to do . . . "Stairway."

When I was old enough to drive myself to Dale's, we played facing each other on two kits, smoked hand-rolled cigarettes, and drank coffee thick as sin. At home, I played on a '60s four-piece Gretsch Round Badge kit. A work of art from the pitch, the sustain, the walnut snare, the attack of the kick . . . I loved it all, all except for the color.

My first kit, a turquoise Pearl Roadshow, only took three months to save up for. But the vintage Round Badge, which is like a white whale to us drummers, took two years. Being no longer in production, along with its iconic cachet, made sellers rare. I initially wanted it in piano-key black, but that one sold within a month of me saving. By the time I had enough coin, the available kit for sale came in Tangerine Sparkle, that my dad and I drove up to Rochester to pick up. The color eventually grew on me, but

I often thought about saving up to get it painted because there was nothing rock n' roll about Tangerine Sparkle.

Carla

Abel surprised me when he told me he planned to close the shop on Columbus Day. When I told him the stores usually stayed open and even took advantage with Columbus Day sales, he appeared lost.

"Look, it's no big deal," I offered. "I'll work so you can" — I searched for the right word — "*observe* the holiday?"

"It's not for me, Carla," he said with eyes looking the most expressive I had ever seen them. "It's for you."

"For me?" I looked left and then right before landing back on him. "What do you mean *for me*?"

"Wouldn't you like to celebrate?"

I had to grin because I couldn't recall a single time I *celebrated* Columbus Day.

"But why not?" He appeared confused. "You're Italian."

On my drive home that day, I thought about it and felt a little embarrassed he had to remind me that an Italian discovered the country I called home. While I accepted my heritage, I didn't know if I could describe it as pride since I didn't take it to the level my brothers did with their green, white, and red "boot" tattoos on their biceps. For one, none of us spoke Italian. In the end, I accepted the day off and celebrated the only way I knew how, by going into the city to buy records.

Taking pleasure in the first days of scarf weather, I decided to walk the forty-something blocks down to SoHo. Exiting Penn Station, the familiar smells of New York City revived my senses from the salt of the pretzel vendor to walking through a vapor of street construction exhaust that somehow smelled odorless and humid. The streets hurried with commuters in office attire and sensible sneakers, as well as loud-speaking parade goers making their way over to Fifth Avenue. I walked down Seventh, and after passing the Fashion Institute, I delighted in a quieter Manhattan on the lazy streets of Chelsea. As I crossed 23rd, I looked to my right to give a knowing nod to the Chelsea Hotel, a beacon of rock history from the days of Mapplethorpe and Patti Smith to the unfortunate bloody Sex Pistols ending.

After stopping at Espresso Thyself for a latte, I wrapped my chilly hands around the hot drink as I continued downtown to Rocks in Your Head record store. Arriving, I walked down the steps into the tight shop with the musty scent of vinyl sleeves and zines, which felt like walking into an old friend's house, even if the cooler-than-me staff kind of scared me. Debating on the new Blonde Redhead or replacing The PeeChees CD my brother accidentally sat on in my car, I eventually decided on both because I couldn't save every penny I had earned since I was fifteen. After, I went across the street to Vesuvio's to pick up a rustic Italian loaf for my dad, chuckling to myself about the Italians who also weren't celebrating Columbus Day.

I walked the streets of SoHo, eventually crossing over into the East Village. As if storing up for winter, I absorbed my surroundings of people and places that looked nothing like Long Island. Everything in the city seemed to have an artistic purpose I found comfort in.

Back on the Island, I waited at the train station for my mom to pick me up. Surrounded by people coming back from the parade, who seemed a little drunk, it was then my mom who took the prize for being the drunkest at Mineola Train Station at four in the afternoon. Almost clipping an oncoming transit bus with only a few inches saving her from spiraling out of control, I let out a sigh because couldn't we just get through one day. I had been naïve, or maybe hopeful was the better word, when I called her from the payphone at Penn. She seemed okay, nice even, which I forgot usually meant she had just started drinking, with the first sips rewarding her with feel-good chemicals. With the first cocktail, she was cool, but as I watched her hunter-green Camry approach me slower than deemed necessary, it was clear her first drink was already a distant memory.

Silently I coached myself not to provoke her and to be careful with my tone, facial expressions, body language, or anything else that could set her off . . . which was usually everything. I buttoned my wool peacoat and tightened my scarf. With the shopping bag dangling from my elbow, I pulled back my mountain of hair away from my face and hastily fastened it into a nonthreatening, low ponytail. As the car approached, I hoped I looked the part of an obedient daughter.

I gently opened the door and lowered myself into the passenger's seat, the air perfumed with booze and a heavy application of Dior's *Poison*. Noticing her in the same ratty sweater that smelled of cigarettes she had worn the day before, as sweetly as I could manipulate my voice, I said hello. As she ignored my greeting, I noticed her eyes slit like paper cuts and her lack of coordination as she stared down at the gear stick in confusion, which meant she was only wine drunk. Wine drunk I could deal with. It was the vodka drunk I knew to beware of. As

I watched her try to figure the car out, she snapped her head in my direction and said, "What?"

"Nothing," I said but then changed my mind because she couldn't drive like this. "Well, actually, do you want me to drive?"

"Why the hell would you drive?"

"You just seem a little" —I stumbled for a second— "a little tired, that's all." I tried to sound sincere and then changed the strategy to upbeat, which in itself I resented. "I had a huge latte at the station." I forced a smile. "So, I'm pretty awake and excited to drive."

"You think I can't drink," she hiccupped. "I mean, drive. You think I can't drive?"

"It's not that. I just thought I'd offer since you were so kind to pick me up from the station," I said, hoping it wouldn't end like the last time I offered to drive, and she ended up punching me in the face, which in her defense was supposed to come out as a slap. Regardless of her intent, I got a black eye I told Abel was from opening a kitchen cabinet too quickly. When I was fourteen, I went to a few Alateen meetings at the church. I didn't stay in the program very long because I was embarrassed about telling my story and resentful for being more different than I already felt from the kids in my school. There was also the word "teen" that bothered me.

"I'm sorry," I conceded as I pulled the seatbelt over my shoulder and mentally made the sign of the cross. Everyone from the name of the father, the son, and the Holy Spirit, I prayed to them silently. I prayed not for me because dying stopped scaring me a long time ago, but for everyone else on the road my sick mother was incapable of thinking of. I breathed deep as we turned onto the busy streets by the courthouse with her unnecessarily riding the brake.

Looking into the other cars wishing I was them, I sighed to myself, once again, this crisis was brought to you by Pinot Grigio.

Pete

Another Monday and another fake band practice. I sat on the couch between Mark, who rolled the joint the two of us were going to smoke in the backyard, and Tony. The three of us, crammed on the small couch, watched MTV, even though the channel hadn't played rock music since, like, 1996.

At twenty years old, I was starting to feel even more confused than I did as a teenager. But for different reasons. By now, I thought I'd have my shit together because twenty sounded like such a scary grown-up age. I mean, I had just voted for the first time. My mom, impatient as always, pressed on for a more impassioned take on the "experience," while explaining the Electoral College to my French dad, once again, proved to be a useless and thankless task.

I looked at Tony, who would become a firefighter like everyone else in his family, and then Mark, who would probably live out of his Pathfinder recording Phish shows for the rest of his life. As for me, I just didn't know . . .

It was the year 2000. The big Y2K had arrived; the year we were either supposed to lose everything because we didn't trust computers to calculate the date, or we were supposed to die. Neither of those things happened, and instead, we got . . . boy bands and music that apparently couldn't be performed without the presence of backup dancers. Just as I was going to change the channel before one of these dumb songs got stuck in my head, my mom's voice rescued me.

"Pete!" she called out from the top of the stairs as Mark quietly stashed the pot under the coffee table.

"Sorry!" I called back, grabbing the remote. "The TV too loud?"

"No, it's fine." She walked a few steps down, which jolted me off the couch. "I was wondering," she said before she cut herself off and twitched her nose. "What's that smell?"

"What smell?" I tried to say casually, knowing damn well she could smell the heady kush dripping with THC crystals Mark had picked up in the lot.

"Pete." She looked at me.

"It's nothing." I was unable to come up with an answer to the thick smell *clearly* assaulting her senses. "Now, what were you saying?"

"I wanted to know if you picked up the film." She looked around suspiciously. "Hi, guys…"

"Hey, Mrs. A," Tony and Mark answered more high-pitched than usual, which pushed my mom to give me one of her faces telling me to cut the shit.

"The film?" I repeated, hoping to change the subject.

"Pete," she said with her head angled to the side. "It's been a week now. Just give me the ticket back, and I'll go to the store myself."

"No, no. I'll do it tomorrow, okay?" I held my gaze to let her know I meant it. "I promise."

"Okay," she said as she walked up the stairs. "And Pete." She whipped her head over her shoulder. "I don't want smoking down here."

"We're not," I said, tilting my head to give her a sweet look.

She fixed her gaze on me and, with a raised eyebrow, said, "Save those eyes for your girlfriend."

5

Carla

Something about the last customer irked me. The way he looked at me was too intense, like he was staring into me in search of something. Or maybe he was trying to be sexy or mysterious. Either way, it annoyed me. As I checked the developing solution in the machine, the doorbell chimed again. This time, it was Mrs. Pascucci, one of my favorite regulars, looking flustered and fabulous in a cropped gray fur coat.

"Hi, honey." Her dyed-red hair glowed under the track lighting. "Can you believe it?"

Her standard introduction: She'd start by asking me if I could believe it, which obligated me to say, "What?" I would then listen—while staggering my reactions at climactic moments—of, say, a luncheon she swore was going to hell because the raffle tickets hadn't come in and the flower centerpieces arrived dead. I always told her I couldn't believe it but knew the pictures would come back the following week when I would see it had worked out to the Chardonnay day-drinking merriment of all.

As she talked about the luncheon, over her shoulder, I noticed this guy Pete I graduated with outside smoking. Tuning her out, I watched him leaned up against his car and couldn't help but wonder what he had been up to.

Pete

Motivated by wanting fewer surprise visits in the basement from my parents, I left the house early to pick up their vacation photos. They could go anywhere in the world with my mom's flying passes, but every year they drove to Montauk. Two weeks out east, they somehow managed to document the trip on three rolls of film. I had gone with them once, and while it was nice, it wasn't three rolls of film nice. I mean, how many pictures could two people possibly take? Having braved a screening of their vacation photos before, I knew I was picking up three rolls of the same exact photo: Dad making the same face of surprise as he accused my mom of not "being ready." And Mom in white shorts, standing in front of various seaside locations laughing and telling my dad to "take the fucking picture already."

They actually invited their friends over to look at these memories. I'm sorry but looking at other people's vacation photos is as miserable as hearing about someone's dream. My dad was smart about it, though, and usually numbed his friends first with a glass of his Kirsch, a homemade *eau de vie* that tasted like rubbing alcohol and got people rocked off their asses.

As I smoked a cigarette outside, I looked inside the shop's windows and decided that photo stores were weird. Like an office no one wants to work at, it had that gray wall-to-wall carpet that probably felt like sandpaper to walk on barefoot and the shelves lined with dusty frames containing photos of fake families. Looking past the makeshift photo studio, I did a double-take because I saw Carla, a chick I went to high school with. And she looked as uninspired at work as I usually did.

Carla

As Mrs. Pascucci left in a flurry of party preparation scandals, Pete walked in past her. I couldn't remember the last time I had spoken to him. He was always someone I wanted to get to know, but he was too cool for me. I knew little things about him...fun facts, if you will. I knew he mysteriously quit soccer in the middle of tenth grade to join track, a scandal, I suppose, in the world of high school athletics. I knew he listened to the weird music Alex's dad listened to; that he smoked-up sixth period behind the school buses with Mark Gallagher and Nick, the janitor who wore Motorhead t-shirts under his uniform. But also, he was one of the best musicians in our school. I guess I knew more about him than I thought...

In eleventh-grade health class, he sat behind me, and I admit to stealing glances at him. There was something about his eyes I liked. Behind the glasses, I could see their paisley shape framed by full lashes that I swear sparkled. His expression, weighed down like honey, was as if he was trying to piece something together in his head; and the color was hazel with touches of green that made them look almost tie-dyed. Having my great-grandfather's blue eyes, myself, I always noticed other eyes and wondered where they came from: a grandmother, a great-aunt, an uncle in prison? I once told him his eyes looked like the tiger eye stone my mom used to wear around her neck, but he got weird about it, and I never spoke to him again. He also had pillowy lips, something Alex brought to my attention one day as we watched him cut through the cafeteria. It was an accurate description, but it still made my face scrunch up because of the word pillowy.

"Let's find a better word," I whispered to her across the table.

Discreetly, we turned our heads to watch as he fluidly walked by, this cute stoner in AP with black-rimmed glasses and messy short hair. Alex then took a moment to deliberate, tapping her index finger against her chin to emphasize she was thinking. "You're right," she finally said. "It is a little ugly. What about luscious?"

She looked at me, and I made a face that said, "No way."

"Okay, we'll get there." She cracked open her Raspberry Snapple. "What about mad juicy?"

"Suddenly, pillowy sounds better."

She agreed. Then her face brightened, and she pointed her finger in the air. "I got it." Leaning forward, she conspiratorially looked left and then right before saying, "What about . . ." She took another dramatic pause. "Kissable?"

"Ooh, kissable," I said, looking at her with an intentional sly smile. "Definitely. Kissable in the boiler room."

"*Always* in the boiler room." We looked at each other with hungry eyes as we visualized our favorite *My So-Called Life* episode.

Pushing aside the mental anecdote that I felt like he could hear, I prepared myself for the annoying questions sure to come about college. Straightening my lab coat, I pushed my shoulders back to appear professional and evolved since high school.

"Pete Albrecht," I said, looking up at him. "Welcome to 24-Hour Photo."

"That's the name of this place?" He looked around for, I guess, a sign.

"Groundbreaking, isn't it?" I said with a smile, catching a glimpse of those eyelashes blinking through his glasses. "Picking up?"

"Uh, yeah." He rubbed the back of his neck. "For my mom. Um, my parents, I mean."

"Okay," I pivoted toward the pick-ups. "Same last name, I assume?"

"Uh, yeah, it's Al—"

"I remember your last name." I glanced over my shoulder. "I just said it."

"Oh yeah," said Pete. "Sorry, I sort of just woke up, and I need coffee. I have the ticket if you need it."

"It's fine. I believe you."

My fingers filed the best they could through the A-F bin, each stuffed envelope disturbing my padded fingertips trying to heal under the ragged Band-Aids. Behind me, he fidgeted as he tapped his fingers along to "Strawberry Fields Forever." I recalled his quiet confidence. Like, he strode to his own rhythm. But he seemed shiftier than I remembered in high school, which had me wondering if I had made him feel uncomfortable. I didn't bring up his juicy lips or eyes or anything, but maybe I had been too relaxed by calling him by his full name. Should I have pretended to not know him? I hated it when people did that.

"I see three rolls here," I said, placing the envelopes down on the counter. When I looked up at him, he was staring at the photo-developing machine behind me. He looked at it as if he had never seen something like it before, staring with his jaw wide open in shock.

Pete

God, she made me nervous. I mean, I did have a little bit of a crush on her in eleventh grade – okay, and in fifth grade too. Fifth grade was brutal, though, and I could never admit to crushing on her. We had to like the popular girls who wore expensive jeans and compulsively flipped their hair. Since I played soccer, that's who I socialized with, even if I didn't find them interesting. When my friends asked me who I liked at school, I lied and said Jessica Schechter because I couldn't admit to liking Carla Bucchio because she was kind of out there. She once told me my eyes looked like a precious stone, and it freaked me out. It was the first time a girl had ever said something of substance to me, and I didn't know what to do with it.

In eleventh grade, though, when she sat in front of me in health class, it was more than a crush. I wanted to know her, talk to her, share things with her I felt *maybe* she'd get; things people in our dumb school wouldn't allow themselves to even *try* to understand. But she seemed to be totally in her own world, so I took what I could get. I liked when her dark hair swept across my desk or when she'd turn around to pass me a loose leaf, and I'd catch her looking at me. And it wasn't like I had never noticed her eyes before either; nautical-stripe blue that peeked out from behind her bangs. She did her own thing, though, and spent her time with Alexa Sherman, the punk rock Betty to her Veronica. They were always laughing about something, probably at our school, and I wanted in on the joke. Then senior year happened, and I started dating Allison.

When I walked into the shop, I saw she still had that super-cute Phil-Spector-girl-group look going on. As she filed through the envelopes, I noticed her fingertips wrapped in Band-Aids. Did she play guitar? I wondered. Having lived through my own calluses I used to pick off with my teeth, I got it, but I just never knew she played. As I was about to ask her about it, I noticed what was coming out of the photo-developing machine.

Standing in the family-friendly establishment, I looked on in a mix of horror, amusement, and confusion to the pornographic photos cranking out right behind her. As the photos spit out of the top and trailed down the machine's display window and into an envelope, I saw a mouth on a dick in the first picture. The second one had the same dick (I presume?) in other places. There was a butt here and there. Some boobs and, to finish it off, an explosive *branlette espagnole* — look it up.

"Alright, here they are," she said as my attention locked on the machine. "Do you want to look at them first?"

Immediately, she noticed my stare and, in an even tone, said, "That's our photo developer. Usually, people under the age of nine are that interested in it, but I guess it's fun for all ages."

When I didn't respond, she seemed to get a little impatient, looking at me like I was stupid. "Whatever," she said, giving up and turning around to put back the pictures she had taken out while looking for my parents' order. A moment later, I was still looking when she interrupted my shock. "Okay, it's not that interesting, Pete."

"It all depends."

"Depends on what?"

"On what you call interesting?" I then motioned my eyes for her to look over.

"I don't get it."

"Well, do you always develop pictures of . . . fellatio?"

Carla

"What!" I turned toward the machine when I heard the word fellatio, a word I *didn't* expect to hear that day. "Oh my God! Oh my God! No! We don't!"

"It's okay," he said, trying to calm me down as I ran to the back, unsure of what to do. "Do you have any loose paper around?" he called out. "We can tape some up to cover the window."

"I think so," I called back. "Hold on, let me see."

Completely frazzled, I grabbed a roll of paper towels from the kitchenette and ran back to the counter, worried another customer would come in.

"This was the only thing I could find." When I noticed him behind the counter, I said, "What are you doing back here?"

"I thought you could use some help, but sorry, yeah," he said nervously.

When I looked at the machine, I saw he had taped up a few blank envelopes to cover the display window. I put the useless roll of paper towels on the counter and brushed my bangs to the side to cool my forehead, feeling like I had survived an attack.

"No, it's fine that you're back here," I said with relief. "Thanks for your help. I'm just so embarrassed."

"Don't be," he said unphased. "It's nothing I haven't seen before."

I didn't know why, but this took me by surprise. At first, I assumed he meant porn because guys are gross, but then I remembered hearing from my family friend Tony that he was still with Allison Kellner, and then, okay, I got it. I never understood them because they were such a random couple. He was this guy with obscure interests, and she involved herself in things like student government, wore silver Tiffany necklaces, and carried tiny Kate Spade bags my wallet wouldn't have even fit in. But they obviously had something in common because it had been a while, so I guess he had seen or rather participated in the same activities as the guy in the photos.

"That's great, Pete," I said in a mordant tone.

"Sorry, that was weird." When he passed me to return to his side of the counter, my shoulder knocked into his arm, and we clumsily tried to get around each other. "Anyway, do you want me to stay until your boss or this creep comes back to get the photos? I can call into work and tell them I'll be a little late."

"No, it's fine." I let out an exhale, still collecting myself from all the excitement.

At the counter, I rang him up, keeping my eyes down on the register the entire time. With my eyes lowered, I told him the cost. While he sorted himself, I faked interest in things around me, like moving the stapler from one side of the register to the other and running my finger between the buttons to grab the matted dust while my Beatles tape moved onto "Lucy in the Sky with Diamonds." When I finally looked up at him to take the money, I found his eyes waiting for me, which sent flutters down to my stomach. They seemed to be smiling, so mine smiled back. We stood still for a moment after I slid his change over the counter, my hands shaking a little as our eyes seemed to slow dance.

"Anyway." He took a deep breath, seeming to reset the moment. "It was good seeing you" — he looked to the side before adding with a smile — "pornographic pictures and all."

"You too," I said, feeling my cheeks get warm. "See ya around."

"Yeah."

I watched him leave, walking toward the door, the cars bustling in both directions out on the busy street. Just as he opened the door, I called out to him.

"What's up?" He turned around with a partial smile.

"You forgot your pictures," I said, pointing to the bag still on the counter.

"Did I?"

And as we stood there looking at each other, I wondered what was happening.

Pete

"I still don't get it," Allison said with an unexpected frankness on the phone that night.

"Get what? What's there to *get*?"

"Well, why did you offer to help her so much?"

When I didn't respond because the question confused me, she added, "I mean, it's nice and all, but you don't even know her."

"Well," I said, glad she couldn't see my exasperation. "I'd hope if you were ever in that situation, someone you barely knew would offer to help out."

"I'd never be in that situation, Pete," said Allison. "Because I go to school and don't have to do things like work at One-Hour Photo."

"24-Hour Photo, you mean," I joked, hoping to lighten the stupid conversation while ignoring her elitist comment.

"I don't know; you just sound weird. That's all."

I didn't know what to say, so we sat on the phone in strained silence. *Did* I sound weird? As I tried to think up new words to say to make her feel better, I almost said, "Oh, thank fucking God," out loud when I heard the receiver click and the unmistakable hum from the kitchen phone.

"Pete?"

"Yeah, Mom."

"Dinner's ready."

"Hi, Mrs. Albrecht," Allison said.

"Hi, Allison, you know you can call me Anna," my mom said as I imagined her eyes looking off to the side in light irritation. "We're not in high school anymore."

"Okay," Allison said, sounding uncomfortable as she pushed my mother's name out of her mouth.

"Pete?" My mom continued.

"I know; I'll be right down."

"Yeah, but not in ten minutes, though; we're having *baeckeoffe*," she said, which always made me laugh when she pronounced the Alsatian meat and potato casserole with her New York accent. It came out sounding like "Bake Off," like she was going to throw some shit down over death-by-brownies at the PTA.

"*Baeckeoffe*?" I questioned. "But it's not Monday."

"Shit, now you sound like your father." I could feel her smile through the phone because I knew she loved that I inherited my dad's quirks. "José didn't click-in, did he?"

"No," I said. "I'd let you know."

"Alright, well, don't be too long. We're waiting."

When the phone clicked, Allison asked in a teasing voice, "Who's José? Your mom's boyfriend?"

"He may as well be," I chuckled, imagining my mom with José, who incidentally also did her taxes. "But no, he's my mom's trip trader. She's been waiting to hear back from him because she got all Zurich for next month, and she's trying to trade them out for turnarounds so she can be home for dinner."

"Whoa, weird flight attendant lingo."

"Anyway." I ignored the haughty timbre in her voice. "Let me call you later. Like in an hour?"

"I have study group after dinner, and then we're going for coffee. So, I'll call you tomorrow, okay?"

"'Kay," I said, relieved by her softened mood. "I love you. You know that, right?"

"I know," she said. "I love you too. It was just a long day, and I guess I just really miss you. I don't know why I was like that. It *was* nice what you did."

"Just forget about it. We'll talk tomorrow."

Walking through the foyer en route to my kitchen, I stepped over a large package we had received that day from France. Since my mom hadn't gotten a CDG trip in a while, my grandmother sent a package with things my dad swore the house couldn't live without. In the box, she sent glazed *pain d'épice* cookies from Gertwiller, bar soap from Marseille in whatever scent my grandmother felt like sending. This time it was a bulk shipment of hazelnut, so we were going to smell like Nutella for the next year. There was also the latest Houellebecq novel, boxer briefs for my dad and me, and Doliprane that my mom has told my dad repeatedly we could get in America…only here, it's called Tylenol.

Every night we ate in the kitchen while watching *Jeopardy!* My mom liked to call out the answers, and when she was wrong, she'd dismiss the correct responses with an, "oh, fuck it!" My dad would then look at my mom, his potty-mouthed New York wife, like she was this rare and exotic bird. She's not exotic, I liked to tease him; she's just from Queens.

As I washed the dishes at the sink, I couldn't help but think about that afternoon. As I poured over the exchange for the hundredth time, I recalled little things like the manner in which she moved the stapler around her workstation to give the impression she was busy or her wide-eyed surprise at the naked pictures cranking out of the machine.

I wondered if I had freaked her out by my indifference to the activities in the photos. I guess I hadn't realized how sleazy it sounded until after it came out of my mouth. I mean, I'd had a girlfriend for a few years, so it made sense, but maybe she didn't know that. Maybe she thought I was referring to porn, and that's how I spent my post-high school years. Gross. I didn't need porn when I had my imagination. Well, that, and leftover Guess? ads from the '90s.

Then there was that moment at the end when she looked up at me from the cash register, her eyes blinking slowly and with intention as if each blink counted. It was only until I was halfway to the door that I realized I'd forgotten the pictures. I didn't know why, but I decided I'd come back and get them the next day, which when I thought about it, made absolutely no sense.

Maybe Allison was right. I *was* acting weird.

6

Carla

G oing out. I dreaded going out. Not old enough to legally drink, not sophisticated to know *what* to drink, and loathing meaningless small talk with strangers made the whole thing sound miserable. But at twenty years old, I figured I had to at least pretend to care about my youth. Mrs. Pascucci scared me the other day when she told me to enjoy it to the fullest so I wouldn't have regrets later and end up cheating on my first husband. So for the sake of my future first husband, I agreed to go out with some girls I sort of knew in high school who had come into the store. They wanted to have a *Sex and the City* night and told me to wear a wrap dress if I had one. I didn't. And I also didn't drink Cosmos or have complicated relationships with old, rich men who refused to take me to Paris. But I agreed anyway because it was Thanksgiving Eve, the alleged "biggest party night of the year," and I was starting to think I really was missing out on my wild and irresponsible youth. All I really wanted to do was get coffee with Alex at the gothic Witches Brew coffee house over by Hofstra, but she decided last minute to stay at school in Illinois.

I had an expired ID. Handed down from one of Alex's sister's friends, it claimed I was twenty-four-year-old Shannon O'Brian from Williston Park. Standing in my bedroom with a towel wrapped around me, the beads of my shower dripping onto my pistachio-green wall-to-wall carpet, I had to find something to wear to artfully convey the deceit. I had ratty vintage sweaters, striped shirts from the '90s, and oversized band t-shirts, not to mention black hair. None of it screamed *Sex and the City*. None of it screamed Shannon O'Brian.

My brother Lorenzo and I shared a small build, so I tiptoed into his room to find something. Opening his drawers, I found his clothes organized by purpose and color as the springtime scent of our family laundry detergent wafted up through the oak. I dug past his cheeky French Connection t-shirts and grabbed one of the many black tank tops he owned. Then, back in my room, I pulled out the Bedazzler from under my bed to stamp rhinestones all over it. I held it up to review my work, the clear crystal beads catching the light, while thinking of my brother, who would have freaking killed me if he knew I had bedazzled his Armani tank top. This is why people hate little sisters, I chuckled to myself. I paired it with the tightest jeans I had and then put a lot of crap on my face, like electric blue eyeliner and jet-black mascara. Being a moisturizer and Chapstick kind of girl, I barely recognized myself after my makeover. Still, it wasn't *Sex and the City*.

With my overnight bag thrown over my shoulder, I called out to whoever was listening, "See you in the morning!"

Driving to one of the girls' houses in Searingtown with Le Tigre blasting from the crappy speakers of my Honda Civic, I made a last-minute decision to get coffee. Stepping out into the parking lot, the cool November winds pressed against my chest, prompting me to pull my coat tighter around me. I walked into Starbucks, which felt inviting and smelled like warm butter and roasted espresso beans. It made me want to cancel my night in exchange for one of the velvet armchairs in the corner.

As I walked through the store, I looked on with gentle envy at the other customers settled into their laid-back night. Then my energy felt suddenly anxious with a heaviness that seemed to propel me forward. As if pulled, my attention and focus drew to the counter. When I looked over, staring at me with heavy-lidded eyes, like he knew something I didn't, was Pete. Instantly, I felt nervous. I couldn't tell if it was because I looked like an ice skater or because our last conversation involved the word fellatio, but my heart pounded fiercely through my rhinestones as I approached the counter.

"Carla Bucchio," he said. "Welcome to Starbucks."

"Is that what this place is called?"

"Groundbreaking, isn't it?"

Pete

Doomed to be the most annoying night of the year with all the college kids back in town, I couldn't believe it when she walked in. She looked kind of hot too. As she eased toward the counter, I couldn't help but feel totally lame in my bright-green apron.

"I didn't know you worked here," she said.

"Yeah, for about a year. How come I've never seen you in here?"

"I usually go to Parkway Deli."

"Yeah, that would make sense." I contemplated . . . "It's right by–"

"Work," we both said.

"Yeah." She chuckled as we let a few seconds of silence settle between us. I didn't know what to say. I had so many questions about what she'd been up to. Was she in school? Was she in a band? Did she have a boyfriend? I fumbled with the compilation CDs for sale next to the register and glanced up at her. Still looking at me, she slightly leaned forward and said, "Aren't you going to ask me what I want?"

"Ask you what you want?" I repeated, my eyebrows pressed in confusion as I stared back at her.

"Yeah, take my order?"

"Oh, yeah, right!" I jumped. "Sorry, don't mind me." I grabbed a cup that immediately slipped out of my hand and fell on the floor. I glanced at my coworker, Jake, who shook his head at how unsmooth I was.

"Wait," I said. "What size do you want? Let's start there."

"Large?"

"It's Venti," I teased, grabbing the cup. "Large means nothing to us here."

"That's right, I forgot." She playfully rolled her eyes. "Is it annoying having to say that all day?"

"Kind of," I said as we exchanged smiles.

"So, I'll have a nonfat latte in the *largest* cup you have."

After ringing her up, which I didn't want to but had to with Jake lurking over the counter, I made eye contact with him to switch over to the register. She then followed me to the next counter, smacking her lips and looking around.

"Hey, so, uh, do you play guitar?" My eyes gestured to her fingers as I firmly pressed the espresso into the portafilter.

"I do," she said, looking down at them. "I mean, I just started. It's nothing serious, though."

"I don't know," I said. "Those calluses look pretty serious to me."

"Yeah, maybe." She looked away nervously. "I think my fingers have finally formed a protective layer against the strings. It was brutal at first, but now I think they're used to the abuse."

"They're hard-earned, so whatever you do, don't pick at them because then you'll have to start all over," I said before realizing I sounded totally patronizing. "But yeah, you know that. Sorry."

"I thought that once I got them, I'd be in the clear." She shrugged. "But now my fingers are numb, and I can't feel where they are, or they slip off the string. It's all about finger memory now."

"You'd be surprised what great memory your fingertips have. I learned something in, like, eighth grade, this little arpeggio, and picking up my guitar the other day, I played it almost perfectly." I looked at her. "Well, almost. But it was like my fingers picked up where they had left off. It was pretty cool."

I poured the milk into the metal frothing pitcher and took my time foaming it, something I usually rushed. Customers began filing in as well as the cups, with Jake's instructions handwritten in our Starbucks code. Lined up on the ledge for me, I pretended I didn't see them.

"I know. I'm trying not to pick at them, but it is tempting because the skin gets a little . . ." She paused for a moment before saying, "crusty." She then looked away.

"You don't like that word?" I asked, studying the almond shape of her eyes.

"I don't."

"I don't like the word 'literally,' but mostly because it's abused."

"Yeah?"

"Yeah, for instance, I overheard someone saying the other day that they literally died," I said, shaking my head in recollection of the linguistic faux pas. "And I wanted to be like, well, then how are you ordering coffee right now? You're dead."

She laughed and nodded her head in recognition. "Yeah, I think I've heard that word misused before too."

"And you don't want to be that asshole —"

"Language!" Jake snapped.

"That *a-hole*," I said in a lowered voice, "who says, 'actually what you meant was that you 'figuratively died.'' You know?"

"Oh my God, yes," she said with eyes that totally got it. "But anyway, what about you? Are you still playing drums and, like, every other instrument?"

"Yeah, I guess I sort of do play everything," I admitted, feeling my cheeks blush a little. "But I'm not doing it as much as I'd like to." I released a sigh. "It's just that no one's around. I mean, some guys are back in town this week, but they're busy with family shit, and I'm..." I almost mentioned the full Thanksgiving itinerary Allison had planned for us, but for some reason stopped myself. "Anyway, no, I'm not really playing at the moment."

"That's too bad because I remember you were really into it."

47

"I was," I said, looking into her eyes. "I mean, I still am. And what about you; you're still into girl punk if I'm recalling correctly."

"I am." Her eyes twinkled in appreciation. "Among other kinds of music I listen to. And you? You still listen to Phish?" She arched an eyebrow and let a sly smirk escape from the corner of her mouth.

"I do." I smiled. "Among other kinds of music I listen to."

To alert me to the increase of orders, Jake began slamming the cups down on the ledge and calling out each one with an irritating, "Order's in!" As I poured the milk into her coffee, I let my eyes steal a glance at her and found her looking at me.

"Order's in!" Jake called out again to my complete disinterest.

I secured the lid on and handed her the cup, unsure how to close out a conversation I didn't want to end. Usually, when people I knew came in, this part, the farewell, unfolded naturally with the handing over of the coffee, but this felt different.

"Well," she said with her hands wrapped around the cup. "It was nice seeing you again."

"Yeah, you too." I looked at her. "Oh, and careful, I think it might be a little hotter than usual, so maybe give it a few minutes before you drink it."

"Okay."

"Order's in!" Jake barked.

"On it!" I said through my teeth, now wanting to punch him in the fucking face.

Carla appeared amused before noticing the other customers standing without their coffee. She looked at me and said, "I should probably go." She then took a few steps back before saying, "Okay, well, bye."

If I hadn't known any better, I would have thought that she, too, was struggling to end the conversation as she lingered in eye contact.

"Anyway," she said, appearing to snap out of it. "Take care, Pete."

"You too."

As she turned away from the counter, getting closer to the door . . . the line of cups demanding my attention . . . I had to think quickly, which didn't make sense why. With my girlfriend home from school, who had recently told me that she decided to go on birth control and who I was spending four glorious days with, I didn't know why I had to think quickly about anything. Logic told me to just let Carla go, but common sense annoyed me sometimes. In defying everything that told me not to, and risking having to answer to Allison, I called out, "Carla!"

"Oh, good Lord," Jake griped. "I'll start the orders, man. Just move."

"Yeah?" she said with a suppressed smile as if she wanted me to call after her. She then looked to the side nervously before saying, "What's up?"

"Maybe we could get together and jam?"

"Okay." Her expression brightened. "But only if you don't call it that."

"What?" I leveled my eyes at her and with an amused grin and said, "You don't like that word either?"

Carla

I didn't know why my family even bothered observing Thanksgiving. I didn't recall in any version of the Thanksgiving story when the pilgrims and the Native Americans sat down to carve the manicotti and braciole. Every year it was the same at our house. There was always the labored discussion on whether to bring the "leaf" up from the basement to elongate the table for Great-Aunt Bernie and Uncle Alfred. Calling it a leaf, however, was misleading. It weighed about the size of Uncle Alfred, which I discovered when it slipped out of my hand the year before and came slamming down on my foot. That year, it was also my turn to go all the way to Glen Cove to pick up the mozzarella and prosciutto, you know, other essentials in the Thanksgiving feast.

All this movement led up to the big meal where my family took a break from screaming over each other and not listening to the other person talk to sit and eat. There were only the sounds of chewing and forks scraping against the wedding china, with no one noticing me pushing my food around my plate. The silence would break mid-way when everyone's teeth were stained red from the wine and an argument would ensue over a look passed over the table, or this one accusing that one of not blanching the broccoli rabe, or someone was spoiled and didn't know real hardship because they didn't serve in the Korean War. Someone usually stormed off, and the night ended with my mom passed out on the couch and my dad and me in the kitchen cleaning up. He'd wash, and I'd dry, and at some point, he'd turn to me and say, "It was kind of a crappy night, wasn't it?" And I'd say, "Pretty much. A real Bucchio Thanksgiving." We'd then laugh, wondering why we bothered every year.

After having a cup of coffee with him, I retreated to the basement to practice some quiet, fingerpicking techniques I was learning. Less intuitive than free strumming with a pick, it allowed less room for error. I practiced my PIMA, which Alex on the phone earlier said sounded sexual. I tried to explain to my horny best friend that it was an acronym for remembering which fingers to use to pluck a string. For example, *P* stood for my thumb; *pulgar*, which I remembered from high school Spanish. Then *I* stood for *indice*, which meant index finger; *M* was *medio*, and *A* was *annular*. I got the PIMA down, plucking across the strings in sequence, but when I tried to get my fingers to dance around with PAMI or PMAI, I got sweaty. My fingers burned from pressing down on the practice C chord, and in frustration, I gave up, letting my mind wander to Pete. The day before, I wrote my AOL screen name on the side of a Starbucks cup for him since he said he wanted to *jam*. Only if he didn't call it that, though. Jamming was for bands with liquid-sounding wah-wah pedals who wore hemp necklaces. But that wasn't the real problem, and I knew it. I alternated back and forth from wanting to hear from him and not because the idea of playing with him, this musical whiz-kid, for some reason freaked me out. So much, in fact, I couldn't stop thinking about it.

Pete

Fuck. Fuck. FUCK. Everything was going according to plan, but of course, something had to happen resulting in complete and total mass destruction. Allison laid out a clear Thanksgiving Day schedule, or rather, the "Thanksgiving Feast," as she repeatedly referred it to. The feast would be at my house, which also included my dad's *choucroute* that he insisted on creeping into the American holiday. Usually one of my favorite dishes, but the sauerkraut, when mixed with the cinnamon sweetness of Thanksgiving, made the house smell like dirty diapers.

For dinner, Allison prepared pre-approved subject matters like when I was going to reaudition for Juilliard (never…and she knew that), as well as selected cultural topics of interest. We then went over topics where she felt my opinions were controversial, like who our president was since Florida was still deciding (totally fucking shady) and the Subway Series (the Mets were *clearly* robbed). After clean-up, "Coffee and Pumpkin Pie" was scheduled to be observed at Allison's house, with the same restrictions applied.

"Fine," I said. Fine to fucking all of it because . . . and I would say the fact rather crudely . . . I was totally being led by my dick. I followed the plan, kept the conversation contained to approved topics, didn't smoke anything, and cursed a lot less in exchange for condomless sex. But then Allison found it. Using my bathroom upstairs, she saw the Starbucks cup I left on my desk. The fucking Starbucks cup with Carla's info written on the side. And it happened right before "Pumpkin Pie and Coffee." FUCK.

I froze up as she stared at me in my bedroom, holding the cup.

"Who is *SHEBANGBANGS*, Pete?"

Fuck, I thought, tilting my head back. "It's nothing," I said, trying to sound convincing.

"Is this" —she then scrunched her face in total disgust— "*porn?*"

"No!" I held my hands up in defense. "Not at all! It's supposed to be ironic. Like," I started to say and then gave up knowing she wouldn't have found the humor in Carla cleverly pairing the Ricky Martin song with the Nancy Sinatra classic, and not to mention Carla had bangs. Super fucking cute, but yeah, those details would not have amused Allison. At all. Had it not said *SHEBANGBANGS*, I may have gotten away with saying it had to do with going over to a coworker's house for PlayStation 2, a topic that had a magical effect of making girls lose interest. But I couldn't. I also couldn't be honest since she freaked out the last time I saw Carla.

"You *hate* the internet, Pete," she said, waving the cup in my face. "What is it? It's artificial communication that goes against your constitution as a human who is incapable of communicating into a plastic box."

"Yes," I said, agreeing with my own words. "Yes, to it all."

"But your constitution has somehow changed for *SHEBANGBANGS*?"

"No! I still fucking hate the internet. But seriously, let's just forget about it, okay?" I said apologetically. "It's nothing. Really." But she wasn't having any of it. "I'm sorry?"

After making a show of throwing the cup out in the trash in the backyard when it really should have gone in the orange bin, she stormed out of my house in muted fury. In the wake of the front door slamming, I walked into the dining room with my family staring at me. My mother sharply eyed my father to not make a single comment because mumbled side remarks in French have this way of pissing people off. I knew my dad would have thought the entire thing was bullshit, and I planned to fill him in on it later over a shared smoke in the backyard. Family members who didn't find any of it to be bullshit, however, were Aunt Carol, whose husband, my Uncle Steve, had recently left her for a hotel receptionist, and my feminist cousin, Amy, home from The Evergreen State College. Both looked at me like I was the source of the problem, a total douchebag who represented the male patriarchy.

Happy fucking Thanksgiving.

7

Carla

By the end of February, I usually grasped with desperation for any sign of spring; longer days, the pointed shape of teeny buds on the branches of bare trees, and if I wanted to push it, willing myself into believing it's maybe a drop warmer. It had been a cold and meaningless winter, and I was seeking any sign of change. So far, though, 2001 wasn't any different than the year before.

It was my day off, and I was heading to the music store on Jericho Turnpike to see if they had a community bulletin board to find people to play with since I never did hear from Pete. I walked into the shop that had that old-fashioned feel to it with the metal music stands, lessons squeaking behind closed doors, and the tinkering of instruments heard left and right. Looking up, I admired the spectrum of electric guitars hanging on the wall. One lined up after the other; the pastel-painted guitars looked like the almond candies my parents got at weddings, while the primary-colored ones looked like a rainbow of glossy acrylic paints in art class.

"You need help with anything?" a voice from behind me said.

Startled, I jumped and turned to see a clerk looking at me. Around my age, with grown-out hair he tucked behind his ear and an eyebrow ring, he looked like he worked at a music store.

"Which one's calling you?" He read my face.

Tapping my pointer finger against my pressed lips, I scanned the selection before deciding. "The green Strat," I said, feeling my eyes pulse with enthusiasm. "For sure."

"Ah," he said in approval, "the Fender American Professional Strat. You got good taste."

"Expensive taste."

Music store staff used to make me nervous. Had it been a few months ago, I would have never had a guitar pulled down for me. And if I had even touched one, it would have been the most accessible one, and I would've strummed a few chords while scanning the room to make sure no one was listening. The sales guy brought it over, nodding in approval as he ran his hands up the fretboard.

"She is a pretty one." He handed it to me. "I can amp you in over there?"

I had to think about it for a second. I wasn't sure I had the chops yet to have the entire store hear me through an amplifier. But since the store had mostly flustered moms replacing slimy clarinet reeds and repairing tattered violin bows, I figured I'd take advantage of the disinterested audience. I followed him to an amp five times larger than the thirty-five-watt I had at home and stared at it, this thing that looked like it'd blow us all away.

"Don't worry." He smiled. "It's not as scary as it looks. But if you want, I can plug you into something smaller."

"You know what?" I said. "I'm fine."

"Cool. I'm Cliff if you need anything."

I took my coat off and settled onto one of the stools scattered around the store, and before plugging in, I appreciated what I had in my hands. The color of a martini olive, I had the preferred guitar of Jimi Hendrix, Kurt Cobain, Bonnie Raitt, and at that moment, me. I ran my hands over its smooth edges, feeling its hips and glossy lacquer finish that felt like soft butter. Grasping the maple neck that fit comfortably around my hands, I gave it a few strums to get acquainted with it and feel out the differences against my Telecaster.

I flicked the power switch on, which let out a furry-sounding hum, alerting the other shoppers. I then slid the cable into the input jack, which for a second released an unpleasant scratching sound that I resolved once the plug was fully inserted.

Sliding my fingers up the neck, I started with a basic three-chord pattern before transitioning into some bouncy bass note strumming. I then played around with a little melody I had been working on, adding in little bluesy fills here and there. I looked around, curious for reactions to see if my playing had any appeal in the store now packed with families. By the counter, I saw a toddler near his mother, pumping his legs up and down in rhythm, which made me smile. And then, seemingly out of nowhere, I heard off in the percussion room someone playing drums in tempo with me. What the . . .

Pete

It was one of those days when everything seemed hectic and irritating. I had just gotten back from Boston, a trip that took longer than usual because I was on the lookout for black ice. Before I left, my mom freaked me out with a story she read about a fatal accident involving a car spinning out of control due to black ice. For the occasion, my dad lent me his four-by-four, but I was still nervous because those long stretches of highway up to Boston meant passing one eighteen-wheel tractor trailer after another where maybe not spinning out of control was the preferable outcome.

Back at home, I was safe and unharmed by the evils of black ice, yet I felt flustered. My room was a mess from leaving in a frenzy, the disarray driving me fucking insane. I also had laundry to do and was hungry, but the best thing for me was to pound out a few rounds on my drums before my parents came home. If only I could find my sticks.

The truth was, I didn't have a great trip visiting Allison. Since we never really recovered from the great Starbucks cup scandal, something I still never fessed up to, she found little ways to get back at me. For example, she became friends with total assholes. Before this trip, I actually liked her friends at school, but there was suddenly this new crop of friends she wanted me to be impressed with. I didn't know where the fuck these people came from; all I knew was they sucked.

She was talking all weird too, like she was trying to get rid of her Long Island accent; something I always thought was cute. But now, she was talking in this aristocratic tone by over-annunciating consonants, pronouncing vowels correctly, and not letting the last letter of a word trail off like it should.

"Where the hell are my sticks?" I screamed at no one.

When I figured I was not going to find them, certainly not in this irritated state, I got in my car to go to the music shop. When I got there, though, I had to keep driving around the block until a spot opened. It was after three, which meant the shop was bursting with kids there for lessons and moms looking confused. I loved watching moms at music shops. For one, most moms hated being there. But maybe I'm just speaking for my mom. For Christmas and my birthday, my mom usually sent me in to get my own presents. My dad, however, liked this one store on Hillside that's now a florist where he'd go in and flirt with Lisette, the French lady that owned it. *Sacré, Papa.*

My third time driving around the block, a spot finally opened. Cranking the truck into the tight space before a van charging down the turnpike could clip me, I maneuvered a jerky, three-move parallel park.

I walked into the store, and the scene was exactly how I envisioned it: moms and kids everywhere with clerks charging around and stepping over toddlers. But what I didn't expect was to see her. I admit to adding SHEBANGBANGS to my AOL buddy list and felt my stomach drop the one time I saw her online, knowing she was just on the other side of her computer. I felt like a dick not contacting her and wondered about her. A lot. But now, here she was working out this sexy blues riff. Lost in her own vibe, she appeared oblivious to the hysteria surrounding her.

I couldn't let the opportunity slip by, so I went into the drum room and got behind the closest kit. With the amps and gear stacked around her, we couldn't see each other. The only thing connecting us was the melody, which from a small misstep in her playing, expressed her surprise by the addition of drums. I continued the same beat, as if to tell her to trust me, and she responded by picking back up where she was, eventually adding in some stylized fills I admit I was impressed with. We played intuitively and in sync.

And it was the best conversation I'd had all year.

Carla

A small crowd began to form after this mystery drummer started playing along with me. The toddler with the pumping legs was full-on dancing with his arms flailing in the air. The exhausted moms relaxed and stopped what they were doing to move along to the music while their preteen kids looked on with intrigue. With the drums daring and encouraging me to experiment, I took it a note further, even when I wasn't sure. It was obvious this drummer had years of experience and formal training because it felt like we were talking while my fingers responded instinctively. I felt a release of butterflies through my stomach when I saw how much delight it gave the people in the store. Even the staff were bobbing their heads.

The mystery drummer and I received a generous applause, prompting me to bow my head in appreciation. *Thank you,* I mouthed to the people looking at me in unfamiliar admiration. I turned off the amp and leaned the Strat against it, taking a deep inhale to allow the nutrients of the experience to settle in. If I got up too soon, I'd be dizzy, so I took a few moments to gather myself. A mother with a small child resting on her hip then came over and, flashing a bright smile, said, "Are you two in a band? What are you called?"

"Me and that other person?" I pointed my thumb behind me in the general direction of the percussions. "No. I actually don't know who that was. That was all improvised."

"You're kidding?" she said in astonishment, looking at her child as if he, too, should be amazed. Instead, he looked at her and then pointed to the cars passing by outside.

"No, I really don't know who was playing drums."

"That's just incredible. It sounded rehearsed!" She squinted her eyes and looked up over the amps. Balancing on her toes, she said, "Oh, I see your mystery drummer! Yoo-hoo!" She called out, waving her hands to whoever was over there. "You should go say hi!"

Curious myself, I held on to the surrounding equipment to slowly get up, feeling a little more balanced than I had moments before. I aimed my focus to the corner where the sound was coming from. There, I saw Cliff, and talking to him was none other than Pete. *You've got to be kidding me.* I watched him, noticing the long-sleeved thermal under his t-shirt pulled up, exposing his toned drummer's forearms. He nodded along to whatever Cliff was saying while a little kid took over the drums behind him.

I didn't really know how to react, but the one thing I knew not to do was approach him. I had embarrassed myself already by writing my info on the side of a paper cup, only for him to totally blow me off. I decided to grab my things and thanked the excited mom for her kind words.

"Wait!" Her face fell in disappointment. "Aren't you going to say something to that guy?"

"I really have to go. But if you talk to him, tell him I said thank you!" I said while quickly walking away.

With my coat draped over my arm, my bag hanging off my shoulder with the flyers crunching inside, I ran toward the door. As I pressed it open and immediately felt the blast of cold winter air on my face, I heard Pete.

"Carla!" he called out.

"Wait! Please?"

I kept walking.

"Oh, come on!"

I pretended not to hear him, letting the door close behind me. I then stepped up my pace, but suddenly it felt like the sidewalk had slipped from under me. Out of balance and overcome with the panic of surprise, I flew onto my back. The contrast felt severe going from the warmth of the store and the encouraging customers to lying flat on my back with the frigid, wet sidewalk bleeding through my sweater.

Damn black ice.

Pete

It was even better than I had imagined. Seminal, like we had just germinated something...if I could be totally rock nerdy about it. She must have been fucking with me when she said she had just started because her fingers told a completely different story. Once we stopped playing, about forty minutes later, I had to go talk to her. After handing my sticks to the kid who looked at me like I was the coolest guy in the room, I made my way around the kit only to have Cliff, this guy I knew who went to Herricks, corner me. *Not now, man.*

As if pressing play on a cassette, Cliff spoke in run-on sentences, unaware a conversation is an exchange between two people. Not that I wanted to add anything since that would only ignite more conversation that I would have to nod along to. I wasn't usually this rude, but I had to get to Carla. I kept glancing over to see if she had gotten up, noticed me, or was walking over, but all I saw were the moms. Cliff carried on, and I listened and nodded. And I listened and nodded some more. It was when I saw her leaving the store that forced me to cut him off.

"Look." I pat his shoulder firmly. "I gotta go. I'll catch up with you later." Not waiting for an official close to our conversation, I ran after her.

"Carla!" I called out. From the slight reaction, a subtle flinch when I called her name, I knew she heard me but was still heading for the door.

"Wait!" I pleaded. "Please?"

She kept walking.

"Oh, come on!" I yelled.

But she kept going, clearly wanting nothing to do with me. I guess I deserved it after blowing her off like I did. The front door of the store slammed in my face as she ran out into the cold without her coat on. When I went to follow her, I didn't see her running anymore but instead lying flat on the cold pavement. Fucking black ice. I carefully walked over and crouched down with my hand out to help her up.

"I'm fine," she said in resistance.

"I know you're fine," I said flatly. "But I thought you could use a hand. It looks kind of cold down there."

Grabbing my hand with reluctance and an eye roll I was meant to see, she let me pull her up.

"You forgot to put your coat on," I said, in which she just looked at me.

Once she got up, we stood there on the sidewalk. Unsure what to do next and with my own coat still in the store, the frosty air cut through my thermal like a razor blade. I rubbed my hands up and down my arms to keep warm. Hoping she'd say something, I kept looking at her, but she gazed off in the distance as if I wasn't there.

"So, ummm," I said, trying to get her to at least look at me. "You're getting really good."

"Getting?" she said, finally looking at me. But not in the way I was hoping. "As if that's not at all patronizing."

"No, I mean," I started to say but decided to just resign right there. "Look," I said as sincerely as I could. "I deserve this. I never got back to you. I'm a total asshole. Can you at least let me explain?"

"It's fine, Pete." She looked away impatiently. "Really, forget it. I should get going."

I shifted back and forth, my shoulders scrunched up to my ears, trying to get warm. The sun was setting, and I knew if I didn't say something now, I'd have blown it forever.

"Have dessert with me," I said plainly, trying to catch her eye that looked everywhere but at me.

When she looked up at me, her face scrunched up in confusion. "What?"

"Have dessert with me," I repeated. "Please?"

I could see her considering it, almost unable to resist the odd request.

"Look," I continued, "I really want to talk to you, but I can't fucking think when it's this cold. It's getting dark. And I'm hungry. So what do you say?"

I waited for what felt like an eternity for her to respond as a truck charged by blasting cold, dirty air over us.

"Alright," she said in a tone that implied she was giving in. "But only because it's so weird. Who eats dessert at five o'clock?"

Carla

I waited on the sidewalk for Pete to grab his things inside. Watching him through the shop's windows, I saw him bolt past Cliff. He then came out seeming a little jumpy, as if at any moment I was going to change my mind. *It's fine*, I wanted to tell him, *I'm not that much of a bitch.*

Out in the cold, I shifted awkwardly, unsure where to rest my eyes as he bundled up. Reaching inside the sleeve of his coat, he pulled out a chunky knit scarf and matching hat. Pale like wheat with flecks of dark brown and sky blue, he wrapped it around his neck twice and finally pulled the hat over his ears that had a pompom perched high like a birthday cake topper. "So I was thinking," he said as he pulled his zipper up, "we could walk?"

"Walk?"

"Yeah, it's not far, but that's if you're okay, actually." He looked at me, concerned. "That was some fall."

I ran my hand up my back to feel for bruises. With it a little tender from the fall and the wind chill factor minus five degrees outside, walking anywhere sounded certifiable. But looking at him wrapped up in his winter attire out there on the street, pompom and all, I guess I was curious.

"I'm okay," I said, hoping to sound unmoved. "Let's walk."

He held his arm out for me to hold on to, a gesture I only accepted to avoid falling again. With our arms linked, we walked cautiously down the street. It was one of those moments that if I saw a snapshot of it earlier that day, I wouldn't have believed it. Why would I be walking arm-in-arm with Pete Albrecht on the street? But as it was happening in real-time, it made sense. We passed storefronts, nail salons, a convenience store . . . all without speaking. I kept my head down, looking at my faded black Converse sneakers, and focused, maybe a little *too* intently, on each step.

After about ten minutes, he broke the awkward silence and said, "It's right up here." Next to the Entenmann's bakery outlet was a little European café I must have driven past thousands of times. He held the door open for me, and once inside, the warmth of the bakery consumed me like a hug. My family only went to the Italian bakery on Willis, but looking in the wraparound display case, I saw the familiars like the *pignoli* cookies and *sfogliatelle* we always bought too many of when we had company.

I looked over at Pete loosening his scarf while he eyed beyond the counter toward the back. His eyes then brightened when a young guy, tall and robust with thick hair pulled back in a ponytail, eased out from the kitchen.

"There he is," he said when he saw Pete. Walking around the counter, he reached his arm out, and the two guys gripped hands, pulling each other into a tight hug. "What's goin' on, my brother?"

"Not much. Trying not to freeze to death."

"Well, you came to the right place." The guy laughed as he shot a thumb toward the kitchen. "I'm roasting back there."

He then looked at me and then back at Pete, clearly expecting an introduction.

"Oh, hey, so this is Carla." He placed his hand on the sleeve of my coat and then looked at me and said, "And this is Miguel. One of the greatest bakers-slash-bassists you will ever meet."

"Nah, don't listen to this guy," Miguel said, blushing a little. "He just wants free shit."

"Nice to meet you," I said, laughing at his comment. "You make everything here?"

"Not everything, but most of it," he said with a modest shrug. "So," he looked back at Pete for a moment, "you from around here?"

"Yeah, Pete and I actually went to the same high school."

I felt Pete looking at me as I spoke to his friend, so I aimed my focus back to the pastries in the case.

"Hey, man," Pete then shifted his focus back to Miguel, "why haven't you been over to play? It's been forever. Now it's just Tony and me, and, like, fucking Mark when he decides to show up."

"You practice too late, man. I can't be getting to your house at, like, ten. That's when I go to bed if I'm gonna be here at four in the morning. I'm not even supposed to be here now. This is late for me."

"That's right. You said that. But damn, it's a shame." Pete shook his head, looking at Miguel in admiration.

"I know." Miguel sucked air in through his teeth as if it was painful. "But what are you gonna do?"

Practice earlier? I wanted to suggest but didn't. The three of us then looked at each other, waiting for someone to advance the conversation. "But what can I get you guys?"

Pete looked at me. "What looks good to you? Oh . . ." He turned to Miguel. "Is the espresso machine still on?"

Miguel nodded.

"Great. I'll have a double espresso." He then turned to me. "Do you want coffee?"

"Sure." I looked at Pete and then to Miguel, whom I felt more comfortable talking to. "Do you make cappuccino?"

"Of course."

"I'll have that with nonfat milk if it's not too much trouble," I said before scanning the pastries. "And maybe a cannoli?"

"You got it." Miguel nodded. "What else?"

Leaning down to look in the case, Pete said, "Also a pastel de nata, bolos de arroz." He looked at Miguel and grinned. "Don't laugh at my accent."

"I didn't say anything," Miguel said with his hands held up. "You wanna bring some baguettes home for your dad?"

"Oh yeah, shit, thanks for reminding me."

"I'll leave 'em up here for you at the counter, but the rest I'll bring over to you," Miguel said. "Go grab a table."

We passed the espresso counter and walked a few steps through the empty dining area. Nestled in the corner between a wall and the window was a small table with two wooden-backed chairs facing each other. Pete gestured to the table. "Is this good?"

Casually, he pulled my chair out and then started to peel off his outerwear as he rolled his neck therapeutically in both directions, making cracking sounds that made me wince. I took my coat off and hung it on the back of the chair and sat as Pete took his time settling in. I noticed his gestures were deliberate and almost graceful as he carefully folded his scarf and placed his coat on the back of his chair. I had been sitting already for several minutes by the time he finished. When he finally sat, he was still wearing his snow hat.

"So," he said.

"So," I repeated and then pointed to my head to remind him of his hat.

"Oh yeah." He looked a little embarrassed. "It's so warm I forget I'm still wearing it." After he pulled it off, which shot his dark hair in different directions, he looked at me with playful suspicion. "You think my hat's funny."

"No," I smirked. "I think it's cute."

He studied the hat and agreed. "It *is* kind of cute, isn't it? But I don't know. Maybe I should wear something more rugged, more manly to brave the cold." He set it back down and shrugged. "I just grab whatever's in the hallway closet."

"I remember your Mets snow hat you wore when we were kids."

"With the orange and blue pompom?" He seemed surprised. "You remember that?"

"I do." I said, hoping I didn't come across totally creepy for remembering his fifth-grade snow hat.

"I still have it, you know." He paused. "And wear it, even if it is a little nerdy."

"I don't know," I said. "I think it's cool, especially the pompom."

"Well, then it's settled." His eyes met mine, offering a smokey stare. "The pompom stays in the picture."

We looked at each other, and together we laughed. I remember liking his laugh; hearing it behind me in Health class when our teacher told us ludicrous stories we all thought were bullshit. Pete's laugh was full, deep, and a little gruff. But mostly, it was convincing, like he truly saw the absurdity or humor in something. I was feeling comfortable, but then in a sort of self-sabotage, I reminded myself we didn't know each other and pulled my eyes away. I stared at the wall with its painted flower mural while Pete looked out the window over my shoulder. Miguel then came with a tray, setting it down in the center of the table.

"You guys are sharing, right?" he asked the table.

Pete's eyes consulted mine. "If that's alright with you?"

It was. I wrapped my hands around the cappuccino Miguel set on the table, bringing it closer to my face to let the steam warm my cheeks.

"Alright, guys, enjoy. And if you need anything, just call out. I'll be in the back," Miguel said.

We both thanked him, looking at him — our safety anchor from each other — longer than necessary as we watched him walk away. Not knowing where to place my eyes since neither of us was talking, I stared into my coffee until he suddenly asked, "So, are you in school around here?"

"No, I'm not actually," I said in a guilty tone as if admitting to it. "I probably should be, though." I caught his eye, assuming to get the familiar look of pity, but instead, he nodded along as if it made sense. "What about you? You go to Post or something?"

"No," he responded less apologetically than me. "I'm not in school either."

"Really?" I said, slightly taken aback. "That surprises me, actually."

"Why's that?"

"I don't know. I guess I figured you would have gone to school for music. Or even gone away to, like, Berklee or something."

"Thanks." He looked away, scratching the back of his neck. "That's nice of you to say, but I'm not that good a musician."

"Really?" I raised my eyebrows. "I think you're pretty good, but what do I know about music?"

"You know plenty," he said, appearing uncomfortable. "I just applied to Nassau and went for, like, a second."

We sat for a few moments, not speaking, feeling the weight of each other's uncertain answers. I wondered if we shared the same fear of not having a real plan. At almost twenty-one, we *probably* should have been working toward something, but I could tell his reasoning had more to do with lack of interest where mine was that I just didn't think I was worth the tuition.

"Can I change the subject?" His eyes returned to mine.

"Please."

"So, I have a few random questions I like to ask fellow rock *enthusiasts*. Not a test or anything." He smirked. "Given your clear interest on the topic, I thought maybe you'd be up to it. You game?"

"Shoot."

"Favorite Beatles album?"

"*Rubber Soul*," I said without having to think about it. "You?"

"*Revolver.*" I nodded in agreement because that would be my second if *Rubber Soul* didn't feel like the home I always wanted; its oaky, backwoods sound reminding me of a cabin I had never been to.

"*Rolling Stone, Spin,* or other?"

"Out of the two, I'd pick *Spin,* but I like *Q* even if it costs almost fifteen bucks at Tower Records."

"British rock press." He raised his eyebrows. "Nice."

"And you?"

"*Rolling Stone* and also the *Voice,* even if I think Christgau is fucking brutal in his reviews. Everything I like gets a ticking bomb, or he deems not even worth a review in his wacky rating system, which I guess has its own entertainment value."

"Yeah," I said, knowing about the picky rock critic. "He hates Babes in Toyland."

"Babes in Toyland," he repeated. "Girl groups have the best names." He slid the plate closer to me in acknowledgment of me not eating. "Okay, so since you read *Q,*" he continued. "Blur or Oasis?"

"Elastica." I offered a sly smile.

"Touché."

"You?"

"Hands down, Blur," he said. "Damon's new group Gorillaz is what's really taking us into the new Millennium. Well, that and *Kid A;* none of this boy band crap."

"Agreed." I thought with quiet surprise that he didn't only listen to weird hippie music.

"So," he then said. "We obviously listen to different shit, but what was the album that did it for you where you were like music is essential to survival?"

"It's kind of a long answer."

"I like long answers." His eyes looked at me again in that way.

"Okay, so for my eighth birthday," I said, going for it, "my parents got me Billy Joel's *The Stranger* on cassette. I wanted it because 'Only the Good Die Young' was a Color War song from camp that summer, and I planned to only listen to that one song and maybe, I don't know, 'Scenes from an Italian Restaurant.'"

"Okay."

"When I got sick of the songs, I decided to let the tape just play. It was the first time I had actually listened to an album entirely through." I looked at him. "As ridiculous as that sounds."

"Anyway," I continued. "The first track on side two is this pretty little song called 'Vienna,' and in my opinion, it's the best song on the entire album with lyrics that felt like they were about me." I took a deep inhale. "I mean, I haven't done much travel and feel like, I don't know, I might not make it to Vienna, but heck, I'd take California."

"Well, the song did its job, didn't it?" His eyes smiled at me.

"What do you mean?"

"If you felt the lyrics were written practically for you, then Billy Joel wrote a great song."

"He did." I crinkled my nose in agreement. "So I'm not done."

"Oh." He raised his hands apologetically. "Please, continue."

"So, from there, you know, this grand revelation of listening to *entire albums*." I laughed at myself. "I started listening to all my tapes, and on the Pretenders' *Pretenders* album, I listened beyond 'Brass in Pocket' and came across *the* song that made me want to be in a band."

"Which was?" he said, leaning forward, his arms resting on the table as he hung on my every word.

"'Mystery Achievement,' of course," I said as I imagined the killer opening bass line. "And that was my gateway into girl rock like Blondie B-sides, The Runways, then on to 7 Year Bitch, Sonic Youth, which was then *another* gateway into indie girl rock like Helium, Geraldine Fibbers."

"So, the Pretenders album was your rock enlightenment?"

"No," I said with a tinge of impatience. "It was *Live Through This* by Hole."

Looking like I had just put him through the spin cycle, I watched him try to connect the dots from Billy Joel to Hole, which I could tell he fell short. Not wanting to burden him with the details, I summed it up, "*Live Through This* is basically my *Rumours*," I offered, which appeared to make sense to him as his eyes lit up in reference to the classic Fleetwood Mac album. "I don't know. My aunts were obsessed with it."

"Not your mom?" he asked, squinting his eyes, trying to catch some piece of information.

"My mom doesn't listen to music," I said. "And you, what album did it for you to see the error of your suburban ways?"

He looked at me with amused and curious eyes as he laughed at my comment.

"Well?" I said, basking in the satisfaction of his response.

"*Bitches Brew,* hands down," he responded. "I didn't know what hit me after I listened to it." He looked off in recollection. "Sometimes I wish I could go back in time and hear it again for the first time to feel those goosebumps up my arm again and to feel disoriented yet clear, as if everything suddenly made sense."

"I've never heard it," I said. "It's a jazz album, right?"

"Yes and no. So it was released only three months into the '70s; it was like this kiss-off to the traditional jazz standards of the '50s and '60s, where it's as much a rock and funk album as it is a jazz album. There are electric guitars, keyboards, those muscular echoes on his trumpet. They fucked with the French editing technique called musique concrète, where recorded tracks were fine-sliced and *then* pieced together. Like, literal pieces of tape containing pure genius were processed with effects light years ahead of its time. They were then assembled to create this architecture of sound. You know what I mean?"

"No." I stared at him. "I don't."

"Well, this kind of technique was unheard of for jazz at the time since recordings were done live," he continued, trying to explain it to my blank face. "But nerdy analysis aside, it's made me feel okay with being, I guess, different somehow. And I know everyone thinks they're different, and maybe I'm some self-absorbed asshole, but this album just made me feel okay." He looked away for a second before reverting his eyes back to mine. "As for seeing the error of my suburban ways" — he tossed his eyes up for a second — "I think I'm still learning."

After letting myself get comfortable, he brought up his girlfriend, which felt like he had dropped a brick in the middle of the table. I guess I assumed he wasn't still with her, which immediately made me feel dumb and shocked me back into my defensiveness.

I felt weird...because if I didn't know any better, I'd think I was on a great first date with someone else's boyfriend.

Pete

Looking at her from across the table, at first, I could tell she was uncomfortable because she barely ate. But after some conversation, she was cool. She had this dry yet animated way about her. I liked the way she talked with her hands and spoke with her eyes. I felt good about being with her until I totally nerded out on the *Bitches Brew* thing— *musique concrète!*—come on! I made a mental note to have more accessible responses in the future.

"So don't get mad, but I think you're an amazing guitarist."

"Why would that make me mad?" Her eyes bled into mine.

"I don't know." I stumbled a bit. "It's just, um, you seemed, well, annoyed when I brought it up before."

"Well, just don't sound so surprised. You don't have to be in a *jam band* to know how to play an instrument well."

"Of course not, and I'm sorry, really, if it came out that way. It wasn't my intent." I took a long pause and then said, "Also, I really am sorry I never got in touch. I still feel like a dick."

"Oh," she said dismissively. "It's fine. Besides, I probably needed those extra months of practice."

"But the least I could have done was stop in your store to talk to you. It's just that the holidays came around, and I had to do all this shit with Allison, and then I just went up to see her, and whatever. Things just got super busy. But I'm sorry."

And instantly, her manner changed. Her body that was leaning toward me pulled back. Her hand placed across the table, sitting inches away from mine, slipped back into her lap. Immediately, I regretted bringing Allison up. Not that I wanted to hide that I was in a serious relationship, but it seemed to suck the air out of the conversation. She withdrew, retracted the warm eye contact I had been enjoying up until that moment, and tucked her hands under her legs.

"What time is it?" she said, looking off into the distance as if focusing on something important over my shoulder.

"About 6:15."

"Already?" She jumped up. "I have to get going. I have to help my family with dinner."

She opened her bag and reached for her wallet when I put my hand out to stop her. "Please. It's on me."

"It's fine, Pete," she said, trying to still sound casual and friendly.

"Really." I stood up. "I insist. I dragged you out on this cold night. Upset you *again* . . . "

"I'm not upset," she said, looking down.

"Right, of course, you're not. It's just, let me." I echoed the soft timbre in her voice. "Please."

"Okay," she almost whispered, lowering her wallet back into her bag.

"Hey, so." I was hoping to sound natural. "What are you doing tomorrow?"

"What?" Her eyes trailed off in disbelief as she stifled a laugh.

"What are you doing tomorrow?"

She didn't respond. She just looked at me with intense eyes, waiting for me to continue my thought.

"Let's start over."

"Start over?"

"Yes. Will you come over so we can play together? Notice I didn't say jam this time?"

Ignoring my joke, she continued looking at me with steely eyes.

"No phone numbers, phone calls, AOL bullshit. Just be at my house at 8:30. Tomorrow."

She remained silent, looking at me like I was crazy. So I stared back, looking at her like *she* was crazy. How were we *not* going to do this? She then focused too much attention on putting her coat on, pulling her five feet of hair out of the back. When I thought she was going to completely blow me off and walk out, she turned back to me and, with a look that said she knew she was going to regret it, said, "Are you still on Grant?"

And that was that. I had one girl less pissed off at me. Now, all I had to do was answer to the other.

Carla

Saying yes to him, I knew immediately it was going to be one of those things that would either lead to something great or something I would deeply regret. There wasn't going to be a middle ground on this, a passing anecdote I'd recall one day. There was something very "turning point" about the whole thing. Metaphorically, I pinched my nose and dove off the diving board because we were about to explore something together, but what, exactly, I wasn't sure.

8

Pete

The next day at work, I couldn't think about anything else. The entire day I had been mentally composing little drum phrases I knew she'd have a melodic response to. While watching the espresso drip the last order of my shift, I got nervous about Allison. I didn't tell her about any of it because I didn't think I had to. *Yet.* I did, however, invite Tony to come, not because I thought he could really add anything since both our levels surpassed his but should this lead to something, musically, of course, I could say he had always been there.

I knew I had a problem when I was already defending myself.

Carla

Before heading out to Pete's, I had the kitchen to myself to clear dinner while my family disbanded to different corners of the house. With the radio tuned to Oldies 101.1, I pretended I worked at a roadside diner somewhere warm and exotic. Singing along to "Love Is Like an Itching in My Heart" by The Supremes, I gazed out the window as I washed dishes. Looking past my reflection and at the snow flurries starting to fall, I wondered about changing my clothes. It seemed like a dumb thing to be concerned about, but what do you wear to play music with a guy you don't know if you like or not?

"What are you doing?" My mom's voice stung me from behind, making the hair on my arms stand. I turned around to find her holding an empty glass in her hand and peering at me with eyes that needed to sleep it off. I tried to make my face as soft as possible.

"What do you mean?" I responded.

"Do you know how loud you are being? You're slamming things around in here." She then turned her focus to the radio. "And why are you listening to music so loud at this hour?"

"Slamming things around?" I said, which came out more defensively than I had wanted it to. "A plate I was rinsing off slipped out of my hand in the sink. It didn't break, though." I walked over to the radio and turned the volume dial until it clicked off. "Sorry about the music."

"You know what, Carla." She swayed from side to side. "You have an answer for everything, don't you? And frankly, I've had enough of it."

"I don't. I'm just responding to your question."

"And you're gonna continue the disrespect. I never spoke to my mother the way you speak to me, you know that?"

"I'm sorry," I said, hoping it sufficed.

She looked around the room for something else to find fault in, but the kitchen was spotless as if it *was* an actual restaurant. "I just have to say, I don't like your attitude these days. I find you extremely disrespectful," she said, looking at me in disgust. "It's like you're not even here. What the hell is going on up there?"

Having already lived through lengthy conversations about the disappointment of the person I had become, I knew there was no response to satisfy her with. I had to play the situation right, though, if I wanted to get out of there...but every response tested and failed. If I apologized, I was placating her. If I said nothing, I was a bitch. If I tried to stay positive, I was being flippant. If I tried to apply the logic that no one spoke to me anyway, we would go around in circles until we were talking about something that happened in 1998.

"I'm sorry, work has just been busy. I don't mean to be distant." I mentally crossed my fingers.

"Well, he has you working too many hours. Why don't you learn to speak up for yourself sometimes? God damn it." She then turned to the counter and filled her glass. With her focus off me for a second, I inched my eye over to the microwave to see it was now 8:25.

"You know what your problem is, Carla?"

"What's that, Mom?"

"You're so quiet, but you come off like you think you're hot shit, like you're better than everyone."

If only that were partially true, I thought with lowered eyes. Claudio then walked into the kitchen and, seeing the stand-off between my mom and me, said, "What's goin' on?"

"Just your sister again," my mom said in exasperation as she took a sip from her stemless glass.

I looked at my brother, who knew about the practice, and with my eyes magnified, I begged him for help.

"What are we gonna do with her, huh?" He forced an upbeat tone, looking at me apologetically for mock-siding with her. "But come on, Mom, watch TV with me and Lo. They keep playing a commercial for that *Women of Camelot* movie you wanted to see."

"I *do* want to see that."

"I know, I know." He walked my mom out and turned back at me and mouthed the word, "Go."

I ran up to my room and, keeping the white mohair sweater I already had on, sprayed some Vanilla Bean body splash under my pits and brushed my bangs down. With my gear already loaded in the car, I quietly grabbed my coat and slipped out the back door.

I was at Pete's less than five minutes later. Before turning the car off, my heart raced from both escaping my mom and in anticipation of our first practice. Watching the flurries swell into full-on snowflakes on my windshield, I sat in the cold car waiting for "I Must Not Think Bad Thoughts" by X to finish as I tried to absorb the advice. My hands shook a little as I pulled the keys out of the ignition.

Gripping my guitar case, I walked across the freshly fallen snow on his driveway, taking small steps, careful not to fall again.

Pete

It was about 8:20. I waited in my basement with my foot tapping and my eyes alternating between the clock and the door. To think about something else, I reached for my needles and yarn on the coffee table. As I began casting my next project, I contemplated who would be the first to arrive. Part of me was hoping it was Carla, but Allison would have flipped if she knew I was alone with her in the basement, which was why the other half of me hoped it was Tony. The whole thing was a mind fuck I couldn't understand.

As I snaked the yarn ferociously around the needle, I created more problems in my head to find solutions to, like if I should have put out snacks. Girls liked snacks, right? My mom had fat-free Snackwell cookies in the cabinet, but I didn't want Carla to think I thought she was fat; in fact, she looked a lot thinner than I remembered in high school. There was also my dad's *charcuterie*, and as natural as offering a spread of cured meats was to me, I had experienced enough crooked faces in my time to know American kids thought it was weird. Well, except for Tony, who usually asked if I "got any prosciutto up in this shit." The goal for the night was to keep things as normal as possible. Although the combination of Tony and me didn't exactly offer an iron-clad guarantee.

I heard the side gate, the handle, letting out a creaking sound that never made me anxious before. I put down my needles. When the footsteps began their descent down the concrete stairs, I didn't know what to do with myself. It was then I changed my mind. I wasn't part-hoping it was Carla; the hope was resolute. I resolutely wanted it to be her. I had worn my faded yellow Devo t-shirt to show I didn't just listen to jam bands, but I had to cover it with an off-white fisherman's sweater my parents got me in Ireland because I was freezing. I got up and walked toward the door, dramatically watching the handle turn. But when it opened, it was just Tony in the doorway stuffed in his puffer coat, looking cold and confused.

"Hey, man, come in." I brushed some of the snow off his coat. "Is it coming down hard?"

I looked up the stairs to my backyard and, in the floodlights, could see large flecks of snow steadily falling.

"It's just starting to pick up. It was still flurrying when I left my house, but now it's fully snowing." Tony took his coat off and hung it on the coat rack my parents insisted on. I didn't understand its purpose since I figured that was what couches were for until the first time I had friends over on a rainy night.

"What's going on?"

"That's what I was gonna ask you." Tony walked over to his bass that leaned against the wall and thumbed a few strings before turning back to me. "Why are we getting together tonight? It's Thursday. We got a show or something?"

"When do we ever have a show?"

"I don't know, man. This is just out of the norm is all I'm sayin'."

"I should have told you on the phone, but we have a guitarist coming to play with us tonight."

"Okay, but that still doesn't answer my question. Even when we do find people to play with, it's always on Monday. Who do we have comin'? Fuckin' Slash, who's only available tonight?"

"No, Tony." I looked at him with a tired expression. "Slash isn't coming to my basement tonight. I think he might be busy with the Snake Pit."

"Nah, man, he's getting G n' R back together," said Tony, looking at me like I was so out of touch.

"Whatever. My point is he's not coming."

Before I could tell him who *was* coming to let him air out any dirty comments, he noticed my knitting gear and said, "I'm still waitin' on my hat, ya know." He gestured to the small basement window starting to collect snow. "Coulda come in handy on a night like this."

"Your head's too big." I flicked my chin upward. "It'll take me a year."

"We got a wise guy over *hea*." He gritted his teeth and playfully jutted his shoulders forward.

"But no, really," I said, setting a more serious tone. "You didn't pick your yarn out yet."

Then we heard the side gate creak open, shortly followed by footsteps that I swear sounded smaller than Tony's. Rubbing his hands together in anticipation, he said, "The mystery guitarist arrives." He then lifted and lowered his eyebrows suggestively.

"That's the face you make when you think you're going to be playing with Slash." I grinned.

"Nah, nah." He straightened his face out to a more neutral expression.

Standing side-by-side, in line with the door, we looked at each other as if we had never answered a door before. Like a pair of morons, we waited for the knock, our eyes darting back and forth to one another. For a moment, we didn't hear anything, and Tony looked at me as if I should deliver an explanation. I didn't know; I shrugged. My heart was pounding so hard I wondered if he could hear it.

"Oh man," Tony said, shifting his weight. "It's like I can't even take it anymore. Who are we playing with tonight?"

"Well, it's not Slash, so stop nudging me like that."

Then, ever so softly, there was a meek knock on the door, and the two of us shouted, "Come in!"

The door then creaked open, and there she was, wearing a light-blue wool coat and white earmuffs. Her cheeks blushed from the cold, and the freshly fallen snow on top of her raven hair looked like coconut flakes.

"Hey, guys," she said, looking suspicious. When she realized it was Tony, she stretched her arms out. "Tony!"

"Carla?" Tony turned to me. "*That's* our mystery guitarist tonight? After all that?" Tony walked over to her to give her a hug. "Hi, sweetie, how's it going?"

"I didn't know you'd be here. I'm so happy to see you!" she said in his arms.

"Me neither," he said over her shoulder, aimed in my direction. "How's everyone?"

She released herself from the hug but kept her mitten-covered hands resting affectionately on his big arms. I took the opportunity to hide my knitting gear under the table. "Family's the same," Carla responded to Tony. "Yours?"

"Same," Tony said, and together they nodded in some kind of unspoken understanding. "Tell them I say hello and that my ma has been meaning to call yours."

"So," I interrupted them. "I, uh, hope it's okay that I invited Tony to play with us tonight?"

"Okay?" she said with delight as she began to unbutton her coat. "It's great." She then scanned the room, eyeing the equipment I already had.

"Anyway, I brought an amp, which I left in the car because I figured I may not need it?"

"No, you don't need it. Everything works, so pick one. Here, why don't you plug into this one?" I pointed to a Fender 65 Twin Reverb. "This isn't all mine, by the way." I felt the need to add. "People have a habit of leaving their gear down here. And that amp you're about to plug into used to be my neighbor's."

"Okay," she said, appearing to be both overwhelmed and unconcerned by the origins of the equipment. "Sounds good."

I was rambling and thought the best thing was to shut the fuck up and let them set up while I smoked a cigarette on the couch. I was so nervous while she was, as usual, so relaxed and cool. As I waited, focusing in and out of their conversations as they went on about things like "Sunday Sauce," I smoked, purposefully avoiding eye contact with Tony. I could feel his eyes burning into me, like he was on to me. For what, exactly, I wasn't sure. But he was on to me.

After another fifteen minutes and another smoke, it got quiet, and I could feel them waiting for me. "You ready, man?" Tony said, plucking a few notes on his bass.

I stamped out my cigarette and turned around, but when I saw her standing there with her *gratte* over her shoulder, I couldn't believe it. With her eyes down to adjust the volume, her hair dangled over her orange Telecaster; the hue was vibrant and nostalgic like Sunset Boulevard in the 70s. Looking up, her flash of blue eyes smiling at me and motioning to my kit of the same color, she said, "We match."

"I see that." I was careful not to express too much excitement over aesthetics. "Anyway," I said, clearing my throat. "Shall we?"

Still avoiding Tony's eye contact, I pulled my sweater off over my head and settled in on my throne, giving my neck and shoulders a few rolls before giving my kick a few pounds with my foot. I looked up, and there was a collective nod passed among the three of us to indicate we were all ready.

Carla got things going with some blues chord progressions I attached a simple beat to. Immediately we synced up as she kept her eye on Tony, slowing her pace to gently guide him into the groove. Once he was in, I figured to just let the music go where it needed to go, like at the music store. I watched in awe as her fingers danced up and down the neck. I listened as her melody lines did some time travel, almost like an autobiographical tour of her influences with chord changes that sounded familiar and sweet.

Playing around, she worked in some soloing I could tell she was still getting used to but created a nice sound that was a little bluesy and—she'd kill me if she heard me—at times, a little jammy. I then worked in some repetitions by settling on a beat, keeping the timing steady and precise on my snares. I watched her fingers respond, and from there, we built the sound together. It started feeling like a melodic conversation, notes rife with meaning as she moved closer and closer to my kit. Even though there was this sonic energy between us, I wouldn't look at her and kept my head down, using only my drums to communicate in this primitive phase of our acquaintance.

Two hours later, with the minute hand inching toward eleven o'clock, we drew the session to a close. I tossed my sticks on the floor, pressed my shoulders back, and inhaled deeply through my nose since I didn't recall breathing the entire time. Parched and sweaty, I looked over at her. She was no better than I was as I could make out the shape of her pulling the neck of her sweater to let air in.

After slipping my glasses back on, our eyes met.

"Hi," they said to hers.

Looking back at me, not moving as if hypnotized, her eyes blinked, "Hi."

From there, I couldn't move. I couldn't speak. And I just absorbed her, watching the profound rise and fall of her chest as she looked into me as I was looking into her. Her eyes then flickered with gratification and pulled away.

"Bravo, guys!" said Tony, spread out on the couch, a can of soda in his hand.

Oh shit, I thought as I looked over, Tony's still here.

Carla

Basements for band practice were supposed to be dank and creepy, with bugs festering and hatching in dark corners. Pete's basement, though, was immaculate with finished details, like the thick, beige wall-to-wall carpet and built-in shelves painted in an ivory semi-gloss lined with rows and rows of vinyl and CDs. With equipment lined up everywhere, there were amps in all sizes and brands, guitars both fancy and ones beaten up, cords tidily coiled in dairy crates, and effect pedals that intimidated me. I had to find my place in this world that I still didn't feel I had enough talent to be a part of. The sparkly orange Gretsch, however, made me feel like I may just be in the right place after all because how was it even possible?

I settled in with the amp he had offered and then placed my focus on my true love in the room: My Telecaster, a total babe, if I may say, who practically winks at me when I flip the case open. When Pete turned around and saw me, he looked stunned to see me with the orange guitar. I knew his delight was for the color, but I couldn't help but like the way he was looking at me.

I thought I'd be nervous, but the second I had my guitar on with Pete behind the kit, all my discomfort about playing with him dissolved. We instantly found each other, playing around with melodies, dipping through valleys, and making a few twists and turns before landing on this super-cool-sounding, steady rhythm. I glanced over at him to see him with his glasses off, his hair messier than before, and his body moving soulfully in rhythm with his eyes down and deep in thought. Without realizing it, I had gravitated closer and closer to him, with my shoulders pulled back and my chest feeling like it was absorbing him. It was like I couldn't get close enough to his sound I already felt bonded to. I may have been terrible at communicating with actual words, but with my guitar, I could express myself through the music.

When I got to my car, I sat in it, practically vibrating over our time together. I had no idea something like that could even happen. And who knew if we were any good or not, it didn't matter. I didn't need to qualify the experience with a critique because, for the first time in my life, I felt like I was on a wavelength with someone else. This was the kind of experience you would read about in, like, *Rolling Stone* with famous musicians. Not from two kids in a basement on Long Island who had just reconnected years after not even being friends in high school. If I had smoked, I would have lit a cigarette because this was much better than the three times I'd had sex. It was also better than a crush.

And to think I was worried about what I wore that night.

Pete

"Now I *know* why you wanted me to come tonight," Tony said as soon as we heard the side gate close. "Allison would freakin' murder you if you hadn't."

"No," I said defensively. "That's not why. I don't even know what you're talking about."

"Oh, you know exactly what I'm talking about, homie."

"Don't call me homie."

"Whatever you say." He was clearly not buying it. "You a dog, man."

"Okay, I'll take homie over that." I winced at having to choose between the two.

I blew off his theory with a wave of my hand and said, "Let's listen to music because I can't handle TV right now."

"Alright, but none of that oldies shit you like."

"Well, I'm not putting on Slayer if that's what you had in mind." I got up and walked over to the shelves to browse through what I had.

"Hey, what's wrong with *Slaya*?"

"For one, I don't have anything by them." I scanned the shelves thinking of a compromise between Slayer and Tony's claim that I listened to "oldies," which I think was supposed to mean the Kinks, Chuck Berry, Count Basie; some records in my regular rotation I'd usually turn off as soon as he arrived.

"Anyway, let's go back to your problem."

"I don't have a problem," I said distractedly.

As I half-listened to him, I made quick assessments of my collection and Tony's needs. What did Tony need at this moment? Was it King Crimson? No, too sentimental. Well, for me anyway. Zeppelin? Too easy. Zappa? Too unpredictable. Nirvana? Too loud. Tori Amos? Just kidding. I wasn't trying to blow his mind or anything but wanted him to hear something different and change his mind that I was someone who qualified to be called "homie." After being with Carla, whose eerie beauty put me in a trance-like state, Sonic Youth's *EVOL* was calling to me, but Tony would *not* have known what to do with that. I decided on Yes's *Fragile*—the more pop and upbeat of my favorite prog-rock albums. I knew I made the right decision when "Roundabout" kicked in and Tony stopped talking and did an air drum thing that didn't make any sense.

I have found people can be so rhythmically irresponsible when they air drum. First off, the imaginary kit is usually spread out too far in front of them so that if they were really playing, they'd barely reach the kick; the crash cymbals are usually too low, the high hat is in some odd place, and there is never a time signature. Okay . . . maybe I was overthinking it. Anyway, my point was, I did good on *Fragile* and Tony stopped calling me homie.

Once the novelty of the album opener wore off, I grabbed my practice drumming pad to work out how I was feeling with my hands. Easing in with a Swiss army triplet, I then went straight into a double drag tap, a rudiment I played when I was nervous.

"Really, man." Tony nudged me. "What are you gonna do?"

Looking up from my pad as I continued to follow the beat, I considered what he was saying and looked at the floor as if I was going to find my answer there. "I guess I do have a little bit of a problem on my hands."

"A little?" He chortled. "That's an understatement."

I put my sticks down and turned to him. "Okay, look. Don't make me regret asking," I said cautiously. "But—"

"But what would I do?"

I nodded.

"Well, if Allison is as crazy—"

"Hold on!" I held my hands out to stop him. "I never said she was crazy. Rephrase, like, immediately."

"Alright, alright," he started. "If she's as *concerned*..." He looked at me to see if that word was okay to use. I nodded it was. "If she's as *concerned* as you think she will be, if I were you..." He looked at me again to make sure I was following. "I'd tell her..." I leaned forward in anticipation, waiting for this sage advice he was about to give.

"You'd tell her what?"

"I'd tell her ... to Get. The. Fuck. Ova. It."

"God damn it, Tony!" I swatted his shoulder with my hand.

"Well, I'm sorry!" He threw his arms out. "What do you want me to say? What I saw tonight was fuckin' destiny or whateva you wanna call it. And if you pass this up, I'd say you're a fuckin' idiot, okay?"

"It was something else, wasn't it?" I looked at him. "She's really good."

"She is. I had no freakin' idea she was that good. I bumped into her brother Lo at Ceriello's a few weeks ago, and he told me she was playing a little, but he didn't say she was killin' it. But that doesn't surprise me. She doesn't get credit for nothin' in that family. Being the youngest *and* a girl? Forget about it. It's like she's not even there. And Carla's mom? Fuckin' brutal, man."

"That's terrible," I said, surprised. "Is she okay?"

"I guess. I mean, it is what it is."

"Wow." I felt completely naïve about unsupportive families. "I really had no idea."

"Don't worry about it. She's tough. She's Italian," he said as if that solved things. "And hey, I'm just gonna come out and say it because you won't, but Carla is kind of a fox, which is why this shit is about to get complicated."

"Oh, stop. It's not about that," I said, wondering if I even believed me anymore.

As much as I tried to discredit Tony's claims, he was on the nose with all of them. Carla *was* an incredible guitarist, and if I passed up this opportunity, I would be a fucking idiot. And yes, she was kind of hot. But it wasn't her looks that made me want to play with her. At first, okay, I was intrigued, but after that first practice, I realized my attraction to her was going to be more of an inconvenience.

Carla

I walked into work early the following morning feeling both groggy and wired. I had never been hung over before, but this was how I imagined it. I stayed awake the night before, staring at my thoughts through closed eyelids. Processing the details, like the faint burnt smell of the space heater; the way his glasses fogged up when he put them back on; the extensive vinyl collection I was almost scared to look at in case he had terrible taste. As for my part, I was somewhat satisfied with my playing but knew where I could improve with a smoother transition or a more challenging riff. But Pete, he was just brilliant; there was something about the way he played I found, well, kind of sexy. He didn't play with his ego by smashing his sticks across the kit, something I knew he was capable of. Instead, he was almost delicate, a word I never thought I'd use to describe a rock drummer. I noticed how he would land on a static beat and settle in with it, and through repetition, he would slowly evolve and build the sound with me like a real collaboration.

As I leaned over to check the developing solution in the machines, I suddenly became anxious. Anxious if it was ever going to happen again. We left off saying we would get together some time, but without exchanging numbers, I worried we were going to have to wait for another chance run-in. Fate had already nudged us together twice that I felt hoping for a third was pushing it. He also had a girlfriend, so I had to tread lightly and wait for a sign from him. When I realized the machine wasn't plugged in, I lowered myself to the ground. On hands and knees pushing the heavy plug into the socket, I kept my eyes closed to avoid looking at the glue mousetrap in the corner. As I grunted in effort, pushing the plug further in, the doorbell chimed, and I screamed, "Just a sec!"

When I glanced over my shoulder, I found Pete leaning on the counter, looking almost as tired as me. Balancing myself up from the floor, I tried to read his face.

"Hey," I said guardedly.

"Hey."

I immediately softened when I saw his eyes smile through his glasses. I smoothed my crinkled lab coat down and approached him from my side of the counter.

"So that was great last night," he said.

"Yeah." I slightly blushed. "It was."

"Wanna do it again tonight?" He looked away for a second. "And you know, Tony can come too."

"Um, sure."

"Cool," he said matter-of-factly. "See you then. 8:30 again."

He walked out of the store, the bell chiming behind him. And there it was. There was my sign.

9

Pete

Three months later, we had a band. Not jazz ensemble or practice. But a band. We didn't let our disparate tastes divide us. We let them challenge us, like how can we make this work without sounding like total dog shit with a fuzz box? With our rivaling influences, though, let's just say it wasn't always easy.

I finally told Allison, who, as expected, hated everything about me making music with a girl. When I explained we *did* want Tony in the band, but he didn't have the skill, she said, "For a basement band, Pete?" which made me laugh.

Carla and I got together every day. Hold on: every day except for Sunday, when she went to church with her grandmother and then had to help her family prepare to eat pasta all day. I went a few times, and while her family was warm and generous to me, I noticed they talked around her almost like she wasn't there. The older uncles called each other WOPs — without papers — which to my shock, *no one* found at all offensive, and Carla did the dishes and sort of stayed out of the way.

One night, she had to drive me home after I drank Uncle Leo's basement wine that apparently got people pregnant. Even in the haze of having one too many, I turned to her and said, "You know I see you, right?"

She laughed. "I see you too, Pete. And you're blitzed."

"No, you know what I mean," I said, trying to be serious but was pretty sure I had one eye closed.

"I do. Now get some sleep. I'll IM you in the morning," she joked.

"Please don't," I griped. "You know how I feel about that shit. It's artificial communication." I then leaned my head back against the seat and gazed out the window, remembering a quote I loved. "'Don't use the phone,'" I said. "'People are never ready to answer it. Use poetry.'" I then rolled my head toward Carla, who appeared entertained. "Jean-Louis Lebris de Kérouac."

"Okay, *Kerouac*," she said, still grinning as she reached over me to grab the door handle. The smell of her sweet hand cream she put on after we practiced permeated my senses, and a brush of her hair dragged across my arm as she returned to her side. "I'll see you tomorrow?"

"*A demain, mon petit chat.*"

The following day at my house, we had a serious discussion about lyrics. Mainly that we needed them. Otherwise, we really were a jam band, a term that made her face prune up like a raisin. Naturally, I thought she would take care of this because she was going to sing. But when I brought the topic up, she looked at me like I was crazy.

"We're *both* writing the lyrics," she said pointedly as she lowered herself next to me on the couch.

"Wait, really?"

"Really." She gave me a supportive smile. "I feel like you have more to say."

"Well, I always have more to say, but I don't know. I guess it never occurred to me, being a drummer." I then thought about lyrics and how they always mystified me. Prose, and even poetry, had a sequence, almost a formula to follow, but with lyrics, it really felt like no-man's-land where they're either great or just plain awful with little room for an in-between.

"Give it a go," she offered. "You may surprise yourself."

"Okay, but" — I held my finger up — "I'm not writing fucking love songs."

"Then don't." She laughed.

"Bathing in the sea, sunsets, standing on mountains, forever, and all that corny shit," I said, shaking my head recalling the songs that tortured me when I worked at Cedarhurst Paper. "Well, hold on," I added. "There are some exceptions like "The Last Goodbye" by Jeff Buckley. Now *that's* a great love song."

"You think that's a love song?" She widened her eyes. "It's about saying goodbye."

"No." I shook my head. "You have it all wrong. It's the last goodbye because they're going to stay together, so there will be no more goodbyes. You see?"

"Or it's the last goodbye because they've said goodbye so many times that this is the last one." She then looked off for a second to consider it. "I mean, I'd like to be optimistic and see it with your romantic vision." Her eyes glinted in my direction. "But the lyrics don't lie, especially when he flat out says it's over."

"If you insist." I turned my head toward hers on the couch. "My point is, though, when done improperly, love songs can be terrible in rock music, which I fear I'd contribute to."

"How about then" — she pressed her cheek on the couch, leaning in closer to me— "you write the worst rock song ever written."

The worst rock song ever written? I liked that. That night I did the assignment. I didn't even get stoned beforehand. Sitting at my desk with the green lamp that made me feel like Mr. Belvedere, I set out to write the worst rock song ever written. Like some corny-ass love song that would make people's eyes roll out in gory disgust of my *feelings*. But what came out on paper wasn't some proclamation for my girlfriend but things I didn't want to be feeling...but couldn't help. It was as if the words were spilling out of my pen while my fingers were unable to keep up with my thoughts.

The next day in my basement, we sat on the floor and exchanged lyrics. Sitting side-by-side, we read each other's words as if walking the halls through each other's imaginations.

As she flipped through my pages, she pressed her palm down on my words as if absorbing them. She then looked at me with clear eyes and declared, "I knew it. You *are* lyrically gifted," which made my cheeks feel a little warm because gifted? Let's not get crazy. "You have a real knack for turning a phrase. You really know how to cleverly express love and confusion, not to mention these pastoral images about romantic summers past." She flipped through the pages again and read more before looking back up at me with pleased eyes.

If I was emotional, then she was otherworldly. As if from a notebook of black magic and sorcery, her lyrics evoked vivid imagery that danced across the page in brushes of imaginary color. My lyrics were based on experiences, unintentionally looking back, while hers looked forward to adventures and places she had only imagined. I looked at this odd and beautiful creature, who had a dreamlike aura around her, who then turned to me and said, "So now the question is, who is going to sing these wonderful words?"

Oh, for fuck's sake.

Carla

I knew eventually one of us would have to sing. I guess I got so excited about the writing assignment that it didn't occur to me who would be doing what. When I sort of suggested to him that he could sing, trying to get him to do it like I got him to write the songs, I didn't have as good of luck.

"No," he said without giving it even a single thought. "I am not going to be the dickhead, beating the drums and fucking singing. Do you know how lame that looks?"

He had a point. It did look kind of dorky when drummers sang. But this was where it got complicated because *I* wasn't a singer. I had no business thinking I could get in front of people with something to say. It went against who I was as a person. Singing original songs with only him felt, I don't know, really personal. Almost like kissing. Clearly, we'd have to find another way.

"I'm not saying this just because I'm trying to get out of singing," he said sweetly. "But I think you'd be great." He then looked at me, waiting for a response, but I felt embarrassed by his confidence in me. "No?" He tried to establish eye contact. But the conversation felt like it was getting bigger than I wanted it to, so I got up.

"I don't get you." I changed the subject as I walked over to his vinyl collection.

"What do you mean?"

"Well, I've been eyeballing your records for some time now, and how do you have The Germs *GI* and then, like, *Ill Communication* on vinyl?" I looked at him, almost accusing him of having good taste. "And what is this?" I pulled out a CD and held it up. "*OK Computer*?"

"What do you mean?" He walked over to me, looking sincerely confused.

"Well," I scoffed, pointing to a CD called *Junta*. "You listen to *Phish*."

"Why are you saying Phish in italics?"

"What?" I laughed.

"I listen to a lot of things. For one, *OK Computer* is totally our generation's *Dark Side*, so everyone born between '75 and '83 should own it. But really, I'm not wed to one genre." He took the Germs record out of my hand and studied it. "Well." He thought for a second. "Okay, not exactly. I don't really listen to these guys. My cousin Guy left these here when he visited from Paris a few years ago. He's really into that post-glitter early punk stuff. Both New York and LA." He thought for a second and shrugged. "I mean, I like some, like The New York Dolls' first album. Oh, and some X, but '70s punk is more his thing."

"You like X?" I said, somewhat surprised because . . . he listened to *Phish*.

"I do." He looked at me like he was waiting for me to get to my point.

"Okay, but what about all of this other stuff, though? It's just so *random*." I held up Al Green's "I'm Still in Love With You," as more proof.

"My dad used to take me to Mr. Cheapo's on my way back from music lessons and let me pick a record from the used bins." He leaned in closer to look at it and smiled. "This one's a favorite." He glanced at me. "Do you want me to tape it for you? I mean, unless you have a turntable."

"I have a turntable."

"Take it then."

I looked down at it again and read the title, *I'm Still in Love With You*. On the cover was a relaxed Al Green dressed in all white, sitting on the same wicker peacock chair we had on the porch. "I like the title," I said. "But I don't know, Pete, this sounds like a love song."

"I told you there were exceptions." He looked at me, his eyes turning amber in the streak of light coming through the basement window. "Anyway," he said, getting back to the point. "So based on your logic, if I like Phish, that means I can't like anything else?" His eyes trailed to the left, a look I learned he made when he was slightly annoyed. "That just defies self-interest. I mean, it's not like you discovered my secret back catalog of fucking Backstreet Boys B-Sides. All this stuff I listen to derives from either jazz or the blues. It's all connected."

"I know, but that's not what I mean." I felt a little silly when he put it so plainly like that. "It's just . . ." I scratched the back of my head, unsure of how to articulate myself since he did make a valid point. "How can your ears handle such conflicting tastes?"

"I don't know. I guess I like what I like without having to get my ego involved." He shrugged his shoulders. "I don't need to conceptualize myself with, like, white boy dreads to listen to Phish or, I don't know . . ."

"Wearing Buddy Holly glasses to listen to Indie Rock?" I teased.

"Okay. Okay." He smiled. "You made your point."

It made sense what he was saying, but I think I just liked pushing his buttons a little. As I turned back to the shelves to peruse the rest of his records, one popped out at me. In front of a turquoise backdrop, a woman wore nothing but bellbottom jeans and a little doll to cover her bare breasts.

"What's this one?" I presented the record.

"That one?" he said with a mischievous grin. "Well, that one is French love making music."

A little embarrassed by his response, my cheeks felt flush, and with a grimace, I said, "Do you *like* French love making music?"

"Not typically." He looked at it, still grinning. "But this one is a classic. It belonged to my dad. He's a huge fan. None of that Johnny Hallyday shit."

Completely lost by the references, I stared at him, waiting for him to explain.

"Serge Gainsbourg?" His eyes met mine.

"I'm not familiar with him," I admitted.

"I'm not surprised. In France, he's a household name. Like, fucking Elvis." He contemplated the comparison and appeared to change his mind. "Maybe not Elvis. It's hard to find an equivalent because Serge crossed over many decades and genres of music. He didn't do just one thing or have one schtick like Elvis. He was a composer, a songwriter. He did rock, pop, jazz, and even reggae." He thought to himself. "He did a reggae remake of 'La Marseillaise,' the national anthem, which most people don't know was actually written by an Alsatian and should have probably been called La Strasbourgeoise." He then looked off almost wistfully before returning to the conversation. "Anyway, the remake was a total scandal but makes up just one part of his bold contribution to French music history. I can keep going on about the genius of Serge Gainsbourg, but I'll wrap it up by saying many of the artists we listen to are *heavily* influenced by him." He tapped the vinyl in my hand. "Especially this album."

"*Histoire de Melody Nelson*." I read the sleeve, feeling a little sheepish about my accent.

"*Très bien*," he said sincerely.

"It's cool you speak French, by the way." I looked up at him in wonderment. "Did you also take it in school? Were you in Alex's French class with, who was it? Madame Duffau?" I asked, marveling at not having thought of our high school faculty in years.

"No, I was one of the few — three, to be precise — who took German. I did do my senior year community service as a teaching assistant for Madame Duffau, handing out papers and shit, and, like, pressing play on the VCR for her ninth-grade class." He smiled to himself. "She was from Toulouse." He chuckled as if sharing a joke with himself. "With that accent. *Oh lá*. She would look at me like *my* accent was weird . . ."

"Wait, though." I thought for a second. "*Are* you German? Because now that I think about it, your last name kind of sounds like it."

"It does because we're Alsatian."

I looked at him like I had no idea what that meant. "It's okay," he said, reading my expression. "Most people don't. In the plainest terms, we're from a region in France that borders Germany, so it's a hybrid culture of the two countries. The French I speak with my dad has a Germanic flair, which my snotty Parisian cousin—"

"Guy?" I started to connect the bits and pieces.

"Yeah, Guy." He smiled. "He's *interior French*, though, because his dad, my Uncle Thierry is Parisian who thinks he knows more about wine from Alsace than the Alsatian viticulturists, which annoys everyone. Anyway, we like to mess with Guy. My dad calls him *Parigot*, and Guy retorts by telling him he speaks slow, which is his snarky way of calling him a redneck." He shot his eyes up to the ceiling in dismissal. "So to check his ass, we remind him about his precious French military that was supposed to defend the border before the wars broke out. Instead, they scattered like a bunch of rabbits when confronted with the force of the German army, completely abandoning the region and the people of Alsace."

I nodded along while biting my lip not to react because how I got back at my brother was usually by giving him a dirty look. Not confronting him with historical grievances from World Wars . . .

It was then that I realized during our conversation we had moved in closer to each other. With him this near, I could smell him; woodsy and a little sweet, sort of like peanut butter. I kept my eyes down even though I knew he was looking at me, which made my chest feel heavy. I wondered if he picked up on it, so I held the Al Green record against me to hide my physical response to being this close to him. The space between us felt thick and ambiguous as if daring us to fill it. Slowly, my eyes met his, and it felt good to be reacquainting myself with his face. It was weird because when I thought about him, I sometimes forgot what he looked like. It was as if my emotions blurred over his features, making my feelings the only thing I could see. As he looked at me, I noticed his eyes tracing over the shape of mine, the curl of my eyelashes, down my cheeks, and to my lips that I slightly pressed together in feeling self-conscious.

"What," he whispered when he saw a little smile escape the corner of my mouth.

"I don't know," I echoed his soft tone. I then looked down at the floor to pull away from the closeness that scared me and said, "I just don't know what else I'm going to discover about you."

He stepped an inch closer to me where I could hear him breathing equally as deep, and he said, "Well, that's sort of how I feel about you."

Pete

On the phone that night, Allison accused me of not paying attention. I mean, I wasn't, but I didn't want her to know that. To appease her, I dropped back into our conversation about the summer, only to get bored again. After spending the day with Carla, I didn't know what we were doing anymore but knew I didn't have the luxury to find out. To make better use of my pent-up energy, I decided a music exchange between us was mandatory. An exchange of albums that were important to us, and therefore would be important to the band, but an abbreviated list because we did have full-time jobs. The rules: The albums had to be listened to more than once, preferably with headphones, and you couldn't dismiss an album based on the cover. Or genre.

I had a distinct vision for the band. In broad strokes, I wanted the long line rhythms and dance-like breaks of kraut; multi-structures of prog without the medieval shit; the sex drive of the blues; the grit of garage; and set to the foundation of steady cyclical drumming . . . if I could be totally vague about it. But unless you're a cover band, you really can't go into starting a band *trying* to sound like anything; a lesson learned from all the shitty Nirvana wannabe bands we were all subjected to during the mid to late nineties. It was best to just find the music with your bandmates. Saying that, though, we still needed to know where the other was coming from.

The albums I lent her were *Red* by King Crimson, *Silver Apples* by Silver Apples *Orange* by Jon Spencer Blues Explosion (which she had), *Tago Mago* by Can, and *Neu!* by Neu. Oh, and early Serge, giving her a collection of his '60s pop stuff before getting her onto the hard stuff. And to balance out the testosterone bomb I pretty much handed to her, I threw in the badass blues guitarist Memphis Minnie. Then, for some psychedelic folk, I gave her *Illuminations* by Buffy Sainte-Marie, and then to flirt a little, I threw in *Tous les garçons et les filles* by Françoise Hardy.

She then gave me, and less hysterically, might I add: *Emperor Tomato Ketchup* by Stereolab, *Dig Me Out* by Sleater-Kinney, *I Can Hear the Heart Beating As One* by Yo La Tengo, *Dummy* by Portishead, *Pet Sounds* by The Beach Boys, and *The Magic City* by Helium. I already had some of these, so we traded redundancies for the *Beautiful Son* single by Hole (on green vinyl—nice) and *Funky Divas* by En Vogue.

One, neither of us knew how to count. And two, it was pretty much a genre cluster-fuck with our band's influences being post-hardcore indie rock, early punk, lo-fi '60s garage-rock, art-pop rock, blues punk, avant-pop, psychedelia, jazz, prog, krautrock, downtempo, French yéyé and '90s R&B?

Maybe we should have gone back to school.

Carla

The music exchange! Oh my God, the music exchange! It turned out to be *way* more challenging than I thought it would be. I mean, it helped that he already had a lot of the classics like *White Light/White Heat* because what's a band if they're not influenced by the Velvet Underground? Pete agreed. I was relieved when he gave me more than the allotted five because I also couldn't pare down my most influential records to just five. But what I gave him was a representation of what I looked for in a band from interplaying guitars, pop melodies, and retro elements like spacey keyboards, mournful yet sensual vocals, and a responsible use of guitar fuzz. *Funky Divas* by En Vogue I knew stood out from the indie rock and '60s vinyl classics, but their harmonies were some of the best I had ever heard, picking up where my precious Supremes and Ronettes left off.

Pete's face, though, when he was confused, was starting to become one of my favorite things. You could see him trying to intellectualize it like a math problem.

The selection he gave me was definitely out there with compositions my ears had never heard before, but I got it. On the final notes of *Tago Mago,* where I immediately recognized Pete's drumming influence, I took my headphones off and said, "Okay, let's make some really freaking weird music."

Pete

I loved what she gave me, each album representing what felt important to her. I knew where she was going with *Funky Divas*, but I couldn't help but think back at this one time when I was watching TV with my mom. Our arrangement back then was that I could change the channel during Oprah's commercial breaks. Flipping over to MTV, En Vogue's insanely sexy video for "Givin' Him Somethin' He Can Feel" was on. With neither of us wanting to acknowledge the awkwardness by changing the channel, we kept watching as the Funky Divas in vacuum-sealed red dresses enticed horny businessmen. That was the last time I changed the channel during Oprah.

On the album, there's a track called "Give It Up, Turn It Loose," with this hilarious conversational intro where Terry feels like Dawn is distracted during their acapella warm-up of "Yesterday" by the Beatles. At our next practice, I asked Carla if she thought Dawn had ever worked things out with her boyfriend Kevin, who the other funky divas thought had cooties.

"Did she end up giving it up and turning it loose?" I asked.

"Oh my God," she said, looking both pleased and amused. "You really listened to it. I figured you'd thought I was joking."

"You?" I raised my eyebrows. "You don't joke. It's beneath you."

"Oh, stop." She looked down and smiled.

"I used to have a crush on Dawn from En Vogue." I chuckled to myself as I raised my arms over my head, pulling my drumstick from both ends to get a good chest stretch.

"What?" She looked over my kit with a pinched expression.

111

"Nothing."

"You're so weird,"

"*You're* so weird."

After the exchange, incidentally, we stopped talking about what we wanted to sound like and just did it. We were having fun, despite bumping into each other sonically, as we developed a melodic appreciation of each other. We experimented, we failed, we tried again. Sometimes it worked, and a lot of times it didn't, which always had us laughing. This feeling of ease I had with my new friend, my collaborator, I could feel was about to end because things were about to get complicated. Very complicated. Because Allison was coming back for the summer.

10

Carla

Understandably, I didn't see him for an entire week after Allison came back. Alex was also home, but only for two weeks before she had to head back for her summer internship at a weekly music newspaper in Chicago. Even though I secretly missed Pete, which I denied vehemently to the ever-accusative Alex, it was nice to kick back with my best friend. After a lazy afternoon of gossiping around her pool, I realized the time and sped home to get on the computer. Signing on, the screech of the modem dragged on like it was taking longer than usual to connect, and I barely made it. But after closing in on our bid at the last second, we got it!

"We got the four-track," I sang to Pete on the phone, feeling a shiver down my arm from the air conditioner that had just kicked on in the vent above me. "I rushed home from Alex's just in time with only 15 seconds to spare."

"Oh, sweet," he said. "Thanks for taking care of that."

"See, the internet *is* sometimes good," I teased, recalling his hesitation with eBay and my argument that we weren't just going to magically find a vintage four-track at a garage sale somewhere on Long Island.

"Yeah, yeah," he laughed. "But maybe now we'll decide who will actually sing in our band?"

"Yeah, I guess we do need to settle that," I grumbled. "You sure you don't want to sing?"

"I'm sure. But in the meantime, we can record those bass lines we wrote because I don't know if I told you, but Miguel is totally out, at least for the summer because he's leaving for Portugal."

"Oh, that's too bad," I said, trying to sound convincing because I didn't think we needed a bassist. Pete's drumming laid down the rhythmic elements to toe-tapping perfection that I thought a bass would actually take away from it. "Are you okay with that?" I continued. "I mean, who can you blame now if you make a mistake?" I laughed, referring to his theory that when something is off with drums, it's usually the bassist's fault.

"Ah." I could feel him smiling. "You're catching on."

"Anyway, at least my drummer isn't leaving for France this summer," I responded, which came out flirtier than intended.

"Oh God, don't remind my dad. This is our first summer not going to—"

"Ammerschwihr?" I said, giggling at my accent that sounded more Schwarzenegger than I wanted.

"Yes, exactly, Ammerschwihr," he laughed. "My dad gets so cranky. It's like he needs to get his Alsatian batteries recharged, and then he's, like, set for another year. Oh, speaking of . . . hold on, Car."

Car. He started calling me that a few weeks into our daily practices, and even though some of my family members called me that, I liked it better when he said it. Through the phone, I could hear him speaking French to his dad, where I was starting to notice Laurent's accent did sound different than Pete's. He spoke with stretched-out inflections and a slower tempo compared to his son's more common-sounding French. Hearing Pete speak to his dad always made me smile.

"Hey, sorry." He came back on the line. "So what are you doing tonight?"

"Not much. Why? Can you practice tonight?"

"Yeah, we can do that. But my dad wants to know if you want to come over for dinner first. Wait, hold on another sec," he said, as I imagined him resting the phone on his shoulder. As I waited, I looked around my kitchen and saw there was not much going on. It was Friday, the night we had fish, but figured God would forgive me if I forwent *one* Fish Friday in lieu of whatever we'd eat at the Albrecht's. "I don't know what's happening in the world," Pete said when he got back on the line. "We usually eat really light, like fish, or you know, full-out starvation on Friday, and now my dad is saying we're having a barbecue. He really *is* having an identity crisis." Misinterpreting my silence, he continued, "Anyway, I don't know, maybe we're weird. It's just my family's convenient take on religion to get out of going to church."

Smiling at his family's interpretation of Fish Friday and hearing Laurent in the background grumble some comment I knew would be funny, and at the expense of his son, I said, "What time?"

"Whenever you want. We'll eat at seven, but, um, you can come by before if you want?"

"Okay."

"Oh, and invite Alex if she's around."

"Alright. I will."

"So I'll see you soon?" I heard his voice get smaller and closer. The background noise in his kitchen suddenly muted like he had changed rooms.

"Okay." I echoed his tone. "Yeah."

"Okay."

"Okay," I said, feeling him on the other side of the phone. I felt a little guilty when I caught myself leaning in closer to the receiver and lowering my eyes as if I was close to him.

"Okay," he finally said. "Come soon."

"Okay," I whispered.

Two hours later, Alex pulled into my driveway, which was about an hour and forty-five minutes later than I wanted to get there. I mostly wanted to avoid a confrontation with my mom and managed somehow to get out unscathed, only running into my dad. My mom was staying late at the market to assemble gift baskets for some company picnic the next day, and my dad sent me off to Pete's with cured meat he sliced in front of me in our steaming hot garage.

Sitting in the driver's seat of her hunter-green Jetta, Alex snapped her head toward me the second I slid into the cool car. Wearing her tortoise Jackie O. sunglasses, she looked at me with an impish grin.

"What," I said.

"Sheela-na-gig," she sang, looking at my chest.

"What?"

"Umm, hello, you exhibitionist!" she said in her finest PJ Harvey drawl, her blond bob swaying with her lanky body. "Lala, are you not wearing a bra bra?"

"What are you talking about?" I looked down at my pale blue t-shirt. "I am. Well, kind of."

"Your boobs look extra juicy and, like, free." She smirked. "Kind of hot." She then sighed and looked down at her shirt. "God, I wish I had boobs."

I looked at my best friend and smiled. Alex may not have had full ones as I did, but she was naturally tall and svelte and even had a short-lived career as a Delia's catalog model. Her mom was Ukrainian and had an accent Alex liked to imitate, and her dad — her mom would say — was a "nice Jewish boy from Brooklyn." Alex had exotic features with her mom's cat-shaped green eyes and long arms and could wear a t-shirt without a bra, and no one would notice.

"They're not that big. I'm just small." I disregarded my best friend's undying appreciation for my boobs as she flipped through her CD book.

"You *are* freakishly small," she said, "with those teeny shoulders." She then looked up from the book and, with a serious expression, said, "But we're not making ourselves smaller on purpose, are we?"

"We're not." I looked out the window. "I promise."

"You can't starve yourself to a breast reduction," she said, looking at my arms and down the rest of my body, seeming only semi-convinced I was taking care of myself. "And if you got a real one, I'd kill you." She pulled her sunglasses up. "Because then she wins."

"I know," I responded absentmindedly, looking away from her peering eyes that had nothing but disdain for my mother.

"Anyway." Her tone lightened as she lowered her glasses back down. "I'll trade your bodacious tatas for my double A's any day."

"I would have worn a different bra," I said, appreciative of the subject change. "It's just that my more supportive ones are dirty, so I had to use this old Calvin Klein one I got on sale at Filene's that's clearly made for small boobs. It's mesh with no underwire."

"Well, whatever you're doing, I like it." She then turned to me, and through her glasses, I could see her eyeing me with her perfectly plucked eyebrows. "And I'm sure Kissable will too."

"Oh, cut it out," I said, swatting her shoulder. "You know Allison is probably going to be there, and I don't want her thinking—"

"That you and her boyfriend are falling in love?"

"We're not," I said. "It's just music."

"Keep telling yourself that, babe." She grinned wider as she slid a CD into the car's player. "Because I *know* you've been 'Ifing' on him."

I didn't respond, hoping that would communicate that I had no idea what she was talking about. My silence, however, had the reverse effect as she said, "I knew it! You are *totally* listening to 'If' and thinking about him." She opened her mouth in faux shock. "So, tell me, La. If you were Pete's girl, what *are* the things you'd do to him?" She looked at my face as I blushed because she wasn't entirely wrong . . . but still. "Do you close your eyes thinking of him a hundred different ways? His smooth and shiny—"

"Okay," I stopped her. "You've made your point."

"La, it's fine. You don't have to justify your love," she said with a self-congratulatory grin, clearly proud of herself for landing on yet another sexually charged '90s reference. "Personally, I'm happy because anyone is better than my gross little cousin."

"Can you stop saying little?" I begged. "He's a *year* younger than us." I then smirked in recollection of our big night together, the way his retainer felt on my tongue and clicked against my teeth. "And he's not gross. "

"You know he still asks about you." She scrunched her face up. "And he *is* gross. Just because he listens to Pavement doesn't make him cute."

"Okay, we're not getting into this again." I shook my head at the dead argument as she backed her car out of the driveway. Cranking the volume up to the song that defined eighth grade for us, I smiled in recognition of the violin sampling of the Supremes song against the wail of the electric guitar as "If" blasted from the car speakers.

"By the way," Alex said, "is Pete's dad still hot?"

We pulled in front of Pete's house just as the song ended and walked around back where we found Tony, Allison, Laurent, and Pete. Immediately, I was relieved to have Alex with me.

"*Tiens, tiens!*" Laurent said in delight when he saw us. I walked over and leaned in for the double kiss I had grown accustomed to as I felt Allison dart me with sharp daggers digging into my back.

"This is from my dad," I said, reaching into my bag to pull out the waxed paper of sliced meat. Looking as if I had presented him with a king's gift, Laurent's eyes lit up. "*C'est magnifique. Merci, ma belle.*"

We then said awkward hellos to our former classmates — there we were, five people who all went to the same high school and graduated the same year but ran in completely different circles. We all knew each other but, you know, didn't *know* each other. If you had told me and Alex senior year that we would have a barbecue at Pete Albrecht's house with his girlfriend, Allison Kellner, and Tony Delvecchio, we would have commented on the total randomness of it. But two years later, there we were, all connected by the fact that Pete and I were in a band, something else we wouldn't have believed.

To ease the apparent tension between Allison and me, I stretched myself out of my comfort zone and tried to make small talk with her. But every time, she offered me these one-word answers before focusing her attention elsewhere. Giving up on participating in conversation, I turned to daydreaming. Over by the grills, Pete was with his dad. As I pretended to listen to Alex and Tony talk and taking advantage when Allison had announced she was going to her car to get her lip gloss, I snuck glances at Pete. He wore black sunglasses I hadn't seen since the movie *Risky Business* and had on one of his soft, athletic gray t-shirts that rounded perfectly over his shoulders. The two, dad and son, sat with their relaxed Gallic air. I could see where Pete got his lean but built physique and how they both had a fluidity in the way they moved. I looked at Laurent and blushed a little because he *was* kind of hot. Unfortunately, Tony, who doesn't miss a thing, totally caught me.

"I knew it. I just knew it," Tony said as if he had just cracked a conspiracy theory he had dedicated his life to. "Girls love it. They can't resist that shit."

"What are you talking about?" Alex said.

"When guys speak French. I totally just caught Carla checkin' Petey out."

Resenting the cliché and hoping Pete couldn't hear us, I quietly said, "No, I wasn't."

"Yeah, Tony. She wasn't," Alex said, thankfully. "Don't be such a pervert. Not everything is about sex." I looked at Alex like she should talk.

"What. Ever," Tony said, not buying it.

"Alright, it's ready!" Laurent called out, approaching the table with the tray of barbecue. "Who wants a *knack*?"

"Hot dog, honey!" Anna corrected him from the kitchen window.

"Oh, *ça va*," he said, dismissing the translation. "Same *merde*."

Seeing him approach the table with the barbecue, instinctively, I went into the kitchen. Set out on the counter was a plate of grilled white asparagus with my dad's meat folded neatly next to it, coleslaw that looked homemade, and Long Island corn on the cob. Just as I was reaching the table with two platters and Anna following behind with the rest, Allison, who was returning from the crucial lip gloss run, looked at me like I was a fucking bitch for helping Pete's mom.

I nestled in tightly next to Alex like she was my safe place and avoided eye contact with Pete. Other than the stilted hello I had offered him when we arrived, we didn't say much to each other. We kind of moved around each other, nervous to display any of the familiarity we had developed. Once we settled into our places and with plates of food passed and food consumed, Anna asked the table, "Anyone have any interesting plans for the summer?"

Tony and I shrugged. As Alex opened her mouth about to share details of her internship, Allison swept in. "Actually, yes," she said proudly. "Pete and I are spending a week in Montauk."

The cool expression from Pete's parents, who I thought would be more enthusiastic given their history with going out east, caught me by surprise. I then looked over at Pete, and even with his dark sunglasses on, I could feel his eyes trailing off to the side in exasperation.

"Oh, I didn't know that." Anna looked at Pete. "Did you two just decide it?"

"Of course not," Allison said in a slippery tone. "My friend Constance told me it was the new hot place. And being from Long Island, she was totally surprised we didn't vacation there, you know?" She looked at Pete for confirmation. "Remember when you visited the last time and Constance and Perry were telling us how Montauk is going to be the new Hamptons?"

"Vaguely."

"And will Constance and Perry be in Montauk, too?" Alex said, unable to resist, forcing Pete to shoot her a look from across the table.

"They will," Allison responded sweetly. "I love them." She then turned toward Pete's parents and said, "It's not the Montauk you knew back in the day. It's like it's getting a makeover, everything from the beachside shanty motels to the restaurants that are in dire need of some culinary guidance."

"Well, that sounds nice," Anna forced herself to say.

"It sounds expensive," Laurent added as he stabbed his fork into his coleslaw.

I pushed my food around while the rest of the table ate in silence, recovering from "the new Montauk" Pete's parents apparently knew nothing about. Alex then perked up when she noticed a tattoo peeking under Laurent's t-shirt.

"What's your tat of, Mr. Albrecht?"

Appearing pleased with the question, he pulled his sleeve up to display a noble-looking red shield with small gold crowns and a gold stripe cutting diagonally across.

"This is the coat of arms for Alsace, specifically Le Haut-Rhin–"

"Upper Rhine, Papa," Pete interjected and, with a shrug that said to Laurent, "It's just easier."

Pete looked at us and continued, "Alsace is divided into two counties along the Rhine River. There's the Upper and Lower Rhine. But what confuses people is that Upper is actually located south below Lower, which has to do with the direction the river is flowing." He looked at us. "It flows from south to north."

We all nodded in acknowledgment that it could be confusing if you didn't know. Allison then looked at Pete and said, "How come you never told me that?"

"Well, you never asked."

After dinner, the five of us retreated to the basement, where we set up the four-track next to Pete's drums. Tony sprawled out on the couch, and I sat on the floor tuning my guitar. Alex was perusing Pete's vinyl with the same confused expression I used to have. And Allison, sitting with her back straight and arms folded, appeared to be waiting for something to happen.

"This is so fucking great," Pete said as he played with the dials of the four-track.

"Now record something so I can write about you guys," Alex said. "But for now" — she looked around with a sly grin— "I'll settle for something live. Here we are now, entertain us?"

"Oh, shit, you gotta hear them," Tony said from the couch. "They're fuckin' tight."

Pete's eyes met mine, waiting for my response. Alex, of course, picked up on it and said, "No secret eye conversations. Just play."

"Wait, who's doing secret eye conversations?" Allison asked.

"Carla and Tony," Alex said quickly to shut her up before reverting to Pete and me. "Come on, guys. Play something."

Pete looked at me, and appearing to tune the others out, he quietly said, "Sing for me." I then looked around me and back at him with wide eyes, like there was no freaking way I was going to sing right now.

"You think you don't have it in you." He gave me a knowing look as if he could read my thoughts. "But I happen to think you do. And if you're miserable, then fuck it, we'll force Miguel to sing when he gets back from Portugal."

I had to laugh, but still, I felt squeamish about singing in front of his girlfriend. But I had to remind myself it wasn't just his girlfriend there. There was also the most supportive person I had in my life in the room, then Tony, who I knew had a kind heart, and then, of course, Pete. I'd never have a friendlier audience than I did right then.

"Alright," I said, taking a deep breath. "But I can't make any promises."

"Wait, really?" He smiled for the first time that night.

"Really."

Pete

The barbecue, I realized minutes in, was going to be fucking miserable. I guess I was hoping Allison and Car would have gotten along, but I also knew that was my optimistic, or as my dad says, my American side coming out. I wanted to talk to Carla. But I knew I had eyes on me. I meant it when I invited her to come over earlier so we could sort of ease into the barbecue. But she didn't take me up on it for some reason. So instead, we acted like total weirdos, as if our friendship was a secret. Things then took a turn from uncomfortable to apocalyptic when she sang. I mean, I had a feeling she'd be good because she had a nice speaking voice, but not like that. Her voice was spellbinding, the way it just melted into the melody like honey. It was full, dusky, a little monochromatic, and dreamy without shoegazing. It was then, at that moment, it became clearer than ever what I wanted to do with my life: create music with this person.

Unfortunately, Allison didn't quite see it that way.

"You were practically having sex with her!" Allison screamed at me once Alex and Carla had left.

"What the hell are you talking about?" I called out as she hurled a drumstick at my head.

"This wasn't band practice!" she continued. "This was foreplay!"

"Well, now that doesn't even make sense." I peeked over my kit. "Which one was it? Fucking or foreplay because, technically, it can't be both."

"Oh no, he didn't." Tony nodded in disapproval. "You're askin' for it, kid."

"And why, Pete," she said pointedly. "Why wasn't she wearing a bra?"

"Fuck if I know!" Shit, I thought. I wondered if she had read my mind on how great I thought Carla looked, especially in that shirt.

"So you noticed?"

"Yes? No? I don't know," I said in defense, holding my hands up in case she decided to throw another drumstick at me.

"You could see her nipples! What kind of trailer park was she raised in anyway?"

"How could you see her nipples?" I felt uncomfortable saying the word. "Her shirt was blue. Now you're just being mean."

"So you were looking at her nipples?"

"No!"

"Then how do you know her shirt was blue if you weren't looking at her nipples?"

"Oh man, you guys keep saying nipples," Tony said, in which Allison and I shot him a death look. "But on that note, I think I'm gonna head out. I don't want to get a drum thrown at my head if you know what I mean." He carefully crept around the couch and bolted past me. "I'll catch up with you later, man. Take care, Allison!"

Once I heard him leave, I held my hands up in surrender and looked at Allison, who was breathing heavily in a rage. With my hands out, I said, "Here, give me the drumstick and let's sit."

We walked to the couch, and I sat down facing her, trying to hold her hands in mine, but she wouldn't let me.

"Okay," I said to her cheek. "How do we fix this?"

"It's not my job to fix it. That's yours, Pete." She remained stiff, her shoulders positioned away from me, as her fingers played piano up and down her arm.

"Okay." I exhaled and then ran my fingers through my hair and around to the back of my neck, placing a few squeezes to ease the tension. "What do you want me to do?"

"End the band, of course," she said without giving it a second thought. I then heard what an awful boyfriend I was as she proceeded to list off everything I was apparently doing wrong, from being distracted to having only gone down on her twice since she'd been home.

I listened to her talk, but there was no way I was going to end the band; it had been the greatest thing that had happened to me since, maybe ever. I remained quiet to carefully choose my next words, which might have given her the impression I was considering it. As she relaxed a little from her hard stance, she turned toward me and grabbed my hand.

"This is the first time you're home for the entire summer. I want it to be just you and me."

And Constance and Perry, I wanted to add.

I shook my head, took a deep breath, and turned toward her. As gently as I could, I said, "No. I'm not ending the band."

"What do you mean you're not ending the band!" she screamed, her face contorting back into a rage. Accustomed to getting what she wanted, she threatened to leave, looking back to see if I'd stop her. But I wouldn't. "This is why you should have gone to Juilliard," she snapped when she realized I wasn't going to run after her. "So you can play with *other musicians.*"

"Is *that* what would have happened if I went?" I said, unable to resist the sarcasm. "Well, fuck me, now you tell me this whole time I could have been playing with other musicians?"

Unamused, she shook her head and said, "I don't know why you applied if you had no intention of even going."

"Auditioned," I corrected her. "I auditioned, not applied."

She gave me a sharp look.

"And I don't know why" —I held my hands out—"it's so important for you to have a boyfriend that goes to Juilliard." I looked at her, now pissed she couldn't accept me as I was. When she didn't respond, I said plainly, "Look. I'm not ending the band."

"I just don't understand," she said in a softer, almost pleading voice as she walked back toward the couch. "We love each other."

Standing in front of me, I looked up at her as she rubbed her bare knee up and down my hand. "I know we do," I said and reached out to gently caress up the side of her leg.

"Shouldn't we do things that make each other happy?"

"Well, yeah," I began to say and wanted to elaborate but lost my train of thought as she climbed on top of me, pressing my back against the couch.

"Then let me make you happy right now then," she said, beginning to move smoothly and firmly against me.

"Okay," I breathed as I inched her skirt up.

Straddling me, she continued to press herself upon me as she let her breasts rub up and down against my chest. As she moved in this sweet rhythm, I felt some parts of me melting while others were doing the exact opposite.

"I want you to stop doing the band," she whispered in my ear as she unbuckled my belt.

"Al, I'm not going to." I looked up, her honey-streaked hair dangling against my cheek. I then pulled her skirt up over her hips and gently tugged the top of her underwear to convey they should come off. I was hesitant since I was expecting her to make me stop since I wasn't giving her what she wanted. But she appeared turned on by my defiance.

"Stop doing the band," she said again while lowering my pants.

Feeling insanely turned on by not only my girlfriend, who had then begun stroking me exactly how she knew I liked, but also by band practice. For a moment, I let my thoughts travel to imagining myself peeling Carla's blue t-shirt off. I got hot thinking about what sucking on her breasts would be like; how they would feel in my mouth with my tongue circling her nipples that, of course, I fucking saw during the barbecue. How could I not? As Allison continued her soft motions, I lowered her hips closer to me. The faint brushes of her inner thigh made me flinch and sent shivers throughout my entire body. Even so, I told her again I would not be ending the band. She then moved her underwear to the side and slowly lowered herself onto me.

"End the band," she repeated.

With my eyes pulled to the back of my head, my hands guided her hips in moving smoothly up and down. Overcome by the warmth that consumed my waking thoughts, by the fourth, or maybe the fifth time she told me to end the band, all I could mumble was, "What band?"

11

Carla

Something must have happened because ever since the barbecue, Allison was at every rehearsal, as if supervising. Pete didn't seem happy, but I didn't know for sure because we barely spoke. No one wanted to piss Allison off, so it was easier if Pete and I pretended the other one barely existed. Thank goodness for Tony, who kept the mood light and totally inappropriate. Otherwise, I would have felt like I was there to watch Pete and Allison react off each other, with her giving him kisses with one eye looking at me.

Sick of feeling dumpy around her trotting around in denim miniskirts and halter tops she could wear without a bra, I went to practice in a navy blue button-down floral dress I felt pretty in. It fit me looser than I remembered, but it was one of the few dresses I had that my mom didn't purse her lips at.

When I got to Pete's, I immediately grabbed Tony's eyes to give him a look to not comment on it. I then retreated to my new corner, away from the drum kit, to set up. Pete, sitting behind his drums, looked up from his book to say hi to me. As soon as our eyes met, though, I noticed he looked at me a little weird. I immediately wanted to burn the dress.

It became even more problematic after we started playing. When I chose it, I hadn't considered the placement of the guitar strap. To avoid squishing my left boob down like a pancake, I usually positioned the strap around it, which had never been a problem in my t-shirts. But in the dress with its lower neckline, the strap pushed them up and over to reveal cleavage that bounced while I played. We ran through a few songs until I couldn't take the discomfort of the situation anymore, with Pete missing beats and Allison's eyes seething on me. I gave Pete a half nod that practice was over, and without waiting for a response, I clicked my amp off.

"So, Carla," Allison said.

"Yeah?" I turned around in surprise at her acknowledging me.

"I didn't even know you liked this kind of music."

"This kind of music?" I looked at her puzzled as I carefully pulled the guitar over my head. "The music I'm creating? Well, of course, I like it. I guess I sort of have to."

"No. I mean, like, I remember in high school, you were into, like, heavy metal." Her tone was designed to make me feel small.

"Heavy metal?" I repeated, earnestly trying to recall what would have given her that impression.

"Yeah," she said. "I remember the angry rock 'n roll stuff you and Alexa Sherman used to wear to school. Me and my friends were like, whoa ladies, take a Midol." She then shuddered as if she was terrified.

"That must have been my Babes in Toyland t-shirt with the headless dolls," I answered, my eyebrows pinched in recollection.

"So yeah, I guess those shirts can be a bit jarring if you don't know the context."

On the couch, Tony was flipping through the CD book I brought in from my hot car.

"Hey, C," he called out. "I ain't heard of any of these bands."

"Are we surprised?" Allison said.

"Babysitters on Acid by the Lunachicks," he said, reading the CD booklets. "That's fucked up." He flipped the page. "You have a burned CD called Free Kitten Oh Bondage, Up Yours. Uh-oh." He looked at me and covered his mouth to feign shock. "You illegally downloading music? Don't tell Metallica."

"No, well, I mean, yes. But I did buy it. I just have it on seven-inch."

"You have what on seven-inch?" He grinned.

"Shut up, Tony."

"I don't know. You got some questionable shit in here. You have an album called *Spanking Machine* with a song called" — he threw his head back in theatrics — "a song called 'Swamp Pussy!'"

Again, Babes in Toyland, I thought to myself, as Allison looked at me with a curled upper lip.

"And what's a Peel session?" Tony asked with a raised eyebrow. I glanced over at Pete, who was grinning and nodding his head to himself, clearly amused. I then looked back at Tony, who was now smiling at me with gorged eyes as if he had just won the New York State Lottery. "You have a CD called *Boom, I Fucked Your Boyfriend* by MC Luscious?"

"Excuse me?" Allison looked at me even more horrified than when my boobs were spilling out of my dress.

I had to press my lips to conceal my amusement because he got me there. The song was an old dance song Alex and I somehow discovered, which became an ongoing joke between us because the lyrics were so out of control. I would have had Tony put it on because I knew he'd get a kick out of it, but given the present company, it probably wasn't the best song to be listening to.

"Oh, man," Tony said, flipping through the book like it was a dirty magazine. "C, you're into some nasty shit with your seven-inch Peel sessions. You look all quiet and sweet with your little orange guitar, goin' to church with grandma, but nah, I ain't buying it no more. You're, like, horny and shit."

"I think I'm going to throw up," Allison said.

I couldn't help but laugh at how predictable Tony was. I looked over at Pete, wishing he would chime in because I knew he also secretly loved provoking Tony. Instead, he stayed safely tucked behind his drums. Smoking a freshly lit cigarette and reading his novel, he wisely chose not to get involved. I then walked over to the small fridge to get water and thought about Allison and Pete for a second. It was weird. They didn't seem to connect at all that I wondered if they even had sex. They had to have. I then wondered what Pete was like in bed. Eyeing him from over the bottle of Poland Spring I was drinking, I assessed him stretching his arms up over his head. I liked his arms; they were man arms. Defined with lean muscle, they looked sturdy and had a coat of dark hair wrapped over them. I imagined Allison liked running her hands up and down them while they had sex. I would've. I then blushed, wondering if he made weird faces *during*.

"Car," Allison said, which slightly startled me. "I can call you that, right?"

"Um, sure." I eyed the room suspiciously.

"I've been meaning to ask," she said, making a face I didn't trust. "Why aren't you in school again?"

Before I could answer, she cut me off and said in a loud whisper, "Is it *financial*?" Stunned into silence, I stared at my feet, feeling as lame as she wanted me to feel.

"You know Pete got into Juilliard, right?" she looked at him slyly. "The verdict is still out if he's going to reapply because, let's face it, this is wasted talent right here."

"Stop," he mouthed to her, finally looking annoyed.

Feeling like she had slapped me across the face, my eyes shot over to Pete, who then had no choice but to look at me. "No," I said quietly. "I didn't know that." Giving me a look that said he didn't think it was important, I immediately felt stupid. Stupid for believing him when he told me he wasn't talented enough for Berklee but somehow managed to get into freaking Juilliard.

"Don't be mad at him," she said, observing my fallen face. "It was just between us, and well, his parents too."

"Of course." I pulled my eyes away from him.

As I was about to pack my things up with the intention of calling Pete later to put the band on hold for a while, Laurent came down the stairs. This concerned us all because adults *never* came down.

"*Ça va?*" Pete said to him with concern.

"*Oui, oui,*" Laurent said, waving him to get up. "Everything is fine. Come here for a second."

"Well, what's going on?" asked Pete, still looking concerned and seeming reluctant to get up.

"*Allez!*" he said with a huff, flicking his arm up at his son to get up.

When he finally did, we all gathered around Laurent, eager to hear what he was going to tell us. Allison even looked at me, a one-time shared moment, as we both waited for Pete's dad to explain why he was in the basement of his own house.

"I took the tape you guys made a few weeks ago and copied it to listen to in my truck on my way to work."

"Okay," Pete said.

"Well, Tom . . ." He looked at Pete. "You know Tom."

Pete nodded.

"Well, his truck is at the garage, so I've been driving him this week. Well, he heard the tape too and loved it, so I made him a copy. A copy of a copy. On the label, I wrote our phone number in case it got into the right hands."

Pete and I looked at each other and then back at Laurent.

"Well, he played it for his brother who owns The Night Owl bar on Hillside, and he enjoyed the tape too. So he made a copy. A copy of a copy of —"

"Papa!"

"Anyway," he said before stopping for a second to look at Pete. "You can be so impatient sometimes." The father and son exchanged a look. "Anyway, he just called the house saying there's an opening on July 1 to play Sunday night happy hour, and it's yours if you want it."

"Yeah?" Pete said calmly before turning to me. "What do you think?"

Still rattled by him lying to me, I echoed his cool composure and shrugged my shoulders as to say, why not? He then looked back at Laurent, who puckered his lips and mumbled something in French to Pete.

"*Si, si, si.*" Pete nodded, looking back at me and then back at his dad. "So, what do we do now?"

"Just call him back," Laurent responded. "The phone numbers on the counter."

The two exchanged a few nods of approval, a squeeze on the shoulder, and as Laurent walked back upstairs, Pete called out, "*Merci,* Papa."

We had just booked our first show. I imagined this playing out differently with maybe *a little bit* of emotion. What should have been an exciting moment instead looked like we had just received a summons for jury duty as Pete and I alternated looking at and away from each other.

"What is this? A fuckin' funeral? You guys got a show!" Tony offered the appropriate response and performed a series of dance moves that made him look bigger than he was. "Where's the fuckin' enthusiasm?" He then turned to give me a hug, lifting me up in his big bear arms. He then turned to Allison and almost hugged her but appeared to change his mind and turned around to give me another hug.

"Tony!" I gasped in his tight grip.

"It's really great, sweetie," I could hear Allison say. Peeking from underneath Tony's armpit I was stuffed in, Pete and Allison awkwardly kissed each other, as I could tell she was trying to look excited for him. "But don't I get a say here?"

"What's up?" Pete said, sounding like his patience was starting to run out.

"Pete." She looked at him. "That's the day we leave for Montauk."

Pete

Was it just me, or was there something majorly fucked about this summer? It was like there was this weird shift I was trying to navigate through but failed every time. Back in the day, you know, an entire year ago, Allison was happy to spend the day at the Sound with sandwiches we made in my kitchen before I left for Alsace for the rest of the summer. These were the kind of summer activities a twenty-year-old guy who worked at Starbucks and still lived with his folks did. Not going to Montauk with Constance and fucking Perry. If I had it my way, which was a joke to even think about since I was trying to keep two girls happy, I wouldn't have had her sit in on every rehearsal. It was making things weird, and no one wanted to say it. Correction: No one wanted to say it except Tony, who took every opportunity to say it.

"Shit's getting weird, man," he would say under his breath when no one was listening. "You gotta do something."

"Like what?" I would snap back.

Carla remained laser-focused on the band, and Allison took every opportunity to make her feel excluded, something I had repeatedly told her to stop doing. As a result, Carla and I kept our distance with me behind the kit, waiting around like a studio session drummer. But when she came to practice in that dress, I didn't know what was real anymore. It wasn't because it was kind of low cut. Or that it rode up when she pulled the guitar strap over her head, exposing her smooth legs I don't think I had ever seen. But it was the buttons that went down the front. Those fucking buttons were driving me insane, especially the top one that had come undone at some point. They were practically taunting me, these little blue buttons that were like gatekeepers guarding what I couldn't stop thinking about at night. Watching her, even when I knew she was pissed about the Juilliard thing, all I could think about was undoing each and every one of those buttons to watch the dress fall off her shoulders.

When my dad came down, the timing couldn't have been worse because I had a hard-on and was trying to discreetly wiggle out of it. My dad accused me of acting weird and asked if I wasn't pleased about the show. Of course, I was. I had never been more excited in my entire life; I just wished my dick wasn't demanding my immediate attention. Then Allison mentioned Montauk, and that pretty much lowered the sail.

Even though I hated the whole Montauk idea, I felt bad. As much as it would have been easier to be mad at Allison, I couldn't. Because how could I blame her for changing when I was doing the same exact thing?

12

Carla

Leading up to our show on Sunday, Pete and I weren't allowed to practice because Allison wasn't available to babysit us. Pete called me the Friday before and apologized, asking me to come over.

"I don't know, Pete," I said in annoyance. "I don't want you to get in trouble."

"Don't worry about it," he said. "I told her she was being ridiculous, and I mean, yeah, we're still in a huge fight, but I'll deal with it." I could feel his head lower in exhaustion and almost desperation at the impossible situation. "I mean, if you even want to come over," he added, sensing my apprehension. "She won't be here. She's getting highlights, or whatever."

"Fine," I said.

I got to his house, and after a quick run-through of the songs we wanted to do, he felt the need to tell me that he and Allison had worked it out so they could drive to Montauk directly after the show. Great, was all I could think of to say, which came out bitchier than I wanted it to.

Other than that, I avoided small talk with him because the Juilliard incident confirmed we weren't actually friends. Besides, I had other things on my mind, like wondering whether to invite my family or not. I knew my mom would either already be drunk or super judgmental, and I didn't know if I wanted to deal with all of that for my first show. I wished I could talk to Pete about it. But on top of realizing we weren't really friends, I knew he wouldn't have understood since his family was perfect. Also, I felt like if I said the words out loud, then my feelings would become real. I liked that my thoughts remained locked airtight and safe in the caverns of my head where I could pretend they didn't exist.

Before leaving his house, I decided to change my strings out. On the floor of his basement, it felt serene as I looked around in appreciation of the stillness. We didn't have any music on, there weren't any Tony sexual innuendos to recover from, the instruments sat quietly, and Allison wasn't there to make me feel like my presence was an assault. I sat on the floor with Pete nearby, who alternated between writing a letter to Cousin Guy in Paris while laughing to himself and sketching out a drumbeat I could see ticking in his head. I looked over at his paper and saw circles and dashes in shapes that resembled Morse Code that he appeared to understand perfectly.

Sitting next to him, only sounds penetrated the space. The tapping of his pen against the notebook. The neighbor's lawn mower buzzing. An ice cream truck chiming in the distance. I looked at Pete, deeply focused on his drum phrases, his dark eyelashes lowered like thick curtains. Sensing my gaze on him, his eyes flicked up to meet mine, and I quickly looked away.

"Hey," he said softly.

Looking back up, I offered a half-smile before reverting my focus back to my guitar. He placed his notebook on the floor and moved closer to me, so close I had no choice but to look up at him.

"Hey," I responded and looked away dismissively.

I could feel his stare heavy on the skin of my eyelids, begging me to look at him as the weight of his presence pressed into me. Being this close to him confirmed that he did, in fact, smell like peanut butter, a thought that made me giggle to myself.

"What." He grinned.

"Nothing." I pressed my lips together.

"So," he started to say. "I know everything's been kind of weird between us. Allison can get a little *intense*. But as for the Juilliard thing, I guess I didn't think it mattered."

"It's fine . . ." I said and then thought for a second before adding, "But why *did* you audition?"

"Honestly" — he threw his hands up — "I didn't think I'd get in. I did it because Miles Davis went there, even though he only did a year. But when I got in, that's when I really thought about it and knew it wouldn't be right for me. People die to get into that school, and it'd be kind of fucked up to go half-assed, you know?"

"Okay," I said, trying to follow his point. "But why not just go? It's an amazing opportunity."

"I guess what I've always been looking for was a more organic, less competitive approach to making music and didn't want to end the four years hating jazz, hating the drums, which was something both Dale and my French grandmother understood." He paused. "Well, my grandmother, not so much the jazz concern but that the four years would cost almost a quarter-million dollars, which is *unheard* of in France." He laughed. "So there was that."

"Were your parents okay with it?"

"They just want me to be happy." He shrugged as if it was the most obvious thing ever. "I mean, eventually, yeah, they'd like me to go to a trade school or something. I was thinking maybe for landscaping to be able to work outside."

"I'm sure Allison loves *that* idea," I found myself saying.

"Yeah, right," he slightly stuttered and made a face, hinting at the many conversations they'd had about it. He then looked at me and said, "Thanks for listening. It feels good answering these questions because no one really waits for the answers."

"Yeah," I said, knowing exactly how he felt.

"As for us, you know, the band. You know you're allowed to tell me when something's bothering you, or you're feeling, I don't know, *disenchanted* by it all."

"Disenchanted?" I grinned.

"Yeah." He smiled back. "I thought you'd like that. It sounds kind of mystical." He widened his eyes as if imagining a life beyond.

"It does." I chuckled in agreement.

"But I mean, isn't that what we are right now? I know I am because things *are* really weird right now."

"Pete, it's fine." I looked away. "Really."

"Okay, it's fine," he said with a tinge of impatience. "Even though I hate that word because it's so fucking vague, but sure, it's fine."

He then lay on his back on the floor and stretched his arms over his head. I decided it was time to take the opportunity to do something, something I had wanted to do for the past few weeks. Taking advantage of it being just the two of us, I crawled over to him lying on the floor and stretched out next to him with our shoulders almost touching.

"Pete," I said softly as I turned my head toward him.

"Yeah?" He rolled his head in my direction.

"I don't know if this is the right time to bring it up, but it's something I think we should probably talk about."

"What's that?" He looked intrigued, maybe even a little worried.

"Well." I blinked. "We need a band name."

Pete

It was the day of our show. I sat on the couch in my living room and waited for Carla, hoping she'd arrive before Allison. I always pictured the scene before our first show to be, I don't know, a little dramatic, a little rock n' roll. Instead, I was carpooling with my guitarist and girlfriend in her family sedan, as my dad cursed in the kitchen at a camcorder that wasn't working. I guess I imagined we'd need to rent a van to load up our gear and be at the venue for soundcheck hours before. But because we were at the bottom of the bill, we were using the headlining band's drum set, and our soundcheck was scheduled twenty minutes before we went on because no one really cared what we sounded like. If I understood correctly from my dad, The Night Owl was a bar that just happened to have live music a few nights a week, where they hosted cover bands to entertain the bar crowd with familiar songs.

Thinking about it made me a little nervous. I mean, I knew people weren't going to boo or anything because people aren't total assholes, but they could look impatient as they waited for a cover of fucking "Africa" by Toto that was never going to come.

Through the window, flecks of pollen danced lazily in the heat of the setting sun. Seeing Carla's maroon car pull into the driveway, my stomach dropped. I took a deep breath and gave my neck a few rolls before walking out to greet her. I had to take another deep breath when I saw how incredible she looked in her fitted white t-shirt. Walking toward me and holding her guitar case, she squinted as the sun radiated off her cheeks.

"Hey," she said.

"Hey."

"You nervous?"

"Not really." I smiled at her. "You?"

"I'm okay, actually."

I took her guitar case and let her walk ahead of me into the house. I hadn't stopped thinking about Friday being alone with her on the floor. I thought for sure that we'd start making out or something, but knew I would have somehow ended up with both girls mad at me *and* no band, so it was better that it didn't happen. I suppose.

"You want something to drink?" I asked as I set her case down on the kitchen floor. "I think my mom made iced tea."

"Sure."

After pulling the pitcher out of the fridge, I gave the iced tea a stir with a spoon to break up the powder sitting at the bottom but soon realized the spoon was too small to reach.

"Here," Carla said, opening the correct drawer and handing me a long wooden spoon. "You'll end up dropping that little spoon in there, and you'll have to fish it out, contaminating our iced tea supply."

"Contaminating?" I shot her a look.

"I don't know where your hands have been." She looked at me in a way that forced me to suspect, even just a little, that she was interested in where my hands had been.

I poured her a cup of the powdered interpretation of iced tea, which tasted mostly cold with a vague lemon sugar flavor. Despite it being kind of gross with pellets of unmixed powder breaking apart in my mouth, it did feel good to drink in my house without air conditioning.

"So I was thinking." She set her glass down and looked up. "What do you think about not having a set list and just going up there and seeing what happens?"

Surprised by the idea, because she struck me as someone who liked things organized and predetermined, I thought about it. It was daring to go out there with no safety net because we could freeze up. But there was also something sexy about putting our connection to the test like that in front of other people. "Okay." I looked at her and nodded. "Yeah, we could do that."

"It's just an idea." I absorbed her big eyes looking at me. "I mean, it wouldn't be much different from what we're already doing in your basement."

Thinking of the things I wanted to do with her in my basement, my gutter mind was then purified by Alsatian blasphemies, courtesy of my father.

"*Got verdàmmi noch e mol!*" I heard him shout in the hallway approaching the kitchen.

"*Qu'est-ce qu'il y a, Papa?*" I turned my cheek in his direction, in concern over his use of such strong language. "*C'est toujours le . . ?*" I searched for the word. "*Le* camcorder?" I then looked at Carla, who was looking at me in a way I liked. "I don't think I know the word in French." I looked at her.

My dad walked into the kitchen with the camcorder, pushing too many buttons at the same time, which I was sure was canceling something out.

"*Ce truc,*" he started and then noticed Carla at the counter. "This thing doesn't work if my life depended on it."

"Well, let's hope your life doesn't depend on a camcorder," I said, taking it out of his hand to investigate.

He walked over to Carla to give her a kiss on her cheeks while I uselessly pressed the same buttons over and over like my dad did. I, however, didn't have God damn me twice like he did. When I heard the doorbell ring, I handed it back to him with a shrug that said I didn't know either. Walking down the hallway, I turned and called out to whoever was listening, "You know, I'm borderline supportive and embarrassed about having my dad film our first show. It's like, we *should* document it, but again, it's my dad in the front filming us on that dorky-ass thing. *Not* very punk rock."

"Punk rock! Ha!" My dad scoffed. "*N'importe quoi.*"

I opened the door to find Tony doing air guitar, and before I could correct his form because his guitar was up to his neck, I saw that Allison's car had pulled into the driveway.

"Are we gonna rock this shit or what?" he said with his tongue out, wearing wraparound black sunglasses and a NYFD t-shirt.

Seeing my dad over my shoulder in the kitchen, he walked past me. "What's up, monsieur?" Tony's voice boomed down the hallway as I walked out to greet Allison.

"Hey," I said, opening her car door.

"Hey." Her face said, "You owe me."

Stepping out of the car, she was already in vacation wear: a navy hooded sweater paired with white shorts and her hair pulled back into a sensible braid. I felt a pang of guilt for having a different emotional reaction when Carla arrived. I used to like how different Allison and I were; it was cute. Now the dissimilarities were closing in on me. It was like every time I tried to shake the doubt off, like it was all in my head, I'd get another reminder of how we were drifting apart. I could feel the fissures more than before because we *weren't* in high school anymore, and the changes were starting to really show. It felt like it was all going to come down to who was going to survive the next phase together and who would be left behind.

Carla

On my way to Pete's, I sat at a red light and went over the things I was nervous about. At first, it was playing in front of total strangers and Allison, who I knew would be giving me dead eye the entire time. I was also nervous about playing in front of my family, whom I ended up telling about the show. I had long gotten over expecting a congratulation for anything, but I didn't know if I was secure enough to have my efforts critiqued and/or completely ignored. When I left the house, they seemed to be in good spirits, though, even my mom. I didn't dare sneak a sip of the Crystal Light she was drinking, which was something I did from time to time to see if I'd end up with a big gulp of vodka in my mouth. Sometimes it was just better not knowing.

I wore a comfortable white t-shirt that fit me tighter than my usual ones, jeans, and a clean face, for a no-frills look I would have frowned at as a teenager because all my idols wore costumes on stage, from tutus to ripped up baby doll dresses. I pulled up in front of Pete's, where he was already waiting for me at the front door, looking as cool as always in his relaxed jeans and a fitted t-shirt. In 100 percent humidity, I didn't know how he got his thick hair to always look perfectly messy like it did in high school. His hair just naturally fell into place. Whenever I tried to look perfectly undone without the help of a flat iron and products, I looked like Joey Ramone. And a little like Great-Aunt Bernie when she got a perm in the late '80s that smelled like rotten eggs. Not wanting to look like either of these people, I put a light gloss in my hair to tame the frizz and pinned my bangs back, which felt like pulling the curtains open. I liked being able to hide behind my bangs, something that would have come in handy at our first show since connecting with people wasn't exactly my forte. Good thing I was a lead singer in a band, I chuckled to myself.

Allison drove us to the show, and with me in the backseat, I felt like a kid in trouble with mom and dad since neither of them spoke up front. Before we got inside the bar, Pete and I snuck a little smile to each other. Then the rest of the hour went by in flashes of bartenders offering us sodas, the owner showing us the stage equipment, our parents arriving, my mom *not* being drunk, Allison pouting, us doing a quick soundcheck over a baseball game playing on the hanging TVs, the bar stools filling, Pete's dad bringing his own sausage, and finally . . . the house lights coming down.

No longer hiding behind soundcheck — me behind my bangs or us behind cover songs — it was just Pete and me up there. And if we sucked, we were about to find out. I turned away from the glare of the stage lights and looked back at him and said, "Alright, I'll see you on the other side." And just as Pete was about to crack his sticks, I remembered something. Into the mic, I said, "Oh, and we're The Disenchanted."

Pete

If we overanalyzed it anymore, we'd be fucked. So when Carla announced us, I hit my sticks, and we took off. We definitely were not in my basement anymore because that night on stage, I watched someone else front our band. It wasn't the girl hiding behind her hair at rehearsal. It wasn't the insecure girl at high school. She was the lead singer and guitarist of my fucking band.

From behind my drums, I watched as she moved her entire body with the music. Swinging her hips to the beat, she dramatically pulled her arm away to prolong notes while expertly turning toward the amp to extract tasteful feedback. I had no idea she was holding back this swagger. And then something else happened. People who weren't our parents, or Tony, came to the front to dance; dance to our songs we had created out of thin air. The energy between us was palpable, our interplay at its strongest as we experimented with texture by adding fills and breaks we had never rehearsed.

We were booked for thirty minutes and finished our set with three to spare. Not willing to give them up, Carla gave me a nod that said, "Follow me," and started playing the chords to one of my favorite songs. I wouldn't have thought of it myself, but damn she knew how to call a situation with a song that wasn't even hers. "You're Gonna Miss Me" by The 13th Floor Elevators fronted by her voice and playing the harmonica parts on her guitar was a next-level experience.

When the set closed out, I met her up front, and together we bowed. We never discussed doing that, but it felt natural. Thank you, crowd, for not rolling your eyes at us, and thank you for not expecting us to play Toto. Carla then pulled her strap over her head, and before friends and family swarmed us, I reached my hand out to pull her off to the side. I wanted to congratulate her on her first live performance that she killed, but waiting for me already was Allison. Standing with her sweater in her hand and her bag hanging off her shoulder, she looked at me expectantly.

"That was great, Pete." She pushed out a smile, appearing uncomfortable. "Were those new songs?"

"No, we just added shit to some of our originals. I mean, we didn't even practice any of that."

"Oh," she said, unsure how to respond, which in fairness, when you're not a musician who craves moments like that, I understood. "So we should probably get going soon."

"Yeah," I said as I turned my head to look for Carla.

My mom and dad then came over, my dad holding a paper plate of herb sausage I knew he brought from home, which meant he had my mom carry it in her purse.

"That was fucking great, honey!" My mom grabbed me in a hug. "Really, something else." She then turned to Allison and warmly reached her arm out and said hello.

"Hi, Anna," Allison said to my mom.

"Hi, sweetie, how are you?" She then looked at both of us. "I guess you guys are heading out soon?"

I knew better not to respond and to just let Allison regale my mom with the plan as my mind rewound highlights from the show. All I wanted to do was talk to Carla and bounce back and forth with her a bit. I looked around the bar that was getting more crowded in anticipation of the next band and spotted her on the other side, talking to her parents. I then saw my father painfully cutting his sausage log with a butter knife, which had me shake my head in amusement. I could just hear the conversation between my parents with my mom forbidding him from bringing his knives we got two summers ago in Laguiole; knives she called death weapons.

Motioning at him, I said to my mom, "What, they don't have food here?"

"He brought bread too," she said with still eyes.

"Oh, well, that I can understand."

"So" —she rolled her eyes to ignore the lifelong debate my dad and I have with her that there is no good bread in America (because there isn't)— "where's Carla? I want to congratulate her on her wonderful performance."

"Mom." I looked to the side. "It's a *show*. Not a performance. This isn't, like, a High School Theatre Production of *Annie Get Your Gun*." I then looked at Allison, who I got a giggle out of because we saw that play together senior year, but only because we were all forced to write papers on it.

Then the owner, Phil, came running up to me. Shit, I thought. Did we blow something out or use something we weren't supposed to?

"There you are, kid!"

"Hi. Everything okay?"

"Yeah, that was some set! You guys got somethin' goin' there!"

"Oh, thank you. That's really nice of you —"

"Yeah, yeah." Phil waved away my modesty. "Where are you kids booked tomorrow?"

Carla

I didn't know what had come over me. It was like once Pete cracked his sticks, I morphed into someone I'd only seen in a VH1 *Behind the Music* documentary. It was like my body channeled Prince's swaying hips, the showmanship of Nancy Wilson, and the gusto of X's Exene Cervenka. The songs just flowed through me as my body reverberated in rhythm with Pete. I figured the show would have been an extension of our rehearsals, not this energy-packed performance with the audience jumping off their sacred spots at the bar to dance to songs they had never even heard of. I swear there was no hidden meaning behind "You're Gonna Miss Me." It just sort of came to me because I had been listening to it earlier that day. That was all. Really.

Afterward, I wanted to jump into his arms in the exuberance of our first show because, well, we did it! We had worked hard for this, and the reward of people actually liking us was intoxicating, as well as validating that we weren't just wasting our time in a basement. The only person in the world I could share this sentiment with was Pete. But when I saw Allison waiting for him on the side of the stage, I understood my place.

At the far end of the bar, I saw my mom smoking a cigarette with a glass of white wine parked in front of her, my dad drinking a beer, and my two brothers leaning against the bar; Lo in a tank top offensively referred to as a "wife beater" and Claudio in a Yankees shirt I hoped Pete wouldn't see. I snaked through the crowd, thanking the bar patrons who told me they enjoyed the set, until I reached my family.

"Hey!" my dad called out. "There she is!"

With his arm reached out, I leaned into him and then looked over at my mom. Pressing her shoulders back as if preparing herself for a performance, she took an exaggerated deep breath.

"Where did you learn how to do that?" She forced a plastic smile that deepened the lines in her face. "I was so surprised."

But before I could answer, my brother interrupted. "Nah, seriously, Car," Lo said, holding court as if he was going to say the most important thing of the night. "That was pretty good."

"Really." Claudio pulled his eyes off the game and nodded in agreement. "It was actually good. Keep it up."

"Honey . . ." My dad gently squeezed my shoulder. "What can we get our little rock star?" He then leaned closer and conspiratorially said in a lower voice, "You want me to get you a drink *drink*?"

"Thanks, Dad." I smiled at my dad's juvenile expression, his light brown eyes practically sparkling at the thought of "pulling a fast one" on the bar months before my twenty-first birthday. "But I'll just have a Shirley Temple and a glass of water."

My family was shockingly responsive, so fishing for further acknowledgment would be pushing it. With not much more to say, I stayed with my dad waiting for my drink, just happy my mom wasn't wasted. From across the bar, I saw Pete not looking for me, content, as he talked with Allison and Anna by the stage.

Maybe I'm not supposed to be friends with my bandmate, I thought. Maybe it was a romantic idea I had imagined in my head. And *maybe* the big open secret was that all bands interacted powerfully on stage, but when the curtains closed, they were mere acquaintances that didn't need to recap the show together...or tell the other they were admitted into an insanely competitive music conservatory.

When I saw Pete leave with Allison through the side exit without so much as acknowledging me, I admit it stung. But I forced myself to focus on which was more important: my hurt feelings or the band? Only one was going to get me to where I wanted to be in life.

Pete

"Why is everything this summer about her!" Allison screamed at me in the parking lot.

"What do you mean?" I slid my hands down my face in fatigue. "Because I told the bar owner to talk to Carla? Did you notice *I* didn't talk to her, which by the way, is starting to get really fucking weird."

"You know what's weird, Pete?" she said. "Is that you have this whole thing with this other girl, and I'm supposed to just sit and watch it unfold. *That* is fucking weird."

"This whole thing?" I held my hands out in disbelief. "I barely talk to her!"

"You know what I mean," she hissed. "Stop acting like you don't because it's starting to get really annoying. And what was that last song?"

"The cover?"

"Well, *are* you going to miss her? Because she seemed to be screaming it in your face."

"Allison," I said, ready to pull my hair out. "It was a cover. She didn't write the song."

"Yeah, well, she chose to sing it!"

I looked at her like she was being ridiculous, but I knew there was no winning here and said, "Whatever. You're right. Let's just fucking go."

In silence, we drove the almost three-hour drive out to Montauk. There, we spent a miserable week with Allison, who laughed along with Perry's gross, elitist comments about the locals being townies, while Constance looked at me the entire time with confusion. I didn't know why I was there either I wanted to tell her as my girlfriend flirted with her boyfriend.

I called Carla from a phone booth outside a pizzeria to explain why I bagged on her. At first, she was a little icy but then blew it off by saying it was fine when I knew it wasn't. I was starting to wish she'd just tell me to fuck off already. I think it would feel good for both of us. But instead, everything was always *fine*.

After I left The Night Owl, she told me Phil caught up with her, and the two arranged a show for the Friday I got back. He also introduced her to some of his friends, other bar owners, who were also impressed with the set. She collected phone numbers and called them all the next day for advice on how to get more shows. When I got home, she surprised me with a mini-tour of midweek shows in greasy dive bars in the tri-state area.

We were going on tour even if we were wildly unprepared. We didn't have a bassist to blame. We didn't have CDs to sell. My girlfriend was pissed. And Tony, who took up more personal space than any of us, had to come along and babysit. But off we went for ten days in a rusty sky-blue Chevy van that looked like it kidnapped children.

Rock n' roll.

13

Carla

These guys had to stop saying we were on tour. We were not on tour; we were booked at a few dive joints in the Northeast that had weekday openings. The scheduling made absolutely no sense, but I had to work with the availabilities they had on such short notice. For example, we would drive to a gig in Hartford, then drive back down to New Haven to a canceled gig because they had no idea what we were talking about. We laughed about the possibility that I booked the show with a busboy messing with us. We didn't laugh about the gas money, though.

Then there would be a one-day lull before our show in Cherry Hill, New Jersey, before having to be in a suburb of Pittsburgh the next day. The bars were empty; we slept uncomfortably in Laurent's old work van, and some of my cables were shorting out. And there was also Pete who felt the need to quote Walt Whitman's *Song of the Open Road* each time he started up the van. Even Tony had had enough and tried to throw the poem back at him. "Yeah, yeah, we know, man," he groaned. "'Camerado, I give you my hand . . . yada, yada, will you come travel with me and hell hath no fury'; will you fuckin' drive now?" I had never laughed so hard in my entire life.

Then there was Tony who took the whole tour fantasy to the next level. When we pulled up to the bars, he would feel slighted and even confused that half-naked women weren't there to greet us. We didn't have fans. Hell, we didn't even have CDs. So how were we supposed to have groupies? But Tony insisted. Every time.

"What's the deal?" He looked around the empty parking lot as we loaded our gear in. "I saw *Almost Famous*, and shouldn't there be, I don't know, honeys in fur coats and bikinis wanting to chill with us?"

I set my amp down and turned toward him to explain it. Again. "It's ninety degrees out here. We all have beef jerky breath, and we're about to play at" — I turned around to read the sign — "at Chips Ahoy where tonight is Too Much Tuesday with bottomless chips when you order the jumbo fish platter. If I had to guess, I'd say the honeys are sitting this one out."

"Fucking Tony," Pete said with a laugh, carrying his bass drum inside. "You really want to be hanging out with people wearing fur right now?"

"Come on, man. You know what I'm saying," Tony said through gritted teeth at Pete, giving his shoulder a flick. As he walked alongside him carrying a puny cymbal stand that looked extra small in his hands, he said, "Don't even try and say you didn't get into this for the mad honeys. Don't even try to play it like that."

Amused, Pete said nothing and just made that face reserved for Tony comments. A look that said, "What are we going to do with this guy?" And, "Please don't ever change," as he proceeded through the bar's side door.

"I'm, like, in the Twilight Zone with *yous* people." Tony shook his head in disbelief. "I swear to God."

Once in the dark bar, after my eyes took a minute to adjust from the day glow of the mid-July heat, I said to Tony, "Here's what. I can't promise you any *honeys*." I looked to the side in reluctance of even having to use the word. "But, after the show, I'll get us that jumbo fish platter, and since we're not driving out tonight, I'll throw in a pitcher of beer."

"Deal."

That night we played a great show to the twenty people braving fried food on a scorching hot summer's night. No one danced like the crowd on Long Island, but there was a lot of toe-tapping, head nodding, and full applause, which felt like enough, granted it was only our sixth show. We ended the set with "Tony's Theme" by the Pixies, with Pete and me both barking "To-ny! To-ny!" at the end. As predicted, Tony air guitared with his tongue sticking out, and afterward, insisted it was one of our original songs. Even when we told him it wasn't.

At the bar, after ordering our food and beer, it suddenly occurred to me what day it was. I leaned forward, shouting over the second band, and asked the bartender, "Any chance you have a candle?"

Pete

I'll never forget the sight of Carla walking toward our table at the fish shack in Pittsburgh. She held a pitcher of beer in one hand, and in the other was a breadbasket with a candle sticking out of a dinner roll. Walking slowly, careful not to drip wax on parts of our daily sustenance, she inched little by little with the glow of the candle flush against her suntanned cheeks. I couldn't believe she remembered my birthday since I hadn't said anything. Allison got mad since we never celebrated my birthday together. I told her I didn't want to make a big deal of it and then left for tour, which I admit was kind of dick of me. But this year *was* kind of a big deal. I was turning twenty-one.

"Now I know why you're not interested in the honeys," Tony said, as Carla took five minutes to walk to the table. "I hear you, man."

"Hear what?" I looked at him. "I didn't say anything."

"You don't have to. I get it," he said, nudging his chin in the direction of Carla. "Carla is like the OG honey. You don't gotta hide it."

"You know what I want for my birthday?" I took my eyes off her and turned to him. "Is for you to be less observant for the rest of the night because your observations are usually off."

"Nah, I'm not off about nothin'. But you know what, it's your birthday, and I'll keep my *astute observations . . .*" He pulled up an imaginary tie. "To myself." And then a more sincere look washed across his face, and he grabbed my shoulder. "But happy birthday, man. Is it fucked up I didn't know?"

"No, I don't even know how she knows."

"Like I said, she's the OG honey."

Carla arrived at the table and began singing "Happy Birthday." Over the bluegrass band, though, I could only really see her mouth moving. It was weird; I was twenty-one, but now what? I guess that made me a real adult, but I didn't feel like a real one. I was old enough to drink, but for some reason didn't feel old enough or responsible enough to handle my emotions. Emotions that were zipping through me in confusion and psychotic technicolor, reminding me of the two times I had taken LSD.

After she slid into the booth next to me, she and Tony waited for me to blow out my candle. I took a second to pick out one of the many wishes I had in my head. There were so many, most that were too complicated for a hot night in July. So I decided to keep it simple. I wished to have a good night with these guys and to get back home the next day safe and sound. *Voilà.*

Carla

He seemed surprised I knew it was his birthday. It was funny because it wasn't exactly a deep-dive investigation since it *was* on the calendar in his kitchen. When I saw it was July 18, though, I smiled because he was a Cancer. Despite his rough exterior with all the cursing and sarcasm, he really was sensitive and protective of himself, sort of like a soft-shell crab. As if fitting another piece to the puzzle, his sign made sense, like how he moved at his own pace, was thoughtful with little things like cleaning the top off a can of Coke before handing it to Tony, his intuition, and how he overthought things to the point of obsession. I admit to looking up our compatibility in my mom's copy of *Sun Signs.*

At the bar, one watered-down pitcher of beer turned into a second, and turned into a third that was on the house. Surrendering to the freedom of summer and the fact that we had nowhere to be except our van parked out front, I let loose and danced like the underage drinker I was. Once the live acts finished, we talked Pete into coughing up some of his payphone quarters to use for the jukebox. When I heard the opening guitar riff of "Blister in the Sun," I couldn't hold back and let Pete finish putting in the rest of the songs Tony and I had been shouting in his ear. I took a big gulp of my beer and joined Tony on the dance floor to dance to the Violent Femmes.

With the jukebox stocked with everything from Tony's Guns n' Roses to me and Pete's Talking Heads, we couldn't resist dipping into our gas budget to play more songs. It was probably a bad business move to be giving money back to the bar, but it was so worth it to reenact the "Dancing in the Dark" video with Tony, who was surprisingly a fantastic dancer. With him as The Boss and me, a young Courteney Cox, we recreated the video's iconic dance scene. Breathless, danced out, and stomachs sore from laughing, we ended the night with another pitcher of beer we didn't need, and the bartender put free credits in the jukebox so we could listen to Nirvana's entire *Unplugged* album.

After we loaded out, we found Tony passed out across the back seat where I had been sleeping. His large body rolled up into a ball on the bench, he looked as peaceful as one could be sleeping on something half your size.

"Do you want me to wake him?" Pete said inaudibly, brushing his teeth with a small water bottle in his hand.

"No." I looked at him over the back seat. "Let's just leave him. He looks somewhat comfortable."

I reached over the seat and grabbed a balled-up blanket and put it over Tony's shoulders. Then walking around to the back and stepping over Pete's toothpaste spit puddles on the street, I waited as he got himself settled in the van. With his shoes off, he clumsily laid down blankets and pillows, arranging them around our equipment.

I then climbed into the van, and grabbing one door at a time, I locked us in for the night. Crouched in the back, balancing on my lilac Old Navy flip-flops, I took some cream out of my bag to run down my arms to cover up the bar smell emitting from my skin. From the corner of my eye, I observed Pete as he neatly made our bed, and then delicately, he took his glasses off and placed them on top of his snare drum.

"Okay," he said, feeling out in front of him. "This is the part of my day when I can't see shit." He then morphed his voice into a little girl's and said, "Thomas Jay can't see without his glasses. He can't see without his glasses."

Incredulously, I looked at him and said, "Are you quoting *My Girl?*"

"I totally am. My cousin Amy and I would watch that movie over and over in my basement, hoping every time the ending would change. Like, who thought it was a good idea to have the *Home Alone* kid *killed* at the end? Kind of fucked up to watch as a kid."

"It was, wasn't it?" I thought about my own feeling of hopelessness after seeing the movie. It was the first movie I had seen that didn't have a happy ending. Like, he *dies* at the end. It all felt very final at the time, making it hard to resume regular activities after. What was the point of riding my bike, I'd think, when a swarm of killer bees can just take us out? "I used to watch that movie all the time too," I said in retrospective regret that we hadn't watched it together. "Probably at the same time you were watching it right up the street on HBO."

"It *was* on HBO all the time, wasn't it?"

Once he was in bed, I crawled in next to him. As we lay next to each other, I stared at the dark van, feeling a little too drunk to fall asleep. From Pete's shifting around, his long legs banging into things, I could tell he couldn't sleep either. Still wearing my street clothes, I tugged at my shorts that were riding up and twisting around my waist. It would have been better to just take them off, but Pete and I were sharing the blanket. Once I got into as comfortable a position as I could, with the grooves in the van's floor digging into my side, I finally got still and began to sweetly drift off.

"What the fuck was that!" Pete then startled me.

"What was what?"

I turned over, and as my eyes refocused, I could see him feeling his face, brushing his hand wildly across it.

"I just felt a tickle on my face."

Leaning slightly over him, I looked as best as I could but didn't see anything.

"There it is again," he said, swatting his cheek.

"Maybe," I said in a slightly teasing voice, "it's a faerie. A faerie giving you a goodnight kiss."

"A what?" he said joylessly.

"A faerie." I tried to conceal my giggling. "You know they say that if you feel a little brush on your face like if you're walking through the forest and you think it's a spider web or something, but you don't see anything, it's actually a forest faerie."

"*They* say that?" He sounded skeptical.

"It's common faerie folklore."

"Faerie folklore?" He then laughed. "You really *are* from another planet, aren't you?"

"Pete," I insisted. "The literature is very convincing."

"The literature?" He turned his head to face me, his eyes flickering in amusement. "I'm sure. I'd almost believe it if I didn't just realize it's your hair. There was this little strand tickling my face."

"Sorry," I said, pulling it around to the other side. "My hair gets everywhere. There's just so much of it."

"Don't be sorry," he said. "I like your hair."

"I like your hair too."

"You do?" He sounded surprised.

I turned my face back toward his and said, "Yeah, I do."

Looking at him, our faces inches apart, I could feel his exhales that smelled like spearmint toothpaste warm on my face.

"By the way," he whispered, "I would've totally watched *My Girl* with you back in the day."

The next morning, I woke up groggy and sweaty, with the sun already burning through the metal roof. The blankets kicked down to our ankles made me thankful for sleeping in my shorts. I looked over to find that Pete had rolled onto my side. With him close to me, I looked at him, noticing how pretty he was when he slept. I faintly touched his eyelashes that practically rested on his cheeks. I thought about Allison, thinking she was crazy for wanting to change any part of him.

As he began to shift, possibly feeling me staring at him, I looked around to see if any of us were smart enough to have a bottle of water, but no one had. I had dry mouth and a headache, which made that loud continuous beeping sound outside unbearable. And then I thought. Beeping sound? What beeping sound? It was then I felt a jolt from under me, like that feeling before a rollercoaster takes off. My body then lurched back with my head smashing into the backseat as our equipment came crashing down on us.

We were getting towed.

Pete

It was the best birthday I had ever had. I couldn't just pin it down to one thing; it was all of it, from the show to the Tony side comments to the disgusting beer. I was relieved at the end of the night when he passed out in the back seat. But not for those reasons. Carla is a fraction of a quarter of his size, which meant I'd have more room to stretch out and maybe get some actual sleep without the fear of a two-hundred-pound guy rolling over and suffocating me. It *was* nice sleeping next to her, though; she smelled like a cupcake.

As we drove back to New York, it already felt too soon, and I wondered how and when we were going to get back on the road again. The next time it'd have to be cross-country to see what the rest of America had to offer our little band. I'd be the impulsive Neal Cassady to Carla's mysterious Jack Kerouac. But of course, without the reckless driving. Or the prostitutes in Mexico. As I looked out the window while Tony drove us over the Throgs Neck Bridge on that cloudless afternoon, I thought about all of the shit we'd get into. Who knew what kinds of situations and people we would encounter, where we would sleep, and when we would shower? I wasn't even sure driving west with New York plates was a good idea since the rest of the country thought we were all a bunch of elitist assholes, but I couldn't wait to find out.

My birthday wish, however, deceived me and knocked me on my ass when I woke up to a cymbal falling on me, as our van was getting towed *with us inside*. There was the loud thud, like thunder cracking a mile away, from Tony rolling off the back seat and onto the floor. My glasses, almost getting crushed by an amp. And Carla, screaming with her hands out to protect herself from music debris crashing down on her.

That day we learned a one-hundred-and-twenty-seven-dollar-and-sixty-six-cent lesson: read fucking street signs.

Carla

When we got back from "tour," we were more motivated than ever. Even Tony was ready to head out again, which was the only way Allison would allow Pete to go in the first place. She was pissed the entire time we were on the road, with Pete having to sweet-talk her at almost every rest stop. When we got back, we weren't allowed to practice anymore. Still, we played two more shows at The Night Owl, gaining increased insight from Phil, who we learned was once a roadie for Emerson, Lake, and Palmer. He had a wealth of knowledge on touring and would spout details as I followed him around the empty bar with my notebook. He told me that, along with contacting venues, we should get in touch with more established local acts who had a built-in audience and try to get on the bottom of their bills. I was nervous at first to be cold-calling these random bands, more so than calling booking managers, but the bands turned out to be helpful.

I focused on the business side, which allowed Pete to spend his last weeks of summer with Allison. Also, word got out that he had a van, so he was constantly helping friends move stoves, couches, and refrigerators into off-campus housing before school started again in the fall. I would check in with him once a day to let him know I had booked another show. Because we weren't expecting much of a payout, and after sending an MP3 of a rough demo we made, getting gigs wasn't as hard as I thought it would be. Pete felt bad I was doing all the work. But, honestly, it felt good being assertive with the busy and, at times, snippy club managers who didn't take me seriously and called me annoying things like sweetheart.

After a few weeks, I had arranged a cute little bar tour that kicked off in October with The Disenchanted booked from Ohio to California. I tried to get us a show in Hollywood, a place I had always wanted to visit because it felt like fantasy fiction compacted into a city but had no luck. Instead, I got us a gig in San Diego. While Pete and I didn't have much time to talk, he did call me after Britney Spears's performance at the Video Music Awards. Instead of the nude catsuit from the year before, she danced on stage in emerald green panties and an eight-foot-long boa constrictor.

"Did you see that shit?" he said as soon as I picked up the phone.

"The snake performance? Yeah, I saw it." I smirked. "I suppose you're all hot and bothered?"

"Hardly."

Hearing the surprise in my voice, he elaborated, "I guess I would have thought it was hot if she didn't look completely terrified during the whole thing...or if the song wasn't totally offensive, something *no one* in the audience seemed to notice."

"I'm a slave for you?" I thought about it for a second. "Yeah, I see your point." I tightened my jaw at the distasteful lyric. "But I think she was trying to be more S&M. It was supposed to be, you know, sexy."

"Well, that just makes it worse." He sounded horrified. "Also, I bet it's 'Slave 4 U' with the number 4 and the letter U totally ripping Prince's 'I Would Die 4 U'," I could feel him bristle at the blasphemy. "The day Britney shreds the holy shit out of the guitar like Prince is when she can rip off his moves, but until then— On his end, I then heard another call coming in. "Shit, Car, I gotta go. It's my mom's trip trader."

"José?"

"Yeah." He chuckled. "So, uh, I'll see you on your birthday?"

"Yep."

It was September, and I was about to hit the road in a few weeks with Pete and Tony. They say you never know when you're living in the good times and only recognize them when you look back; "Glory Days" as The Boss calls them. But I wasn't letting mine pass by. I knew I was smack in the middle of some of the best days of my life.

For my birthday, Pete wanted to take me to a bar and buy me my first official drink, but turning twenty-one didn't automatically make me want to get wasted.

"Weak," he said but complied and picked me up that night to go to Hildebrandt's, one of the last original diners in our area.

Together we sat at the 1950s marble counter top, swiveled on our stools, and ate ice cream. I had just turned twenty-one, I thought to myself as I glanced at my reflection in the mirror, looking for evidence of change. Did that make me a real adult, I wondered as I scraped the bottom of the metal bowl to get the last bit of my peach ice cream. Did drinking alcohol on your birthday make you an adult? Or paying bills? Understanding politics? Having sex all the time? Since I wasn't doing any of these things, maybe I'd just bypass the adult phase and go straight to becoming a senior citizen. When I told Pete, he looked at me with those hazelnut eyes that I'd fall in love with if I stared into them too long, and he said, "Can I come with you?" We smiled at each other before he added, "To quote the great Brian Wilson, maybe we just weren't made for these times." Pete looked away for a moment. "Also, I think you'd make a pretty cute senior citizen." He blinked, his eyelashes picking up the light in the overhead hanging Tiffany lamps. "A mean one, but still, pretty cute."

I may not have known what being an adult meant, but little did I know the very next morning would test the definition by forcing me to see life as I knew it in a completely different way.

14

Pete

It obviously wasn't real, I told myself over and over. As I cleaned my lenses with my t-shirt to make sure I was seeing straight, I stood in my kitchen in complete denial. It had to be footage of some unreleased apocalyptic action flick. It just had to be. But why was it rolling on repeat when the stupid morning talk shows should have been on? I suddenly longed for the soulless talk show hosts licking some celebrity's ass, claiming to love their new movie. I didn't usually turn on the TV first thing in the morning for that exact reason, but I had slept terribly the night before . . . maybe from the coffee ice cream and then the double espresso I had with my dad when I got home . . . and needed something to wake me up. Well, I definitely got woken the fuck up that morning. When I realized my mom was on a trip, I jolted toward the phone to call her, my heart feeling like it skipped a beat when I heard the front door unlock.

"Holy shit!" My mom burst through the door, pulling her roller-board behind her. "Do you see what's happening!"

"Oh my God, Mom!" I ran to her and pulled her into a hug. Squeezing her in her uniform, that navy blue blazer that felt like sandpaper, she wrapped her arms around me where I could feel the fear trembling from her core.

"I was in the employee lot when I found out. I didn't even get on the bus to go to the terminal to sign in. I just came home," she said, sniffling in my arms. "I don't care if I get a missed trip."

"Mom," I said. "I don't think they're giving out missed trips today."

"You don't know the company."

"I'm just so glad you're here. You could have been on one of those planes." I felt my eyes swell with tears as the reality started to set in.

"Pete," she said in a still tone.

"I know," I said with my voice muffled in her shoulder that smelled like her Angel perfume. "What are the odds?"

"Well, not only that but," she said in a clearer voice like she wanted to make a point. "I'm not domestic."

Over her shoulder, I watched the news anchors on TV trying to look calm and keep a professional face in order to not create more panic, but their antiseptic reporting came across as inhumane, as if this sort of thing happened every day. Fuck. Off. I thought, even though I knew there really was no proper way to report something so catastrophic.

Just as I went to reach back for my mom, the phone rang, startling me more than it would have. I thought it might have been Allison or my dad, but instead, it was a hysterical call from my grandmother imploring me to get the family to flee to Canada. She seemed to have an elaborate plan so worked out that I was ready for her to tell me to retrieve the fake passports buried in the backyard. With the phone in one ear, I had my grandmother recalling the story in morbid detail of the blood that washed down the streets of Ammerschwihr at the end of World War II, and in the other ear was my mother crying, the weight of her head pressing my shoulder down. I went back and forth between French and English, saying words I didn't even believe because I didn't know if everything would be alright. When my dad finally walked in—his face devoid of color—he just stared at me because there were no words. There were just no words. I extended the phone to him and gently placed my mom's head on his shoulder and grabbed my car keys.

Passing her house, when I didn't see her car in her driveway, I drove to the photo shop where I saw it parked around the back. In the store, she was sitting with her boss behind the counter, listening to the radio with her hands covering her mouth in disbelief.

"I can't believe what they're saying," she said, looking at me in a daze. "Maybe I'm just not getting it since I can't see what's happening. We should find a TV. Parkway has one, I think."

"No, you don't want to see it." I shuddered at the thought. "Hold off as long as you can because you won't be able to unsee it. It's, like, playing on a loop in my head."

I made eye contact with Carla's boss and helped myself around the counter to shake his hand.

"Hello," he said gravely. Looking at his face and hearing his subtle accent, I paused for a second because that's when I saw it: French face.

"*Bonjour?*" I squinted as I waited for his response, wondering if I had my dad's gift.

"*Bonjour,*" he responded in a tone that said, of course. "Abel," he continued, giving my hand a firm squeeze.

"Pete," I said back. "*Enchanté.*"

173

For Carla's benefit, we switched back to English, but every so often, Abel would speak French because, like my dad, it felt more comfortable to express himself in his mother tongue when emotions ran high. Carla would look at me and give me a nod as if to say it was okay. He then made us a pot of coffee, and the three of us sat in swiveling office chairs, sipping it and staring at the radio as it told us awful things.

Looking out through the shop windows onto the usually bustling Willis Avenue, large blocks of time would pass before a single car drove by. I thought about how Allison was taking the news and how scared she must have been too. I knew I had to head back home soon to see my family and check in with her, but I felt frozen in my own disbelief. Did this really happen? I tried to rationalize to myself over and over. It was then I felt as naïve and small as ever because terror attacks happened all the time in other countries. But never had it occurred to me that it would happen in America, which to my horror only proved just how privileged and bourgeois I'd been all along.

Carla

The days and weeks after September 11, it was hard to know what to do with ourselves. The stink of burning jet fuel with haunting smells of carnage swept up the North Shore and was the first thing you'd smell when walking out of your house. Band practice was on hiatus because we weren't feeling terribly musical, but also because Pete's house had become a haven for flight attendants unable to get home since the airports were closed. Helping his parents with grocery shopping, preparing meals, and even giving up his room, he didn't have time for much else. As for my family, they managed to eat more. Eating while talking about what to eat at the next meal was how *my* family dealt with grief. Well, that, and vodka.

Needing a break from our families and the around-the-clock news coverage, Pete picked me up one night. We grabbed a coffee at 7-11 and then drove down to the marina that faced Manhattan in Port Washington. While listening to *The Bends*, we sat in his car in silence, truly feeling like it was the end of the world. As Thom Yorke cried through the car speakers that everything and everyone was broken, we looked at Lower Manhattan; the smoke still billowing out in large puffs from Ground Zero. Pete kept mumbling about how we were being fucked with somehow by the government and how spoiled we were as a nation. I didn't know what to say because I didn't really know what I was feeling. A part of me wanted to have sex with him or do hard drugs just to feel confused and scared about something else. While the other part of me just wanted to go somewhere and hide forever. Our tour was also coming up, and I wondered when it would be a good time to mention it. But looking over at him in the driver's seat, haunted by tragedy, I decided to wait.

The following day, I came home from work to find Lorenzo's handwritten messages from three different bars we had upcoming gigs at. Home, I sighed to myself as I walked up to my room, holding the messages. I hated being at home more than I had ever remembered. Since the attacks, my mom's drinking got worse, and she started accusing me of being a boyfriend stealer. When I told her I wasn't, she said something that hurt even more than her implying I was a whore.

"Well, it's what you have up your sleeve." She looked at me with vodka-fueled eyes. "I never trusted girls like you because you're sneaky; that's what you are." Her eyes then lowered down to my chest, and with a curled lip, she said, "The only reason he's in a band with you is to get ahold of those." Her eyes burned with resentment. "Don't think it's because you have talent."

Only my mother knew the exact words to say to hurt me; it was a skill she had mastered to an art form. She knew how much time and passion I had put into learning the guitar and that this was her way of taking it away from me. The words stung as I felt my face drip in embarrassment for thinking I was good at something and then in shame for even entertaining the idea of sleeping with him.

Knowing how far into the bottle she was, I left the house to take a drive. Winding down the country backroads of Old Westbury, the trees still lush in their late summer greens, I gazed out the windshield and wondered if I should go if only to finally get away from her? And was it so wrong that he *may* have wanted to sleep with me too? And was it too soon to be having these gluttonous thoughts of sex and rock n' roll after everything that had happened? I had never been so confused about so many things at once. Either way, I had to call Pete. When I got him on the phone, he sounded distant. I asked him what he thought about the tour, and after waiting for what felt like a good minute before responding, he said he had to talk to Allison first.

Pete

"You're still thinking of going?" Allison squealed into the phone.

"I don't know, Allison. I wanted to talk to you first."

"You do know what just happened here in America a few weeks ago, right?"

"I do," I said impatiently. "Thank you."

"But you're still considering going?"

"Maybe." I let out a long exhale. "Maybe it'll be good for me."

"And Carla," she said in an ugly tone. "Let's not forget. It'll be good for her too, I'm sure."

All the peace, love, and solidarity going on left and right after the attacks, I guess, didn't apply here, I thought as I tuned her out. As she yelled words at me, I leaned my head against the doorframe with the phone resting on my shoulder as I observed my dad reading the paper. He wasn't fighting with my mom during all this. If anything, they took even more care than they usually did. My dad making sure she always had a warm cup of tea to wrap her hands around, and my mom playfully giving into his culinary complaints.

"Fine, Laurent," I overheard her saying the other day. "There's no bread in America. Let's just move to France and get fat asses on baguettes and sausage." To which he responded, "*Enfin.*" And then it got quiet, which meant they were probably making out or something gross like that. As I watched him read while drinking a late-afternoon espresso, there was something calming about him that made me want to just be with him. But I couldn't. I was still on the phone getting my ass reamed out.

"I don't know what to tell you, Allison. Carla *is* in the band," I eventually interjected. "I can't exactly go without her; otherwise, I'll just be some dickwad on the drums."

"And Tony? Is he going?"

"I don't know. You were my first call." I heard myself groan in frustration. "I wanted to talk to you first."

"Well, you're obviously not going without him. It's just not correct." I didn't know what to tell her, so I stayed silent. "Oh my God," she said after a minute or so of neither one of us speaking. "You're going to go even if he can't go, aren't you?"

"I don't know."

"Sure, you do," she accused. "I'm just letting you know that this is really unpatriotic of you. We just had a major thing happen here."

"Yeah, and our country's response? Our country's brilliant response is to go to fucking war with a country that had *nothing* to do with it," I said, which had my dad look up from his paper and shoot me a look that he too thought it was bullshit. "Because war fixes everything, right?"

"I don't know, Pete," she said, not wanting the conversation to steer into the geopolitical rant she knew I'd be prepared to have. "My point is that you're still thinking of fiddling around on your drums with this chick from high school. And maybe it's time you grow up."

"I wish I knew what that meant." I scratched the back of my head because it felt like I didn't know about anything anymore. All I wanted was to be in a band with someone who gave a fuck. I had that. I also wanted to keep Allison happy, which felt more and more like a Herculean effort. And if I could have it at all my way, it would be to maybe *not* start my twenties with words like terrorism and anthrax in my everyday vernacular. Was I asking for too much? Clearly, I was.

"You don't know what growing up means." Allison's voice came back into focus. "Well, for one, spend less time with a girl who, I don't know, isn't your girlfriend."

And we were back to this, I thought as I walked outside with the cordless to smoke a cigarette. If I had been more myself, I would have started to get angry, but I was too tired to be angry. A part of me, I guess, did see it from her point of view. But that didn't mean I had to ignore mine. Getting out of this place to play music was something I needed to do; my soul depended on it. Otherwise, I was going to fucking fall apart. And it wasn't like I had a shitload of other options. It was either I continued to split myself into two people, which I was failing miserably at, or just do what I wanted to do.

"I'm going to go," I said.

"Okay, call me back."

"No, Allison. I'm going to *go*."

15

Carla

The next two weeks flew by in preparation for the tour. This time, it was a real tour. Laurent transformed the van into something we could actually travel long distances in. He laid out smooth wooden flooring, built drawers for our cables and pedals, created custom storage compartments with locks to protect our gear we feared could get stolen, and there was even the smallest fridge I think I had ever seen. He had thought of it all...if only he could have built a compartment to contain the tension mounting between his son and me, I thought as I bit my lip, looking at our foam mattress.

"Now, try not to get towed this time." Laurent laughed, looking at us like we were numbnuts.

There was no time to record a new demo, but once again, Pete surprised me with yet another one of his talents. With his apparent production abilities, using the four-track and some other equipment he had lying around in his basement, he did an impressive cleanup job of our otherwise rough demo. Bringing the vocals forward, I sounded clearer, and for certain bridges and choruses, he tripled my voice for a fuller sound. He added flourishes here and there, like incorporating his Fender Rhodes keyboard for nostalgic and dreamy effects; a cowbell for some of the breaks; and even handclaps, which was something I wouldn't have thought of but loved the pop value it gave some of the songs. It sounded so good that I sent it to all the bands and bars I had been in contact with, proud of our new sound. As for the "album art," we used a great photo Alex took of our bright orange equipment, and the inside was a photocopied picture of us playing at The Night Owl. We had two hundred CDs pressed. *Voilà*, as Pete would say.

Pete and I talked about Tony as if he was going to come, but we both knew he wasn't. A week earlier, Tony had popped by my house—something I noticed after the attacks, these random pop-ins became a social norm. He came to check in on the family and me, and he didn't look so good. His family didn't personally know any of the First Responders, but the kinship between firefighters is so profound, they may as well have. Plaintive and reserved—two words I would have *never* used to describe Tony— I could see the impact it had on him as I watched a layer shed from his playful veneer to reveal a stoicism I didn't know he had in him. Not that there would have been any room, but it would have been nice to have him along. And as a bonus, I'd get out of driving again.

We were all set and looked about ready to head out the next day. There was, however, one last order of business to tend to. From my bag, I pulled out an empty CD binder I bought at Best Buy.

"What's that for?" asked Pete.

"I think we should make a CD book with neutral choices. You know, stuff we *both* agree on."

"Oh, yeah, that makes sense." He looked off into the distance, appearing to process the initiative seriously. "Okay."

"Well, yeah, from my Bikini Kill to your *Mahavishnu Orchestra*." I made a face to demonstrate distaste. "There's just no other way."

Pete

It was the morning of our departure, and the sky lamented with low-hanging clouds that depressed me like a rainy day in July. Something about that morning made everything feel lifeless and final, with the grey hues reflecting in misery off the walls in my house. Having breakfast with my parents, they acted like they were never going to see me again. Every time my mom had me within physical reach, she'd hug me in desperation. And for a week, my dad spoke exclusively in French because he swore I'd forget it on the road. He even had me pack my passports.

"I'm crossing the United States," I reminded my parents as I exhaled at the theatrics. "Not getting deployed in Afghanistan."

"Well, thank God," was all my mom could say and then looked at my dad who nodded his head in agreed sentiment.

The night before, Carla and I loaded our gear into the van to decide on the best configuration with the heavy stuff packed in first. It took a few rounds of loading and unloading until we found the best arrangement, in which we then drew out a map to remember.

With the equipment all set, I walked out to the driveway with my duffle bag when Tony's Celica pulled in.

"Hey, man," I said as he opened his car door. "You change your mind? You comin' with?"

"Nah," he said as he laboriously pulled himself out of the compact car. "I wish I could."

In truth, I wasn't sure if he could come at this point since we had taken out the backseat, a detail I felt guilty for not sharing with Allison. Tony reached his arms out, and we exchanged a firm hug as I asked how he was doing.

"Okay, I guess." He shrugged one shoulder and glanced to the side. "Just laying low with the family."

"I guess that's all you really can do these days, right?"

"Is it me," he said, giving me a look like he'd been trying to figure it all out. "But are things still totally weird?"

"Yeah, we're in what the assholes on TV are calling 'The New Normal.'" I rolled my eyes at the fact that every moment had to be packaged and sold into some snappy catchphrase. "But yeah, everything is still weird and probably will be for a long time." I had a feeling our opinions on the war greatly differed, and he probably didn't share my critical views, so I offered, "We're going through some dark times right now, but we'll get through it."

"Yeah." Tony looked off wistfully.

We stood on my driveway for a few moments in the residence of the funeral mood until I broke the silence, and in a brighter tone said, "I'm glad you stopped by, though, because I *do* have something for you." I held my finger up and backed up a few steps. "Gimme a sec."

Running down to my basement to get it, there I also grabbed my backpack and some last stray items and locked the downstairs door behind me.

"I finally finished it," I called out to him. "I took the liberty of picking out the yarn. I thought something to go with your eyes,"

I joked as I twirled the two-toned brown beanie around my pointer finger.

"Oh, man." His eyes lit up as he took the hat from me. "I was just fuckin' with you. You didn't have to!"

"It was nothing. Just a simple double moss stitch," I said purposefully for a reaction as I peeled my backpack off my shoulders.

"Double moss stitch," he imitated as he flicked me with the hat. "Get the fuck outta here."

"Seriously, though," I said, looking over my shoulder as I put the last of my things into the van, "the distraction was nice."

"Thanks, man." He then put the hat on, which I was thankful fit his head since I had to estimate the size. He looked at himself in the reflection of his car window and adjusted the hat, turning left and then right to admire it. "This shit's stylish."

"I'm glad you like it," I said, happy to see my friend smile.

I then turned to the van to give it a final review before looking at Tony. I dropped my arms down to the side and said, "Well, I guess this is it."

"You off now, huh?" He eyed the van in admiration. "I can't believe you're actually doin' it. Next time I see you, you might be famous and not remember little ol' me."

"Little?" I leveled my eyes at him. "And not remember you? Please."

"Even when you're surrounded by *all* the honeys?"

"All?" I rolled my eyes. "I have a girlfriend, remember?"

"Yeah, right." He steadied his eyes on me to tell me to cut the crap. "I give it 'til the Jersey Turnpike."

"We're not taking the turnpike." I returned the still expression that told him to give me a break. "And if you keep it up"—I reached out to rummage my hand over his head—"I'll revenge knit a pompom for you right here. You won't know what hit you." I fanned my fingers in the air. "These hands work fast."

"Yeah, I bet they do, homie."

And there he was again…fucking Tony.

Carla

After picking up my latest pay from work and saying goodbye to Abel's daughter, who would be covering my shifts for three weeks, I waited for Pete out on the driveway. Because my mother disapproved of the tour, it created tension in the house, and no one wanted to cross her by seeing me off. She wouldn't say bye to me; my brothers did it in their own way by telling me to "not get killed out there," and the night before, my dad tapped on my door.

"Come in," I said, pleased to see him as I pulled the zipper on my bag to close it.

"You're really doin' it, aren't ya?" he said with his hands deep in his sweatpants pockets.

"I am." I gave him a look of mock suspicion. "You're gonna give me grief too?"

"Of course not," my dad said as he scanned the remaining items scattered on my bed. "Honey, look," he started, "it's a crazy time right now. The world is in chaos." He shook his head as I could see the latest headlines running through his brain.

"That doesn't mean the family has to fall apart too. We're better than that." He paused to look at me. "We're Italian."

"So I've heard."

"But world events aside," he said. "I'm sorry about what's going on. You deserve–"

Before he could get into it, though, I had to stop him because apologies directed at me made me uncomfortable. Maybe it was because I intrinsically thought it was my fault, and had I done something different, the problem wouldn't have happened in the first place. Or maybe I didn't like taking a power role, but I hated being apologized to.

"It's–"

"I know, honey." He gave me a slanted look. "It's fine."

"But it really is." I forced a smile as he continued to look at me like he wasn't buying it. "There's one thing, though." I lowered my eyes in mild embarrassment of having to bring up the subject. "There's nothing going on between me and Pete."

"I know," he laughed. "Not with those nerd glasses."

He then snuck me two crisp hundred-dollar bills in case of an emergency and gave me one of his dad hugs. With the scent of his cologne thick as maple syrup, I breathed him in and held him a little tighter.

That morning, when Pete pulled into the driveway, seeing him behind the wheel in his fitted grey hoodie with the sleeves pushed up and his perfectly disheveled hair mussed off to the side sent a light flutter down to my stomach. As I dragged my bag off the porch, I thought back to only a year before. I had gone from developing film and *wanting* to learn the guitar to leaving for a makeshift rock n' roll tour with my band. The change was gradual with each practice bringing me closer to this day, but when putting the imagery side-by-side, I had to admit, it was pretty incredible. After we packed up the van with my things, we looked at each other, the moment feeling important under the ominous grey skies.

"So, I guess this is it," he said once we clicked our seatbelts. "Wait, is your family going to come out and say bye?" He looked at the front door. "Or did you do that already?"

"Yeah, we did," I said kind of defensively.

"So, we're all set?"

"All set."

"I guess we're going to leave all this shit behind us, huh?"

"The further, the better," I said with a glassy stare, looking at my house.

"Alright then, let's do this." He nodded, and just as he was about to pull the gear into reverse, he turned to me and said, "But wait, we have our first important decision to make as a band."

"What's our first CD going to be?" We said at the same time.

Pete

Two hours into our tour and I already felt worn out. The weeks leading up to my departure, Allison needed extra assurance. Even though I emailed her an itinerary of every show and even planned out our stops with the times she should expect a roadside phone call, it was never enough.

This was around the time she started calling me totally drunk in the middle of the night to tell me what an asshole I was. I started turning the ringers off all the phones before bed and sleeping with the cordless to not wake my parents up. It would take hours to calm her down as the alcohol wore off, and I'd wake up three hours later and head to work.

I felt like I had no one to talk to. All I told Carla was that I wasn't sure if I still had a girlfriend, which I then contradicted by scheduling phone calls along our route.

Sitting in traffic on the George Washington Bridge with our third CD on, this one Weezer's "Blue Album," I wanted to sing the lyrics along with her. As she sang about sweaters and surfers, she studied the map. Wearing one of her Carla sweaters, a pink and red striped one, her fingers traveled across the small towns and interstate highways. Since pulling out of her parents' driveway, liberation exuded from her core. From the relaxed positions of her shoulders to the way the corners of her mouth curled on the brink of a smile, I could see leaving home for her was imperative, if not crucial. She looked out the window onto the Hudson River like she was at the aquarium, absorbing it all.

In contrast to the looseness of her movements, my muscles felt tight, my neck sore, and my breathing operated at a staccato pace. I wondered if Allison was right. *Was* I a total asshole? Because what kind of boyfriend goes on a cross-country trip with a girl? A girl he fears he might be falling in love with . . .

16

Carla

Sitting in locked traffic on the bridge, I felt both uneasy and excited. Nervous because the news had reported the possibility of copycat attacks where major roadways and bridges were vulnerable. If a bomb went off right now with us suspended by hundreds of feet, I thought, well, yeah, that'd be it. My thoughts on death had changed, and I now feared it. But I guess everything had changed since Pete. I then wondered if we died together, would we go to heaven together? Or since we were over water, would we live a mermaid afterlife together? He'd make a cute merman, I chuckled to myself. Looking down at the water that started to look like a mermaid's tail I watched as the sun burned through the clouds casting its golden streaks across the soft-looking waves I wanted to touch with my fingers.

Our first stop was Cincinnati. For someone who hadn't gone any further than Philadelphia before, it sounded exotic and exciting. Cincinnati. What was waiting for us in Cincinnati? It was even fun to say. Cincinnati! I then looked at Pete driving, who appeared deep in thought. I knew he had a lot on his mind and wished there was something I could do to help, but every time I tried to talk to him, he offered me crisp, one-word answers.

"What do you want to hear next?" I delicately asked as he was getting out of the van at our first rest stop in Pennsylvania.

"Whatever you want." He counted quarters in his palm as he walked away but then turned back to me. "You need anything?"

"I'm fine," I told him, trying to pull his eyes in toward mine to read him, but he wouldn't look at me. "Thanks, though."

Wanting to give him space, I waited before going in, wondering if I had done something to upset him. Since he wasn't saying much to me, the only thing bonding us was music, which placed an importance on the next CD I put on. I could have pandered to his tastes and put on *Kind of Blue* or the one Grateful Dead show I agreed on, but he didn't get to practically ignore me through the entire state of New Jersey to get rewarded with a "thirty-seven-minute 'Dark Star'" (whatever that meant). I reached in the back and grabbed the secret CD book I assembled with stuff we didn't have time to agree on.

Afterward, I went inside. Walking through the pavilion that smelled of fried food and bleach, I was careful not to look for the payphones. I didn't want to see Pete's pained expression, probably explaining that he wasn't having sex with me a whole five hours into the tour. When I got back to the van and saw he hadn't returned yet, I decided I couldn't put off driving any longer and pulled myself up into the driver's seat. I figured it'd give me something to do while Pete brooded to himself.

Up front, I got myself acquainted with the space. It was my first time behind the wheel of something so big, where the wide stretch of the windshield made everything seem magnified. Adjusting the seat, it glided forward about three feet and locked into place, allowing my feet to feel for the pedals.

Once I got familiar with the settings, I sat back and observed the other travelers coming and going at the rest stop. I wondered if they, too, were as excited and scared about the journey ahead of them. Or if their travel companion was totally icing them out. They were mostly families and truckers, and I studied their faces — they all seemed at ease with their travels. Then I saw Pete walking through the parking lot, appearing to mentally replay the conversation he had just had, his eyes squinting in the low autumn sun.

When he saw me in the driver's seat, a slight grin snuck out from the corner of his mouth. "You sure?" he asked.

"Yeah." I shrugged.

I waited for him to get settled in before telling him, "So I picked out something special for us to listen to. But we can *only* listen to it in this small stretch of the trip."

"Sounds mysterious," he said, still sort of grinning, probably at how ridiculous and small I must have looked handling this rig.

"Oh, it is." My hand hovered over the triangle button, ready to press play.

As I pulled the lever down into drive, the song opener of a steam whistle tooting twice followed by a familiar drum phrase had him smirking in recognition.

"You're right," he said as I pulled the van out of the rest stop. "This *is* the only place to listen to this song. A highway near the highway that connects us to . . ." and together we said, "Allentown." If only to get him to smile for even a second was worth listening to the otherwise terrible song.

We got back onto the interstate heading west as we drove through the Pennsylvania we never found. And probably never would find because we weren't stopping there again. Together, we listened to Billy Joel as we got further and further from our hometown of Long Island.

"Wait," he said suspiciously. "We picked this CD out?"

Pete

Dale taught me everything I needed to know about music and what it meant to accept myself. But what he didn't teach me was how to be a touring musician *and* a good boyfriend at the same time. Was it even possible to be both, if you're not, like, Sting, or something? With every phone call learning what a dick I was only confused how I felt about Carla. Did I have feelings for her only because I was being told at every rest stop not to have them? Or were they genuine? Carla, who had the patience of a Resource Room teacher, didn't say a word about the misery that must have been my face and tried to keep spirits up with small talk and shitty music.

When I got back from my phone call, seeing her in the driver's seat for the first time made me smile because it made her look even smaller than she was . . . if that was even possible. When she drove, though, in the simplest terms, it was probably the sexiest thing I had ever seen. Her hands controlling the steering wheel with a firm grip, her shoulders pulled back, and her eyes fixed forward, she had the confidence of a road warrior. Also . . . because the van's shocks dated back to the early '90s and were, therefore, nonexistent, her boobs kind of bounced up and down in her tight t-shirt. I had to turn myself toward the window to keep my focus looking out because, even from the corner of my eye, I could see how hot she looked.

Once we crossed the Susquehanna River and were cutting through deep Pennsylvania, it felt like we had cracked the seal and had entered America. The sky became a massive backdrop, the billboards fewer, and road signs seemed almost scarce. Unlike the Long Island Expressway, which gave you a play-by-play with signs practically every few feet, I noticed long stretches of road would pass with us not knowing exactly where we were. There was something about it that I liked. Living in a world of constant information pelting you like dodge balls, it felt good to not know everything at every moment and to just be.

For our first show in Cincinnati, we played a quick and tight set to the after-work crowd. Some people ate dinner at the bar, some even bought CDs we sold from the side of the stage, but for the most part, no one really cared. That night, the bassist of the band we opened for and his girlfriend invited us to sleep on their floor. Surrounded by our gear we brought in because we couldn't find a wall to back the van against to protect it from theft, I tried to sleep. With Carla's knees digging into the small of my back and the hardwood floor cradling my hip bone, it wasn't much different than sleeping in the van . . . well, except for the beagle sniffing my face.

And then things got weird.

It started with a creak. Followed by another. And then another. And before long had settled into a rhythm of springing squeaks, the sounds of senior year before I got a new bed. I shifted around as I lay on my side in the discomfort of nearby strangers having sex.

"Pete?" Carla eventually whispered.

"Yeah?"

"Can you hear that?"

"Of course, I can." I looked over my shoulder in her direction.

"What should we do?"

"What do you mean what should we do?" I smirked.

"Well," she said impatiently. "They're having *sex*."

"Yes." I rolled onto my back. "They are."

As their passion increased, the bed's hardware got louder, the exhales intensified, and the girlfriend became more aroused as she started moaning his name: Rick. Rick Junior. That's when Carla started chuckling, I imagined for the same reason I was because when there's a junior in your name, it seemed unnecessary in the sexual equation. Like, if she left it off, I doubt Rick Jr. would be looking around the bedroom to see who she was referring to, or a fight would erupt because she was chanting — yes, the moaning had upgraded to chanting by this point — someone else's name.

"Pete!" She lightly smacked my shoulder as laughter snorted out of her nose. "It's totally weird."

"Well, yeah." I turned my head in her direction, catching the glow of her eyes in the light of the microwave's digital clock. "But they should be done soon." I waited a beat before adding, "Unless Rick Jr. here is practicing the Kama Sutra."

"Junior!" she loudly whispered. "Why does she have to say it every time?"

"Well, she needs to be specific," I joked as she muffled her laughter into my shoulder.

Once our giggling tapered off, we lay back on our pillows, looking up at a ceiling fan, waiting for Rick Jr. to get on with it already. When he finally did, I was thankful that he was undisciplined in the virtues of tantric lovemaking. Carla fell asleep first, then the pesky dog, who gave up on my face and retreated to his plaid bed marked Zimmy, and eventually, I dozed off.

Our first show pretty much set the tone for what lay ahead of us. On our way to Bloomington, Carla explained the process that went into booking a gig at an empty tavern to play a show for people who didn't give a fuck. I thought about the emotional sacrifice of having people roll their eyes at you because they can't hear their friends over your band; the fake wooden-paneled rooms that smelled like piss; slobbering dogs named after Bob Dylan not letting you sleep; hearing randos having sex; using a stranger's computer with an Orca whale screensaver, only to learn that the Mets got their asses handed to them the night before by Montreal. Was it all worth it? Just to play rock music in any given American town?

With her, I couldn't think of a better deal.

Carla

Another rest stop . . . another long-distance phone call to Allison, this time in Batesville, Indiana. I didn't know how long Pete could go trying to please someone who didn't want him doing what he was doing. It was like we had a third person on tour with us who seemed to have more say than anyone else in the band.

As I drove, I looked out onto what I had always heard referred to as the Heartland of America. We cruised past dairy trucks of brands I had never heard of, crossed bodies of water with names like Sugar Creek, and saw signs for Christmas tree farms. As we entered the state of Illinois, I asked Pete if he read words in a French accent. When he asked me what I meant, I clarified by asking if he saw the word Illinois the same way I did, or did he see *Illi-nwah*? He smiled and said no one had ever asked him that before and then explained that he sometimes did, like when we passed Le Roy, he saw it in French. *Le Roi.* We then decided to *Frenchify* cities we thought were begging for it, like Des Moines then became *Day Mwah* and Detroit became *Day-trois*.

I then reminded him of when I dressed up as Abe Lincoln for our class Fifty Nifty United States project. He laughed in recollection of the mole I colored on with my mom's brown eyeliner. For his project, I remember he gave his presentation dressed as a vintner, wearing purple-stained overalls and rubber boots which, of course, *no one got*. "Why didn't you just come dressed as a surfer?" or "You totally ruined it. You got the easy state!" were a few comments flung around the classroom, in which a then ten-year-old Pete responded that it was a clichéd stereotype of California. In forced patience, he then explained to our simple class that winemaking was a multimillion-dollar industry, making winegrowers more common and therefore more enterprising than surfers.

"It was either that," Pete said, smiling at a memory he probably hadn't thought of in years, "or a sleazy movie producer. My parents thought a winegrower was more appropriate." I could feel him glance over at me from the passenger's seat. "Oddly enough."

Getting off I-74 to pick up 51 heading north, a sign with an arrow pointing right read Bloomington and the other pointing left read, "Decatur!" I shouted like a Tourette's patient.

"What about it?" He seemed surprised by my outburst.

"I don't know," I giggled. "I remembered this city from my project and always thought it was fun to say."

"Decatur," he repeated. "Yeah, that is fun. Okay, quick, what rhymes with Decatur?"

"Umm." I contemplated for a few seconds. "Elevator. Now you."

"Excavator."

"Terminator."

"Oh shit, we can do names?" He said as if there were actual rules. "Okay then, Ralph Nader!"

"Oh, God." I slightly tilted my head back. "You totally voted for him, didn't you?"

"Well, who did you vote for?"

"I didn't," I confessed. "My one vote doesn't count."

"You're insane." I could feel his eyes widen the way they did when he strongly disagreed with something. "Of course, your vote counts. That's like saying you don't count."

I didn't know what to say to him, so I didn't say anything. I focused on the road as if our straight direction suddenly needed my complete attention.

"You count, Carla," he insisted when I didn't react. "You have to know that."

As he continued to look at me, pressing for a response, I felt myself get a little annoyed because I didn't have one. So I just ignored him because it was easier that way.

By lunchtime, we were in Bloomington. We stopped at a local supermarket, where we immediately noticed the groceries were a lot cheaper than in New York. Then out in the parking lot, with our legs dangling off the back of the van, Pete made us turkey sandwiches he cut diagonally. When I gave him half of mine, explaining that I got full on the baby carrots we nibbled on in the market, he gave me another look I chose to ignore.

After lunch, we decided to park the van somewhere to take a nap, which ended up being more difficult than we had thought. We drove down residential side streets festooned in Americana charm, like our nation's flag draped over porches; rocking chairs that leaned forward and back in the autumn breeze; and pumpkins, ready for Halloween dissection, sat on stoops.

Every parking spot we found big enough and in the shade, though, was in a playground. Nothing is creepier than an unmarked van in a children's playground. As a kid, I remember building entire narratives around vans that crept slowly down the street, exactly the way we were. And to think, all that time I feared I'd end up a face in a Soul Asylum video, it could have just been a rock band looking for parking. In the end, we settled for a bowling alley, which we both agreed was only mildly creepy.

Once we set up our foam mattress, topping it with an egg crate pad and clean sheets that smelled like his parents' house, we stretched out alongside each other. Sharing the comforter this time around, I had to stop thinking about how close our bodies were underneath it and forced my eyes closed. We listened to each other breathe until we eventually fell asleep.

I woke up to the sound of Pete turning a page in a book and biting into an apple. Immediately, I noticed the light outside wasn't as bright and high as it had been before I passed out.

"How long have I been sleeping?" I pulled my shoulders back like I was pinching a pencil in between my shoulder blades as I let out a deep sigh from the stretch.

"About four hours," he said, echoing my hushed tone while offering me a bite of his apple.

"Wow, really?" I then moved closer, looking up at him as my teeth sunk into the rounded edge of the fruit. He watched me take my bite, his eyes heavy on mine. As I chewed, I felt the acidic tartness pinch my taste buds. His eyes smiled as he dog-eared the corner of the page he was on and closed his book.

"Any good?" I asked with a mouthful of apple.

"So far." He nodded and looked at the book. "My mom sent me off with some books people left on their seats on the plane." He smirked. "Because, you know, every great rock story about a band on tour has, like, fucking Osterberg reading fiction recommended by mom. Shit."

I chuckled at his comment and said, "Well, I only brought two books." I then stretched out on my side to face him with my ear resting against my bent arm, my fingers running soothingly through my hair. "But seeing how much downtime we have" — my eyes flicked up to meet his— "I should have brought more."

"Which two did you bring?"

"I brought C.S Lewis' *Prince Caspian*."

I paused for a reaction because, as predicted, he said, "You know that—"

"Yes, Pete, I know." I smiled in the satisfaction of knowing him. "*Prince Caspian* is also the name of a Phish song."

"And a good one too."

"I'm sure," I said, unconvinced.

"And what else?" He shot me a teasing look. "A book about faeries?"

"No," I said in a dry tone. "I didn't want to bring nonfiction."

He then erupted into full laughter. "Nonfiction!" he howled while holding his stomach as the guffaws spilled out of his body.

As I alternated between looking over his shoulder and at him, I patiently waited for him to compose himself from what he saw as comedic gold.

"That's the fucking funniest thing I've ever heard!" He couldn't resist as his throaty laughs practically vibrated the van.

After a few minutes of this, I finally said, "Are you done?"

Offering him a little smirk, I added to my point, "You know, for someone who listens to prog, you have a strange aversion for fantasy since that's what that music is about, right?"

"You're kidding me," he said flatly. "Prog is political. Don't be fooled by the medieval overtures, which in itself is political. Just listen to *In the Court of the Crimson King*." He looked at me and then looked off to consider my point. "Even though Fripp *did* say during recording that they were guided by the presence of a good fairy." His eyebrows pinched inward. "Fuck." He looked at me, feigning defeat. "You may have a point."

"I've been meaning to ask you, actually," I said. "How did you get into all this weird music? It's not like there are krautrock enthusiasts washing up by the dozens on Long Island."

"A friend of mine in Alsace introduced me to it." His eyes softened. "He was into all of this otherworldly late '60s and '70s European rock. My friend would make mixtapes, and we'd listen to them on this mini-cassette player during picnics in the Vosges Forest." His eyes slid over to mine. "Summer of '95. That was a good summer. Even *if* Jerry died."

"Oh my God." I gently placed my fingers against my lips. "Your friend ended up dying?"

"No," he said with still eyes. "Jerry as in Jerry Garcia?"

"You had to ruin a sweet story, didn't you?"

"1995 was a hard year for us Deadheads."

"I don't know how you all managed to pick up the pieces."

"Whatever." He shook his head in playful dismissal. "Anyway, what else did you bring?"

I hesitated for a second before pulling out *Delta of Venus* by Anaïs Nin, where he propped himself up on his elbow and eyed the book. He gave it a knowing grin and then looked back at me with curious eyes.

"So you came on tour with fantasy and French erotica?" He threw his back down onto our makeshift bed and slapped his forehead. "Man, now I'm *definitely* the nerd in the van reading books from mom."

"No," I said plainly. "You're a nerd because you referred to Iggy Pop as Osterberg."

"It's his name, isn't it?"

"I suppose," I resigned. "So, what other books did you bring?"

"Just some fun shit. Let's see, a Bukowski, the Miles autobiography I've read a million times." He thought to himself. "What else? A Gore Vidal I've been meaning to read for a while, and for a little Cold War espionage in comic book form, I brought *L'Affair Tournesol,* which is part of the *Tahntahn* series," he said.

"Part of the *what* series?" I said, amused.

"*Tahntahn?*" He looked at me as if it made perfect sense before his eyes roamed off. "Sorry, Tintin," he said, exaggerating the nasal American accent. "The Adventures of Tintin."

"Whatever, Pete. We don't talk like that."

"You don't?" He reached over to give me a playful poke on my shoulder. "You don't *tawk* like that?" He then turned toward his cubby. "But wait, I also have something for you." He pulled two books out of a small shopping bag and handed me one. "Here," he said. "To counterbalance your French erotica."

I sat up to take the book and chuckled in disbelief because it was pretty much the opposite of a drunken chauvinist Bukowski novel.

"A memoir by Simone de Beauvoir?" I said with a skeptical glare.

"Oh, are you unfamiliar with her work?" he said teasingly. "Well, she's this French—"

"Shut up, Pete." I gently pushed his shoulder. "I know who she is." I didn't want to admit, though, that I had struggled to get through her manifesto *The Second Sex.* But him? I looked at him like there was no way he read feminist existentialism. "Are you, like, trying to *craft* yourself into a perfect guy who's, like, so in touch with his softer side? What, do you crochet too?"

"No," he said defensively, which surprised me since I was totally kidding. "And the perfect guy? I don't see how that could be possible," he added. "I mean, I do listen to Phish."

"You do," I said with pity.

I looked down at the book and felt my eyes swell with sentiment. The idea of him going to the bookstore, which I had a feeling was the independent one forty-five minutes away, surfaced emotions I felt unprepared for. It was like I was *always* thinking of him, so there was something nice about having proof of at least one moment where I knew he was thinking of me. I didn't know what to say, so I looked away, hoping I wouldn't tear up like a weirdo.

"Is everything okay?" he said quietly as I felt him move closer to me. "Should I not have—"

"No, no." I pushed a smile through my emotional response. "It was just really nice, and, whatever. I think I'm just tired, so . . . " I looked at him. "But really. Thanks for thinking of me."

I noticed he then looked away, appearing uncomfortable as we both focused on opposite corners of the van. I wanted to say something, anything, to offset the tension. When I glanced at the books, noticing they had different covers, I said, "Why are our copies different?"

"Oh," he said. "Well, mine's in French."

"Oh my God."

Pete

Perfect guy. Please. I didn't know what she was talking about because I wasn't. In fact, I had a girlfriend telling me every few hundred miles just how awful I was. I also wasn't about to admit to crocheting on a technicality because *technically*, I knit, which is an entirely different beast in the flaxen thread arts.

When I went to Book Revue to buy Carla a tour present, the idea was to get a rock biography of one of her favorite bands on the road. However, I stopped short when I saw *Memoirs of a Dutiful Daughter*; the title practically screamed out at me. Reading the first hundred pages in the bookstore, I discovered that Beauvoir's first short story she ever wrote was about an orphan from Alsace, which was totally cool to see in an American bookstore. But that wasn't why I gave it to her. I noticed the writer's direct yet lightly ethereal way of storytelling by employing metaphors to black magic, witches, and ogres, something I thought Carla would totally dig. But there were other things like the theme of seeking her family's approval and how she made no demands on anyone by staying in the background. It all screamed Carla to me, and I wanted to show her that Beauvoir, despite her insecurities, had allowed herself to become a visionary. Because that's what Carla was to me. I just wanted her to see it too.

Carla

Before soundcheck, while Pete went to look for a post office to send a postcard to Guy, I grabbed a coffee at a café in town. It was the first time in my life it had occurred to me that I had an accent. I always prided myself on *not* having the New York accent and thought I just spoke, well, normal. But after Pete's comment, and then when I placed my order and the girl kind of smiled and asked me if I was from New York, I realized I sometimes do say *caw-fee*.

At the college bar, we began loading in through the side door. The bar swarmed with band buzz as we all seemed to arrive at the same time, rolling in amps around each other and carrying in heavy gear. Walking past me with purpose was one of the guys I had spoken to on the phone in August. Wearing a yellow and white striped boatneck top, he looked like he should be on a yacht in the French Riviera. His hair, thick in a shade of deep auburn, was coiffed in a style that was messy-mod, and his face was as cute as his pictures online. Maybe even cuter.

"Hi," I said.

"Hi?"

"Carla." I pointed to myself. "We spoke on the phone over the summer?"

"Ah, yes! Of course, of course," he said, his eyes brightening in recognition. "You made it. So, how's it going? Your first tour?"

"You remembered," I said, charmed. "So far, we can't complain."

"You're coming from New York." He shook his head. "I feel like I should give you a hug."

"Yeah, we're all pretty much still in total shock, but who isn't?"

"How is it over there?" he said with his eyes glazing over in a mournful expression.

"I haven't been to the city, so I don't have much of a local point-of-view, but our friends' family is in the New York Fire Department, and he said downtown is still pretty much on lockdown with checkpoints. The debris I hear is getting pretty bad."

He then went into his story of where he was when he heard and his immediate reaction to the footage. I nodded my head along to the familiar details. The stories we all had, we held close, like Purple Hearts for the emotionally and psychologically wounded. As Pete said, it was something you couldn't "unsee," making it impossible to be the same person after.

"So, I have to say," he said once the conversation reached a respectful distance from tragedy. "I love that new demo you sent me. We've been listening to it a lot."

"Thanks," I said, accepting the compliment. "Pete did a really good job with it."

"I mean, the first one was good too," he said, appearing amazed at the transformation. "But the songs really pop on the new one." He then looked around him. "So where's the rest of the band?"

"He's right there." I pointed to Pete walking across the stage carrying cables and cords. I would have introduced him, but Pete was in set-up mode, which meant he was in his own world, oblivious to life around him. Unless it was with the sound guy, he wouldn't allow chitchat to weigh him down. I could see Pete's lips pursed as his eyes calculated the space, looking up at the ceiling, the floor, anywhere, for optimal mic placement. He didn't care we were the opening band for the opening band's opening band; it still had to sound right.

"That's it? That's your band?" He looked at me in awe, which in turn surprised me because I thought he had read our bio. "It's just the two of you?"

"Yeah?"

"Did you guys do some major overdubs on those songs you sent me even in the first demo?"

"I don't know. Maybe?"

"It's just that you sound so full, so robust, I guess is the word." The guitarist then looked at Pete again, who was now crawling on hands and knees, as the sound guy gestured in apparent agreement with some finicky detail Pete was obsessing about. "You guys just have such a tight-knit sound. I would have thought there were a few more of you."

"No." I sighed, looking at Pete, who then had a slim flashlight in his mouth while still trying to talk. "It's just me. Me and that guy."

Pete

At the bar, I stood next to her as we watched the headlining band's soundcheck and asked, "What's the name of this band again?"

"Special Ed," she said, looking at the lead singer with stars in her eyes. Oh, God. "Aren't they so good?"

They *were* good with their 1960s Sonics throwback vibe, even if the cute singer reminded me a little of Etienne Daho with his striped top. But seeing Carla's full moon eyes, I wondered if she was laying it on a little thick, maybe to get back at me for my distraction with Allison. Whatever it was, this little scene did nothing to quell my confusion because, on top of everything, I was feeling . . . guilt, uncertainty with love, unexpected intrigue, and now a teeny-tiny bit jealous?

Just as I thought things couldn't get any more emotionally chaotic, a familiar voice from behind me called out, "Hey, guys!" When I turned around, it was Alex, with her pale blonde hair accented by a lime-green scarf that looked kind of cute on her.

"Hi, Pete," she said in a singsong tone as if I was up to something. "Funny to see you outside of Wino Island."

"Stranger things have happened."

We played our show to a packed house of buzzed college kids who seemed to dig us. After load-out, I left Carla and Alex outside to talk to the other bands while I went in to grab a beer. With the house jukebox blasting U2's "Where The Streets Have No Name," I sat at the bar enjoying the moment of the day when I had absolutely nothing to do; our gear was locked in our van, and I didn't have to be anywhere until tomorrow. I almost felt free until I realized, oh wait...I still had a phone call to make.

"Great show," a voice called out behind me.

"Thanks," I shouted as I turned around to find the lead singer of Special Ed looking at me. "Oh, hey."

"Hey," he said with a polite wave. "Just wanted to tell you that you've got a killer style. Loved that steady beat you've got going."

"Oh, thanks," I said, surprised since no one ever compliments the drummer. "You guys were really good too."

"Thanks, but I have to say," he said, leaning in, the music forcing him to talk in my ear. "It was those ghost notes you were just barely hitting that really floored me."

"Oh, wow, you noticed?" I couldn't believe it because I hadn't had a conversation about ghost notes since Dale.

"Sometimes it's what you can't hear that counts as much as what you can, you know?"

"Yes, totally." I looked at him like he was from my planet. "Do you play?"

"No, my dad does, so I know what to look out for." He gave the empty barstool next to me a glance.

"Sit, please." I gestured to it. "Pete, by the way." I extended my hand out.

"Ed." He smiled as he shook it, which made me smirk because, of course, the lead singer of Special Ed would be named...Ed.

As much as I wanted to be a little bit of a dick to him for putting the moves on my guitarist, especially during their set, when he was practically seducing her from the stage, I couldn't because he was kind of cool. And not just because he knew what a ghost note was. But I guess anything was better than a plastic payphone at this point.

After having a beer with him, Ed invited us to stay at his place. When we got there, I tossed my things in the corner of his living room and then asked to use his phone, flashing my calling card to let him know I wouldn't rack up his phone bill.

Once again, I regretted the call to Allison. But this time, it was worse since she could hear Alex and Carla giggling in the bathroom, the sound of the shower not helping *anything*. After accusing me of now fucking both of them, she then agreed she was being unreasonable because, of course...I was fucking groupies. Groupies. *Tu parles*. The jokes were writing themselves at this point. I didn't have groupies, I wanted to scream into the phone as she went into painful blue-balling detail about all the head I was allegedly getting. There were no blow jobs! There were no groupies! There were just these fucking phone calls! When the *hell* would I have time for anything else? Of course, I didn't say any of that and just listened to her.

209

When I finally got off the phone, two hours later, I walked down the long hallway wanting to forget about my phone call and to pick up the conversation I'd had with Ed at the bar. It wasn't every day I spoke to someone who knew the drums as well as I did. But when I turned the corner into the living room, I found Alex passed out on the pull-out couch, and on the floor, Carla was stretched out on her side, her hair cascading over her shoulder. Next to her, Ed serenaded her with an acoustic version of "Crimson and Clover."

Like I said before...Oh, God.

Carla

I wasn't going to lie. It felt nice having a cute guy check me out. And it felt even better fooling around with said cute guy. I didn't even know I had a thing for redheads, but I couldn't help but be totally into it. It was also the first time I had felt stubble tickle against my cheeks and around the corners of my mouth. Who would have thought it would be me hooking up on tour? I thought, chuckling to myself as I tiptoed out of Ed's room early the next morning. I'd had my share of Pete and Allison drama that I enjoyed the escape from it all. I just hoped my escape didn't wake anyone up.

I dug Ed. He was cute with his '60s style, thinking he needed a Vespa to go with that swagger. I just couldn't get around the fact that his name was Ed. I was only twenty-one years old. I was way too young to be into a guy named Ed.

Pete

Leaving Bloomington the next morning, it was obvious something had happened between Carla and Ed. Wanting to ignore it, I tried to talk to Alex, who looked like she was reading into everything. *Argh! Can everyone please stop being so fucking annoying for, like, two seconds?* My mental plea for normalcy, of course, went ignored as Ed and I exchanged awkward goodbyes. He and Carla hugged for an eternity. Alex's writer's eyes consumed it all. And I wanted to throw up.

As we packed the van up, Carla and Alex appeared to talk in code. Giggling about undetectable references and in strange voices that entertained them to the point of absurdity, I almost asked them what the hell they were talking about. Almost.

"Why are you making that face?" Carla finally said as we closed the back doors of the van. She stood firmly in front of me with her arms folded like she wouldn't let me get around her.

"What face?" I said, purposefully avoiding eye contact.

"You've been, like, acting weird all morning."

"No, I haven't," I sort of snapped.

If she asked again, I would have said something rude, so I kept my head down and walked around her. "I don't know what you're talking about." I opened the driver's seat door, pressing my lips closed to appear preoccupied.

"Whatever you say," she said and then looked at Alex. "I'll sit in the back. You can sit up front with him." She tossed her eyes at me before turning around.

Once the three of us settled into the van, I turned to Alex and said, "So we're taking you to St. Louis?"

"I'm visiting my boyfriend," she retorted in a way like I had somehow contested she had one. "So you get me for another few hours. I know how excited you are."

"Thrilled."

I realized that I was being sort of a dick and figured I had to do something to ease the tension. If I didn't, I was afraid it would have all come out, and I just didn't think it was the moment...if there ever was one. So I looked around me and said, "Before we head out, Car" — my eyes scanned the floor with all our crap lying around — "I just want to put something on. Can I have your CD binder?"

"*My* CD binder?" She looked at me with innocent eyes.

"Yes." I leered at her. "Your CD binder." I paused for a second to clarify. "Your *secret* CD binder."

"I don't have a secret CD binder, Pete." She laughed and looked away skittishly. "All the music I have is in the book you and I made together of authorized albums."

Not buying it, I put my hand out for her to give it up. "I know you have one because I have one too. Now come on, hand it over."

Eventually, she gave in, probably because she knew I wouldn't have backed down. Reaching into her cubby and digging through her shit, she produced a secret CD binder, probably containing all the music we wouldn't have agreed on. She handed it to me, and as I had guessed, all the usual suspects were there; the rest of the Kill Rock Stars catalog, Cuddle Core, Billy Joel, CeCe Peniston, Tori Amos, and the *Reality Bites* Soundtrack that had the one U2 song she liked on it. *One* U2 song. She was so weird sometimes. As I flipped through her book, she looked over my shoulder anxiously, where every so often, I would look back at her with wide eyes that told her to stop hovering.

"Ah-ha," I said, delighted she had exactly what I was looking for. The girls were intrigued, but I purposefully put my hand over the top to conceal the title as I snapped the binder shut. "Perfect morning music." I offered a sly smile to my very interested audience.

I clicked the disc into the portable CD player and pressed play, certain it was the first song on The Shondells *Greatest Hits*. And it was. With lyrics as saccharine as I remembered, I couldn't help but explode in laughter. Maybe I was starting to lack some serious sleep because I felt delirious as I replayed elements of the night before. On the floor with my pillow pressed against my head, it failed to protect me from not one but the many rounds of fucking "Crimson and Clover."

I looked at Alex for support even though I knew I was testing dangerous waters by trying to conspire with her, the best friend. As I looked at her, though, a small smile crept across her face as she glided her head back to Carla and said, "Yeah, I'm kinda with Pete on this one."

"With him on what?" Carla snipped.

"Well," she said. "For one, why did you keep asking him to sing it?"

Unamused, Carla sat with her back pressed against our drawers with her arms folded. "I didn't *keep* asking him to sing it." She shot us a look.

"I don't know," Alex said, starting to laugh. "Way to take the lyrics literally because I definitely heard 'Crimson and Clover' over and over last night."

I looked at Carla in the rearview mirror. "'Crimson and Clover?'" I gave her a look like, you're kidding me, right? "What, he didn't know 'Hallelujah?'"

"What's wrong with 'Crimson and Clover,' Pete?"

"Oh, come on," I said. "It's *so* cheesy. What, because he hardly knows you, but he thinks he can love you?" I turned around to back the van out, and glancing at her, I could see she understood exactly why we were laughing.

"It's a great song, Pete," she said.

"It is. But within context."

"I'm sorry he didn't bust out into, like, some twenty-minute and twenty-*two* second Yes song."

"Well, obviously. That would have been impossible," I said flatly. And for dramatic measure, I pressed on the brake and looked at her. "He doesn't have the skill."

"You," she said in contempt, "are *such* a snob."

"Says the girl who almost stabbed John Snyder in health when he asked if you listened to No Doubt." I continued to back the van out, cautiously looking for oncoming traffic. "The poor guy."

"Well, I *didn't* listen to No Doubt," she said, looking at me like what's your point?

"Well, you listened to Hole." And to totally fuck with her, I added, "Aren't they, like, the same band?"

And as expected, and admittedly to my impish delight, all chaos erupted in the van. Loud voices. High voices. Screeching. Absolute pandemonium as I laughed in response to Alex and Carla completely losing their shit.

"What!" they screamed, followed by...*umm no. Not at all! What are you even talking about! Can you believe this guy! That is so fucked up! Courtney shaped a generation*...and blah, blah, blah.

"A generation of what?" I said, unable to resist as they got all crazy again.

"You don't know what you're talking about," Carla eventually said, her eyes turning to slits. "They are *not* the same band."

"Yeah, not even close," Alex snapped. "Phish and Dave Matthews on the other hand? Now *they* are the same band."

"Whoa!" I stopped the car as if that was taking it too far. "Not at all the same. I can give so many examples."

"Oh my God, please don't," she said and then turned around to Carla. "Anyway, back to Ed. We're not laughing at you." Alex reached her hand around to grab Carla's. "We're sorry. It *was* romantic."

"Okay, let's not go that far," I felt inclined to clarify. "It was actually kind of annoying."

"Ooooh." Alex's eyes narrowed in on me. "You're cute when you're jealous."

"What?" I tried to brush it off. "Get the fuck out of here."

She then studied my face as if she was trying to figure something out.

"Jealous?" I kept talking, hoping I sounded unmoved by the accusation. "Please."

She then continued to look at me in a way that made me uncomfortable, like she was piecing together information.

"Whatever," she finally said, appearing to snap out of her investigative work. "Anyway, what's with this stubble?" She then reached her hand under my chin and scratched it like I was a house pet. "What, forgot your razor at home?"

"Yeah," I said, feeling even more self-conscious as I shooed her hand away. "I did."

"It's cute, Albrecht, very cute. But now what I want to know is," she said, turning around to Carla and looking back and forth between us with a suspicious glimmer, "what's in the authorized CD binder?"

Carla

What I love about my best friend is how well she knows me. Alex and I have had telepathy since we were ten. What I hate about my best friend is how well she knows me.

We stopped for breakfast at a mom-and-pop before getting back on the road to head to our next show in Joplin, Missouri. As soon as Pete left to go to the bathroom or to call Allison or whatever, Alex snapped her head toward mine and said, "*J'accuse!*"

When I ignored her, which I should have known only incites her, dramatically, she held her fingers up.

"Two things," she said with her mom's "don't mess with me face." "One, you're eating my toast." She then pushed her plate next to my fruit cup, in which I made a show of biting into it for her benefit. "And two…" Her eyes slid to the side. "Don't think I didn't hear you creep back into bed this morning, you little slut." She then leaned forward and, in a whisper, said, "I almost *died* when the Shondells CD went to the song "Hanky Panky" just now in the van because I *know* you were getting some hanky panky last night."

Turning red, I looked down at the menu as her green eyes burned into me, demanding answers. "That is so ugly," I mumbled, trying to hold back from smiling since that would only encourage her more. "Please don't call it hanky panky."

"My grandma calls it hotsy-totsy," she reasoned as she took a sip of her coffee. "Do you prefer that?"

"Aww, that's kind of cute," I said, picturing Grandma Estelle saying it with her Brooklyn accent.

Glancing at Pete over by the phone booths, I could see him rooted in his conversation, which gave me a few minutes to deliver the juicy gossip Alex was clearly salivating for.

"Alright, what do you want to know?" I whispered. "But be quick."

"Well . . . ?" Her eyes became ravenous. "Did you finally break your second-guy virginity?"

"No," I rolled my eyes, hoping to avoid another lecture about me sleeping with her cousin or her new theory that our sexual exploration really starts with the second person.

"So then...?" She appeared confused.

"We did everything — well, almost everything," I looked at my friend, but after a few seconds of seeing that she still wasn't getting it, I was forced to add, "I didn't, you know . . ."

"Go down on him?" she said directly. When she saw my face, she said, "I'm sorry, you didn't kiss him *everywhere*?"

"No," I squirmed. "I didn't."

"Better off." She shook her head. "You can never get that taste out of your mouth. You need, like, a whole real meal afterward."

She then looked up as if making a grand revelation. "But maybe that'll get you to eat something."

"A whole real meal? Quoting *Kids* again, I see?" I teased my best friend. "Everything you learned about sex you really did get from Rosario Dawson."

"I swear, she is *not* acting in that scene. That's a real conversation they're having." She grinned. "So yes, her…and Dr. Judy, of course.

"But back to you. When you say you did everything 'but.'" She looked confused at first, and then I could see her picturing it. "Ooh, okay, hush and rock. Very nice, Lala, very nice."

"Wait, what?" I looked at her quizzically.

"Never mind. But why didn't you guys just have…?"

"We didn't have a …" I said omitting the word condom because she understood, but also because I kind of hated that word.

"I mean, you have them, though? Right? Like in your bag somewhere?"

"No." I was almost appalled. "Why would I need them?"

"Ummm, well, last night, for instance. Hello?"

"It was better off. I didn't need to sleep with him. And it was kind of fun *not* doing it because he seemed to be into other things." I paused to look at her. "And please don't say hush and rock again." I then felt myself blush, thinking about how insatiable Ed was. I was always under the impression guys didn't like doing that, but Ed proved that theory wrong. It was my first time, and I didn't realize I was missing out on this whole realm of pleasure where I just had to lie there.

"And," Alex said, popping my bubble of blissful recollection. "Because you're traveling across the country alone with a cute guy who is kind of into you, for starters." She looked at me like I was truly a stupid human being. "Have I taught you nothing?" She paused for a second. "No, he definitely brought condoms. He's a guy. He *definitely* thought about it."

I looked over to see if Pete was coming, but he was still on the phone. "Okay." I leaned forward and, in a lowered voice, said, "Before he gets back. One. He's not into me. Two, I doubt he brought anything because we're in a band, and he has a girlfriend." Alex made a show of rolling her eyes. "And three," I continued, "I'm not planning on sleeping with him, so there's no need for, you know."

"Condoms, Carla. They're called condoms."

"Yes," I hissed under my breath. "Those."

"You don't fool me for one second. Neither one of you do. First, there's the approved CD book." She looked at me with a raised eyebrow that said give-me-a-fucking-break. "You two aren't flirting anymore; you guys are living on a farm in Croton with your five kids running around because there is no way you're going to get me to believe that Pete had some musical awakening and approved of *Spanking Machine* by Babes in fucking Toyland."

"No, there's a story behind it," I tried to explain. "He was curious because of something with Tony, and we listened to it, and he actually liked it. Well, he likes Lori's drumming."

"He likes Lori's drumming? Okay." She looked to the side and then at me. "Well, then there's you." She pointed. "Since when do you approve of Can and, ew, Genesis?"

"*Early* Genesis," I corrected her. "And no, I don't like them, but, you know, we have to compromise."

"Early Genesis? Oh my God. You're in a band with my dad," she said, in which I nodded in agreement because Pete and Stu Sherman really did have to meet one of these days.

"But come on, it makes a difference because we're not listening to, like, 'I Can't Dance' in the van," I said, feeling justified. "And besides, why are you so surprised? You know our music. It's a little weird, but our influences meet in their own way."

"Oh please, save it for your bio," she said, which I had to admit made me laugh. "I mean, okay, I can hear both of you in your songs, and it *is* pretty freaking cute, which only demonstrates my next point."

"Which is probably a rephrasing of your first but go on." I took a sip of my coffee.

"My next point is I know you. I know you've thought about sleeping with him. Like, heart-pounding, dripping sweat, legs wrapped around him, those juicy, kissable lips all over your body." She appeared proud of the descriptive imagery she painted for me. "*And* I'm going to say you've thought about it more than once."

"Can you stop writing for one second?" I hid my face in my mug, totally embarrassed by what she was saying. "Not everything is a narrative about sex." I set my mug down to look at her. "And another thing." I raised my eyebrows. "He was *not* jealous, you know, with me flirting with Ed."

"Sure, he was." She looked at me like I was completely hopeless. "And quite miserably so. He knows you guys did more than just flirt."

"No, no, he's just grouchy," I reasoned. "He's been going through a lot with Allison, and sometimes he gets like that."

Her face then straightened, and she looked off with quiet introspection and said, "But you know, there was something—"

It was then I saw Pete hang up the phone, prompting me to knee Alex under the table to stop talking about him. As he walked toward us, he looked pale and even more distant and pensive than he usually did when coming back from the phone. The two of us watched him with guilty looks on our faces as he lowered himself into the booth.

"What?" he said, looking at both of us suspiciously.

"Nothing," we both said sweetly.

Pete

Carla offered to drive, even though it was technically still my turn. Too distracted to even think straight since I almost broke up with Allison in the diner, I took Carla up on her offer. As I made myself comfortable in the back, I looked out the van's side window as we cut down I-55. The Midwest landscape with its flat terrain and stretched-out fields made me feel further away from home than I had ever known. I grabbed one of our maps scattered on the floor to calculate where we were and realized the little service road we had been riding alongside was the legendary Route 66, America's Main Street. From all the books I had read, I knew of it as a symbol of optimism and starting over in the quest for prosperity. I then wondered if that was what I was doing as we traveled on our journey west. Was I in the pursuit of emotional wealth and a new beginning? Maybe. But with each state line crossed, I only became more confused. While gazing out onto the sunny late morning, I couldn't help but feel lonely in this new space of not knowing myself as well as I had thought, a feeling I thought I had outgrown in high school. It was then I noticed Route 66 had also parted with me. Forlorn with no answers in sight, thankfully, there was Alex to rip me out of this meaningless soul-searching. "Pete." She turned to me. "Are you awake?"

Worried I had looked depressed because I really didn't want to talk about it, with alert-looking eyes, I said, "Yeah, I'm awake. Why?"

"Like, you have enough coffee in your system?"

"Umm, I think so," I responded, becoming wary because it felt like a trap. "Again, why?"

"Because we're going to change out this lovely, revolutionary, and acclaimed Thelonious Monk CD you so graciously put on," she said gently, which scared me. "And put on something a little harder."

"Okay." I held my hand out to take the CD from her. "What are you putting on?"

"The Lunachicks, Pete," she said, looking at me like I was an asshole.

Something about changing Thelonious Monk out for something called The Lunachicks sounded like a one-way ticket to sonic purgatory, trapped in a padded room with fucking "MMMBop" remixes. I would have tried to negotiate a smoother transition, but the CD was well into the player before I could even disagree to it.

"It's fine," I said to no one listening to me as the thick distortion of the heavy metal guitar shut me up. It wasn't exactly my kind of music, especially with some of the lyrics being about halitosis, farting, and shitting on people. However, I was surprised by how well they played their instruments since that wasn't always a guarantee with some of the bands Carla liked. But the Lunachicks *did* sound like they knew what they were doing. Fart noises and all.

When the album came to its end, things then took a dark turn in the van. Alex looked at Carla, and with eyes glassed over, she said, "Dewdrops in the Garden."

"Yes," Carla said in a faint whisper.

Looking at her from the back and noticing she too appeared to be in an altered state, I found it only mildly unsettling considering she was driving.

"It needs to be on," Alex demanded with a raised fist. "Like now."

"Wait," I chimed in, the douchebag guy in the back thinking we should implement a voting system here. "So, what's Dewdrops in the Garden?" I tried to sound casual.

"Deee-Lite," they both snapped as if I should have fucking known.

"Deee-Lite as in 'Groove is in the Heart?'" I asked, my voice trembling in fear of their response. Please don't mean "Groove is in the Heart," I said to myself, squeezing my eyes shut and clenching my fists tight to release cosmic flows of energy to *not* hear Groove is in the fucking Heart.

"No, Pete," Alex said as she turned the pages of *her* unauthorized CD book she brought into the van. "Not 'Groove is in the Heart.' Don't be so ignorant all the time."

"All the time?" I squinted. "Whatever. Just, thank God is all I have to say." I felt my shoulders relax and my fists soften in relief.

"This is the album *after* 'Groove is in the Heart,'" Alex said with an evil smile.

"There was an album *after*?"

"Well, yeah." Her eyes rolled to the side.

"Car." I leaned my head back in exasperation. "Come on. Step in. Please?"

"Okay, Pete." She nodded her head in a way that seemed like someone in the van was going to be the adult. "You're right. I do need to step in here." She turned to Alex and said, "Alex. Please put on 'Dewdrops in the Garden.'"

"Ha ha," Alex gloated and then let out a truly diabolical laugh. "Dissss!"

"I'm sorry, but did you just say *dis*?" I looked at her in horror.

"I did, Pete." She turned, looking proud. "I said dis. Dis on you." She then laughed harder at my expense.

"Yeah, well, I think the '90s called and asked for their insults back."

"No, Pete, the '90s called and asked to hear 'Dewdrops in the Garden,' so fucking deal with it.'"

And then it happened. We listened to the follow-up album to one of the cruelest one-hit-wonders before "Breakfast at Tiffany's" took the honor. I found myself mourning the Lunachicks.

"Don't you just love it, Pete?" Alex asked, knowing I absolutely did *not* love it. Every so often, I caught Carla's eye in the rearview mirror, who also looked like she was getting evil pleasure out of my misery.

"Pete," Alex looked at me with a bratty grin that made me internally celebrate being an only child. "What do you think?"

"You don't want to know what I think."

"Come on," she whined. "We value your opinion."

"Yeah, I'm sure." I rolled my eyes. But after the fourth time she asked, I said, "Okay, fine. I'll throw in my two cents. Well, for one, it sounds like it was made on the Muppet Babies Casio keyboard."

"Did you own a Muppet Babies Casio keyboard, Pete?" she said in a condescending voice designed to embarrass me.

"Of course, I did," I said, unwilling to accept the embarrassment. "We all did."

Up front, I saw Carla's shoulders slightly bounce as she quietly laughed to herself because she knew I was right. It *did* sound like the fucking Muppet Babies keyboard.

"And how is it," I said, looking back at Alex, who was still eyeing me like I was trashing "Teen Spirit" or something actually epic, "that you can listen with a straight face, like, without a stitch of irony, to something that sounds like Mary-Kate and Ashley rapping about fucking? I mean, why can't you put on *Broken English* like every other aging riot grrrl?"

"Aging!" Alex said, feigning shock. "Fuck. You. Let's see the shit in *your* secret CD book. What's in it? The Dead at the Winterland '74?"

"For one."

"Captain Beefheart or like, Ween?" she said in some alien-sounding voice to suggest how fans of the quirky avant-rock bands spoke. Actually, she may not have been too far off there.

225

"Sorry, are you going through Avril Lavigne withdrawal?" I snarked. "I mean, it *has* been twenty-four hours since I'm sure you've listened to her."

"I don't listen to Avril Lavigne," she snarled exactly as I had hoped. "Whatever, you listen to The Disco Biscuits."

"What!" I cried. "Your mom listens to The Disco Biscuits!"

"Ooooh." She looked at me with dead eyes. "Burn."

"Children!" Carla called out. "Enough!"

Alex then settled back into her seat, the silence forcing us to focus on the pulsing 1990s house beats that invaded my personal space like a teacher's bad coffee breath. Once the album came to its thankful end, I almost demanded to select the next one. I wanted to torture them back with some of my shit. Maybe some Mogwai or since Alex brought it up, fucking *Trout Mask Replica*, but they'd just talk over it, killing the satisfaction. Tuning them out as they giggled up front about this, that, and a sign that read Kickapoo Creek, I kept my eye on the road noticing Route 66 had returned like an old friend.

Once the billboards started to pop up and the highway widened with added lanes, I didn't need the map to know we were approaching St. Louis. Crossing the Mississippi River with a view of the Gateway Arch, quietly, we all looked out onto our right. Passing our first monument of the trip felt significant, shutting up the car of loud New Yorkers who looked out the window in awe.

We dropped Alex off on Market Street, where I could see one leg of the stainless-steel landmark over her shoulder as I gave her a hug. As I was about to release her, she pulled on my ear.

"What the hell!"

226

"Shhh," she said, glancing behind her to make sure Carla was still in the van retrieving Alex's things. "Listen to me."

"Okay!" I cringed as she continued to tug on my ear.

"Make sure she takes care of herself."

"Okay," I said. "But just let go of my ear. That fucking hurts."

She obliged and then placed her hands on my shoulders. With her eyes bleeding into mine, she said, "I mean it, Pete. She doesn't look good."

"Well, I wouldn't go that far." I looked away for a second.

"You know what I mean," she said through gritted teeth. She then flashed her eyes back to the van to see Carla coming. "Pete, I'm worried about her."

"Okay, okay." I nodded in comprehension of her concern because I, too, started asking myself questions. "I hear what you're saying, and I'll try."

Her eyes softened with sincerity, and with a light squeeze on my shoulder she said, "And don't forget to take care of yourself too."

We then exchanged a look, and I said, "Again...I'll try."

17

Carla

I admit to torturing him a little with Alex and tried to make it up to him by letting him choose the music all the way to Joplin. I assumed he'd try to get back at me with one of his prog albums that resembled a score to a terrible musical or his experimental stuff that sounded like people moving furniture around. Instead, he put on something I actually enjoyed. Multi-spirited, the album evoked the fluctuating moods of travel with liberating rock songs made for the open road, dips into acoustic Americana with fingerpicking and bluegrass guitar work, jaunty instrumentals, and songs with dreamy imagery.

"Do you like it?" he asked me.

"I do." I glanced over at him. "A lot, actually. I wouldn't be opposed to hearing it again if we can."

"We can. It's almost over. There's just one last song."

"Who is it?"

Appearing satisfied with my praise, he answered, "Oh, just some band I read about in the *Voice*."

"Nice," I said before diverting my attention out the window.

What impressed me most as we crossed our country was the open spaces. Far from the parking lot of residences that was New York, we drove across the expansive countryside and traveled toward the sky as if it were within reach. With nothing to do but look out the window, no change went unnoticed as the flatlands rose with green hilltops and towering trees, and the road glided in smooth curves around mountain ranges. I focused back to the music when Pete's album struck a familiar chord with a lyric jumping out at me.

"Prince Caspian?" I turned to him.

"Oh." He feigned surprise. "Yeah ... like your book." He then tapped his chin to give the impression of thinking. "Is this, wait ... is this *Phish*?"

"You tricked me!" I lightly pushed his shoulder. "Some band you read about in the *Voice*?" I looked at him with my mouth slightly opened in aghast. "You are such a jerk!"

"What was it you said?" He squinted in faux recollection. "You wanted to hear it ... *again*?"

"Shut up, Pete."

"Well, look at that. Miss Kill Rock Stars likes Phish." He stuck his tongue out teasingly, appearing a little *too* pleased with himself.

I had to admit he got me. I couldn't help but chuckle along with his ruse that proved his point to perfection about the unfairly judged band because they were kind of good. We listened to it again, and I felt as weightless as the lyrics went. Because if the worst of my problems was learning that I might like Phish, then I'd say I had it pretty good.

At our next rest stop, we got situated in the back of the van to finish the cold cuts from Bloomington. With six pieces of bread laid out, Pete took care in assembling the sandwiches, calculating the cheese to turkey to lettuce ratio for each one. I observed his small, thoughtful movements and pressed my lips together to conceal my amusement.

"Tour is quieter than I thought it would be," he said, probably referring to the long spells of silence in the van. "Well, with the exception of the last twenty-four hours, of course." His eyes glinted in my direction as he handed me a sandwich.

"Yeah, sorry about that." I was about to make a joke that *my* long-term girlfriend was also a handful but wisely decided not to allude to Allison. I took the lettuce and cold cuts out of the sandwich and handed him back the bread since I had already eaten Alex's toast that morning. Seeing my hand held out with it, his eyes became small as he looked at my offering.

"Come on." He looked at it and then at me with a waxy expression. "Just eat it."

"You French are so obsessed with bread," I tried to make a joke.

"Well, this isn't bread," he said, unable to resist. "So I don't entirely blame you, but come on, please eat it?"

No longer interested in the conversation, I put down the bread he refused to take and looked away. As I bit into my cold cuts wrapped in lettuce, I left him to deal with the questions I could feel floating in his head. I diverted my attention, thinking about the distances we'd already crossed and the small towns we'd seen, curious how these new experiences would change us. Like how water makes up our body mass, are our personalities simply molecules of our collected experiences? How would sitting in a rest stop eating turkey roll-ups in Conway, Missouri, make a difference in the people we were to become one day?

"I've been meaning to tell you," I said after swallowing a bite. "I started the book you gave me." I then grinned at him. "She mentions Alsace right out of the gate. Is that why you got it for me?"

"Of course not." He forced a smile as I could see him trying to recover from me blowing him off. "Do you like it?"

"Well," I said. "It's not what I usually read, but there are some great lines that I'm appreciating."

"There are some good ones, aren't there?"

I nodded my head as I chewed.

"I just read this one that I really liked," he said. "'Be loved, be admired, be necessary; be somebody.'" He then sat in the quote for a moment before turning to me. "It reminded me of you."

"It did?" I felt a little defensive. "Why? I'm not looking to be loved."

"Sure you are," he said plainly. "We all are."

"That's a little too simple, Pete."

"It's really not." He pinched his face a little. "It's probably the most universal desire."

"If you say so, but let's take you, for example. I find it hard to believe that you have trouble feeling loved and appreciated."

"What makes you think I have everything so figured out?" His eyebrows pressed together.

"You make me think that," I retorted as I started to get a little annoyed.

"And how's that?"

"For one," I answered, "you had a great upbringing."

"I did…"

"So, you couldn't possibly understand what it feels like to lack love and to want to feel necessary. There wasn't exactly a famine of love. Your family's whole world revolves around you."

"In a way, yes." He looked at me like he was waiting for me to get to the point.

"Okay." I felt defiant. "Then you don't get to include yourself because you've never experienced real heartbreak."

I then got one of his famous side eye rolls, and as he began to clear our lunch, he said, "I wish that were true, Carla." Stuffing the deli wax paper into a plastic shopping bag, he did it in a way I knew was designed to tune me out.

"And maybe," he finally said, speaking in a hurt tone I had never heard from him before. "Maybe one day I'll tell you about it." He paused before releasing a deep exhale. "But not like this."

Pete

From lunch at the rest stop, we drove in silence that felt as tight as my throat. It amazed me that we were still discovering one another, as each new town or sprawling landscape seemed to extract another one of our character traits.

We pulled the van into Joplin and familiarized ourselves with another place we had never been to. Driving down two-lane country roads that turned into wider boulevards, we noted billboards of local businesses and fast-food chains we didn't have on Long Island and exchanged grins when we pulled into the Kum & Go gas station. Having some time before soundcheck, we went to a Red Racks thrift store, hoping to find cheap souvenirs.

In the store that had that undeniable charity shop smell of other people's lives fused into the fabrics of old clothes and furniture, it was gloriously overwhelming. Looking for t-shirts, I made my way to the boy's department while Carla went off to get "tchotchkes." As I rummaged through the racks, appreciating a moment to myself, I thought about Carla practically accusing me of having a perfect childhood and the insinuation that I had no soul because of it. Even though it was total bullshit, I couldn't let it upset me because I knew it wasn't about me. What was more important was what Alex had said, which left me feeling completely helpless. She trusted me with the important task of keeping our friend alive, and I was failing. What we needed was a fat joint to get her to eat and to get me to chill the fuck out. But being in the middle of Missouri on our way to Oklahoma and then Texas, buying a gun would have been easier, so I had to come up with something else.

I filled my basket with soft t-shirts brandishing local Little League team logos, family reunions, and company softball games, with some dating as far back as 1985. Satisfied with my finds, I went looking for Carla. When she saw me, she held up a mug with a rainbow handle that said Joplin across the front. She smiled at me, which felt like a mini peace treaty. I then followed her to the changing room and sat outside in a wicker chair, taking advantage of the space as I stretched my legs long out in front of me. With my fingers woven into each other, I drummed my thumbs against my chest and observed a girl about my age with streaks of purple in her hair. While adult contemporary assaulted us through a speaker somewhere, I noticed she wore the same face I had moments ago. While digging through the unknown, you hope to land on that one gem you never knew you couldn't live without. For me that day, it was a washed-to-perfection navy blue t-shirt that said in 1970s paperback novel font LOVE A STEWARDESS.

I noticed then the changing room curtain ruffled and swayed, with Carla grunting on the other side, sounding like she was struggling with a wild animal.

"You okay?" I called out.

"Yeah," she said, slightly out of breath, as if pulling on something heavy. "I'm just," she continued to grunt, "getting this freakin' thing on."

"What the hell are you putting on?" I continued to look at the moving curtain with intrigue. "A space suit?"

"Sort of."

Sort of?

"Okay," she said. "You ready?"

"Yep."

"You promise to keep an open mind?"

"Okay," I responded with a note of skepticism in my voice.

Slowly, the curtain peeled to the side, and she presented herself wearing a one-piece outfit. One-piece as in the top attached itself to the bottom. *This* was what all the excitement was about?

She looked down at herself in appreciation. "What do you think?"

I didn't know how to respond because I didn't get it. It was *attached*. I also couldn't help but wonder how she'd go to the bathroom in that thing without being totally naked.

"Well?" she pressed.

"Well." I searched for the right thing to say before blurting out, "It's a onesie. Like, I think I wore the same one in 1980."

"Pete." She made the face when she thought I was being ridiculous, which was one-part amused, one-part impatient. "Your mom did not dress you in lilac terrycloth as a baby." She looked down at it again and, in a chipper tone, said, "And it's not a onesie; it's a jumpsuit!"

"Jumpsuit?" I threw my eyes up. "And that word is better, how?"

"Jumpsuits are disco, for one. I mean, check out this cool wrap detail and these little cap sleeves." She stopped admiring it to glare at me. "Stop looking at it like it's a onesie because that's creepy." Still dissatisfied with my response, she added, "Also, it's not going to look like this."

"It's not?"

"Of course not," she said in a way as if I was purely dumb while looking around for something to validate her point. "Here." She pulled out a gold belt from an accessories basket and pinched it around her waist. After poking the buckle into a braid in the belt and tucking the remains around to the back, she turned to me, and I had to admit, it was kind of cute.

That night we played at a cocktail lounge, which turned out to be one of our greatest shows ever. Feeling warmed up from tour, we got out there and, without overthinking it, just went for it. Knocking around and having fun on stage, she turned to me a few times mid-song where even though I couldn't see her clearly, I knew she was smiling at me.

In the spirit of jumpsuits, I settled us into a variation on disco with my double kick laying down a steady bass rhythm. Exploring a mood that was a little dance and maybe even a little punk, she timed in some melodic chord progressions, which got our packed house moving like it was the last party on Earth. We stayed in this space, keeping it punchy as we gradually evolved it into a full dance break that toppled the room like thunder. The walls trembled as dancing feet pounded the sagging wooden floor, bodies sweat up against one another, and arms hung around necks. Feeling the emotions bleed out of every person, it felt clear what so many of us needed right now was music.

I felt uneasy about the state of the world. I suspected all of us in the room were going to pay somehow for whatever new ass-backward policies were being put into place to the advantage of no one but greasy politicians. But at that moment, we had music. Opinions about the war differed, but no matter what side you stood on, it didn't dissolve the fear that unfortunately unified us. On stage with Carla that night, I was pleased to provide one small thing for us all to have in common . . . even if it was just for a fleeting moment.

Carla

We had been lucky with bartenders and members from other bands kindly offering a floor or a fold-out couch to sleep on. But by the time we got to Tulsa, we had to pay our tour dues and sleep in the van finally. At a Love's Truck Stop, after a five-dollar shower and blowing my bangs out under the hand dryer, we parked the van in a tucked-away spot in the parking lot. Settled in comfortable clothes, we got warm under the blankets. As I lay on my side, I nibbled on a bag of baby carrots and walnuts Pete had picked up for me. He told me his grandmother said the combination of fiber and healthy fats was good for peaceful thoughts and colorful dreams with winged creatures. I didn't really believe it since I'd had mostly dreamless nights since we left for the tour but thought it was too cute to pass up, and I ended up almost eating both bags. Pete, however, seemed uninterested in his sweet grandmother's wisdom and noshed on Halloween candy the bartender loaded him up with.

We faced each other, the smell of milk chocolate on his breath, as I quietly admired his facial hair that seemed to have grown in overnight. It made his eyes flicker a deeper gold, and his eyelashes appear fuller. On the floor, we spoke about love and sex and relationships. I hinted at my limited experience and said, like a unicorn, I might be someone who didn't need to mate. "An asexual?" he said, giving me a look that said that was bullshit. "There's no way. You're too interesting."

"Maybe." I looked off for a second and then found myself saying, "Can I ask you something?"

"Depends."

"It's kind of random, but I've always wondered." My eyes scanned over his shoulder before asking him. "Why'd you quit soccer in tenth grade?"

"Wow, I wasn't expecting that." He looked at me in genuine surprise. "Shit, I didn't even think you knew about that."

"Our class wasn't *that* big, Pete."

"I just thought you were too cool for high school current events."

"I was," I quipped. "But really, why? I remember you were, like, the star."

"Okay, I wasn't the star," he said, rolling onto his back. "It was just." He took a deep breath. "I don't know. Some of the guys on the team used to say these things that made me uncomfortable."

"Like what?"

"Just stuff that bothered me. I wasn't into…" He got quiet as if recalling the memory. "Locker room talk, as they call it." He held his fingers up in quotations. "And when coach asked why I was quitting, I told him, and it got weird, and he then arranged for me to join track mid-season." He turned his head toward me. "And that's it."

"Okay," I said, wondering if there was more to the story.

We then sat in silence; our hands rested centimeters apart where I could feel brushes of the hair on his arm tickle against mine. I wanted to slide my pinky over to touch his but knew any slight physical contact would have made me want to pull him on top of me. He then got up and reached for the beat-up classical acoustic we brought along for fun and began tuning it. Since he didn't do it often, hearing him play guitar felt like a special occasion. Pensive with his movements, he fingerpicked with a featherlight touch, moving his fingers softly across the strings as if playing the piano. Singing a song he had probably written for Allison called "Buttons," I listened to the sweet lyrics while contemplating on whether to bring to his attention that what he wrote was, in fact, a love song. His voice was smooth, boyish, sometimes throaty, and totally affective as it pulled me in.

Quietly, I grabbed my guitar, and together we came up with a melody of intertwining guitars and braided vocals we almost whispered to each other. It was there I witnessed his songwriting instincts at play, quick-witted and fluid as the words came out. Though I could tell he wasn't completely sure when he'd let out a little laugh and look off to the side nervously, still, I could see him growing into a beautiful songwriter.

We stayed up later than we should have, singing to each other, eating snacks, and talking about everything from sketch comedy to imagining what the kids in our graduating class were up to. Spending time with him like this in the van was more of the image I had of us on the road. Not the greasy, naked one Alex had supplied.

18

Pete

The deeper into America we got, the more affectionate the nicknames from old ladies became. In Ohio, paying for gas, I was honey. At the diner in Illinois, I was baby. In Missouri, at the bartender's apartment we stayed at, I was sugar. But at the truck stop leaving Tulsa, for some reason, I wasn't anything but an asshole who got weird looks from burly dudes who could have totally kicked my ass.

Driving through the flatlands of Oklahoma, I admired the chromatic angles of the land. Reminding me of an abstract painting of the neoplasticism era; the solid block of blue sky met the grassland in a clean line across the horizon, and a shot of black pavement sliced through the middle. The blocks of color were defined and not bleeding into the other, which felt opposite to the person sitting next to me, where nothing felt defined. I thought about our conversation from the night before. It was the closest, emotionally, we had ever gotten. I had been waiting for this because I thought it'd be my opportunity to ask her some questions I had, but ironically, it was me who held back.

Tuned in to a local classic rock station with Boston's "More Than a Feeling" crunching in and out, we drove yet another long stretch of the American land.

"Did you know," Carla said, looking at the map through her enlarged round red sunglasses, "that there's a Miami, Oklahoma?"

"I did not know that," I said, appreciating the local trivia. "Did you know," I offered a bit of my own, "that there's a Paris, Texas?"

"Really?" she said brightly. "We should totally go to Paris on this trip!"

As she ran her finger along the map, presumably looking for it, I almost said I'd rather go to the real one with her but realized how flirty it would have sounded. Even if my version of Paris was sleeping on my cousin's bottom bunk, eating food that would have probably grossed her out, and hiding from Aunt Odile, who insisted we go to Père Lachaise to see Jim Morrison's grave; my Paris wasn't exactly "frenching" in front of the Eiffel Tower wearing Ed's yellow striped top. As I imagined what it'd be like to be in France with her, through the mirror, the blinking cherry-topped lights of a State Trooper we had passed ten minutes earlier caught my attention. I wasn't sure if it was for us since I was going the speed limit and even did that dumb thing of easing on the breaks when I saw him on the side of the road. As he continued behind us, hopefully about to change lanes and pass us, I felt his presence get closer until I couldn't see him anymore because he was riding our tail.

"Shit," I said, reaching to turn the radio off.

"What?"

"We're getting pulled over," I informed her as I put my blinker on and edged into the right shoulder.

"Okay," she said as she calmly opened the glove compartment to take out the paperwork. "I'm sure it's nothing."

"Yeah." I felt more nervous than I should have as I reached for my wallet in my back pocket.

Once both vehicles were at their complete stop, I unrolled the window. Through the side mirror, I watched the officer approach as I felt my heart pound against my chest. I didn't know what was supposed to happen in these situations since my points of reference for getting pulled over by the cops were limited to *Terminator 2* and *My Cousin Vinny.* With my choices being annihilation by a death machine sent from the future *or* going to trial on suspicion of murder, let's just say the comfort wasn't exactly overwhelming me.

With his boots chewing into the ground, his nearing the van felt menacing until we were face to face, his steely blue eyes peering into me unimpressed.

"Good morning, officer," I said, deciding to leave off the Miller, which I read on his name tag.

Solid and resolute in his fitted uniform, he looked at me and then surveyed Carla, who had since taken off her sunglasses, put on a sweater, and tied her hair back. Officer Miller took a quick scan of the interior of the van before demanding, "License and registration, please."

Ready with them in my hand, I passed them over and watched him study them.

"Long way from New York, wouldn't you say?"

"Yes, sir."

He looked again at my face and continued to cross-examine it with my license photo taken when I was seventeen. His eyes fluctuated back and forth between my face and the photo, which started to make me nervous.

"I'll be right back," he finally said, holding a stare that seemed more assertive than necessary for what I had to assume was a random checkpoint.

As he walked back to his car, the two of us stared straight ahead not speaking, like we were in the principal's office. Once I heard his door close, I whipped my head over to her and loudly whispered, "What the fuck is happening?"

"I don't know." She looked skeptical. "I mean, he hasn't even told us why we've been pulled over. Aren't they supposed to?"

"I have no idea." I raised my shoulders. "I've never been pulled over."

"Shit, me neither." She looked at me. "I don't know what our rights are." She paused a second before saying, "And why was he looking at you like that?"

"You saw that too," I murmured.

We then turned our gaze to each other, our eyes glued on the other as if the answer was going to somehow manifest if we thought and stared hard enough. What felt like longer than it probably was, I flinched when I heard Officer Miller's door open and close again. "Shit, he's coming back."

The officer returned, lightly beating the documents into the palm of his hand, still looking at me like I was a total dirtbag. "What brings you to Oklahoma, Mr. Albrecht?" I didn't like the way he didn't have to glance down at my license to recall my name, which hinted he might have run some reports on me in his car. However, I was impressed with his pronunciation of my last name because, seriously, no one ever fucking got it right.

"We're in a band, officer," I said, certain my answer would greatly dissatisfy him. "We played in Tulsa last night and are now on our way to New Mexico."

He then leaned forward to get another peek inside the van, where I could smell the coffee he must have been sipping on in the car. As he looked, I did feel at ease because, as far as I knew, there was nothing out of the ordinary: our own to-go coffee cups, the CD binder, maps, and Carla's messy side of papers, loose CDs, her flip-flops, and a protein bar wrapper. If there was anything to get a ticket for, it would be the pigsty that was her side, and I wouldn't blame him one bit. His eyes then met mine, and he said, "I'm gonna need to inspect your vehicle. Please step out of the van."

I had no idea if this was in violation of our rights, and in the movies, the perps — shit, was I perp? — always demanded a search warrant, but if I learned anything from *My Cousin Vinny* was that New Yorkers weren't exactly celebrated in the Bible Belt, so I agreed to the request.

"Also," he said as I gingerly unbuckled my seatbelt like my mom did after she came home from the nail salon. "If you have any drugs or paraphernalia, you best tell me now." He then held my eyes in a firm grip and added, "Or anything *else* you think I should know about."

After giving him my word that we didn't have drugs in the van, I contemplated over what he meant when he said if I had anything *else*. I couldn't think of anything worse than having drugs other than, I supposed, weapons of some sort? But it didn't matter because we didn't have any of that shit. I met Carla on the other side of the van, giving her a look that said it would be fine. I felt better about our position, that was until a *second* cop car arrived on the scene . . .

The two arriving officers talked to Officer Miller in a way that wasn't inquisitive enough for my comfort. They didn't just happen to drive by and were checking out what was going on; they had been called for backup, it seemed. Stretching a pair of latex gloves over their hands, the officers then helped themselves into the back of our van. On the curb, we heard them jostle things around, which annoyed me because I knew things weren't being returned to their proper place. They then proceeded to take our gear out. Starting with our bags of mics and stands, then our amps, and then my floor tom...until our entire stage set-up was on the side of I-44. While harboring in the agony of my Gretsch soaking in direct sunlight, I watched as they ran their hands along the rims and shells and held my snares up to give them a good shake. *Please don't do that,* I wanted to say as my eyes bled at their mishandling, *that's a legendary piece of equipment.*

"Is there any way to take this apart more?" an officer called out to me.

Horrified by the question because he couldn't have been serious but seeing his face that expected a response, I said, "Yeah. The rims come off, as do the tension rods and lugs, but you'll need a —" before I could finish my sentence, Officer Miller returned, and in his hands were my French and American passports.

"Mr. Albrecht." He got closer. "You wanna tell me about these?"

"Those are my passports, sir," I responded, only then realizing how the pluralization made it sound shady as hell.

"I see that. You wanna tell me what a twenty-one-year-old is doing with two passports?" He held them up as if he found some great piece of evidence. "I told you to tell me everything."

"I apologize, officer. It didn't occur to me to tell you I had my passports," I said, hoping I didn't sound sarcastic. With my confusion mounting from them asking about taking apart my kit because what the hell would I be hiding in those little nooks? A joint? It seemed like a lot of manpower for something so small. But now the concern over my passports? I looked over at Carla, who was talking to two female officers who I could hear explain what we were doing on the road.

"I'm waiting, Mr. Albrecht."

"I have dual nationality, sir," I said with my voice slightly quivering. "My mother is American, and my father is French but naturalized as an American citizen."

"Albrecht." He glared at me. "Doesn't sound very French to me."

Jesus, I said to myself, thankful it hadn't slipped out of my mouth in front of my God-fearing audience.

"My family is Alsatian." I immediately regretted saying it because of how exotic it sounded.

"Alsatian?" he repeated. He turned around to his colleagues, who were still conducting the search through our shit, and with a chuckle, said, "Any y'all heard of Alsatian?"

"No, sir," I heard coming from the van before Officer Miller turned back toward me, giving me a nod to continue.

"We're from Alsace, a region in France that borders Germany, which is why my name sounds German. The region is a hybrid of the two cultures," I explained before adding, "sir."

"A *hahbread*, you say?" He then shot me the look I gave to Carla when she got into her fantasy talk shit. "Well, I'm gonna call this in and see about that *hahbread* you talk of."

Following behind him was the female officer holding Carla's driver's license. Unsure if I was even allowed to talk to her, still I inched my way over and said, "This seems a little excessive for a routine check, don't you think?"

"Yeah." She looked out at our stuff on the side of the road. "They were asking me really weird questions like telling me to give them a sign if I was in danger and then how long I've known you and then stuff about your family."

Surprised by how much focus was on me, with no more questions about drugs, something seemed off. We stood next to each other, waiting as the officers tried to piece together what they felt was some kind of mystery. And then it struck me like a punch in the head. I slowly turned to Carla and said, "Oh my God."

"What." She dug her eyes into me.

"Car."

"What!"

"This isn't about a broken headlight or some bullshit like that."

"Okay, then what do you think it is?"

"Think about it."

"We don't have time, Pete. Just spit it out."

"Well," I started to say, as I quickly glanced over at the busy officers. "We have New York plates, which already is begging to be pulled over."

"Okay."

"We're driving a sketchball van," I continued. "And the driver" —I pointed to my chest— "has a full beard."

"Pete." She looked at me with impatience. "Get me there faster."

"It's fucking 2001, not 1971. Bearing in mind what just happened, beards aren't exactly á la mode right now if you get what I'm saying."

"I don't," she hissed.

"Well, we might as well have a fucking Allah Akbar bumper sticker on our car."

"They don't make those." She leveled her eyes.

"Car." I placed my hands on her shoulders. "We're not being pulled over for a broken taillight or whatever. We're being pulled over on suspicion of terrorism ... a fucking month after September 11."

Carla

I knew Pete's flair for the dramatic, and if the female officers hadn't basically asked if I was being kidnapped, I would have called him out for starting to lose it. He may have been right, though, since I'd heard on the news about these kinds of suspicions happening increasingly after the attacks.

I think what made the weeks following 9/11 so difficult to digest was not having anything in our mental or tactile memory to compare it to. We rely on past experiences to trust and make sense of things, and on that day, we didn't have that. For a large majority, what we had seen was brand new information that we struggled to piece together with logic. That, and the endless influx of information and speculation, had put so many people on edge.

However, with Pete's growing distrust for the establishment, I knew the interrogation had struck an even more resonant chord with him.

In the end, our gear proved not to be explosives, Pete's passports checked out, and being Alsatian was not being a member of al Qaeda. Then, with the enthusiasm of an SAT proctor, Pete explained the region's history of the alternating occupations that left the inhabitants conflicted between the two cultures. In Strasbourg, he explained, the elites and intellectuals could afford to remain loyal to France, while outside the city, artisans and laborers leaned toward the German culture, notably the Germanic dialect. "As of today, though," he concluded to his surprisingly captive audience, "there's harmony between the two cultures, which makes the region" — he looked at Officer Miller — "a hybrid. *Voilá.*" After that, they let us go. With their expressions softened, they wished us good luck with the band, and I think Pete even sold them on the choucroute. "Sausage and sauerkraut," one officer said with an approving nod, "sounds good to me." Pete looked like he was going to cry.

After taking an hour to load up the van again, we headed back out with me driving and Pete chain-smoking in the passenger's seat. To keep my own mind from wandering into the dark corners of what could have happened, I took deep breaths and focused on the road. We passed by towns with cute names like Henryetta and Beeline, and the clouds stretched across the sky like vanilla cotton candy. Once we crossed the Red River—its surface so still, it looked like you could ice skate straight across it—we were in Texas. We pulled off at the first exit in Denison to get Pete a battery-operated razor. And in the parking lot of Wal-Mart, he shaved his beard into a plastic bag.

Several hours into Texas, we drove without music or conversation. The tension felt as dense as the desert air we were easing into as we left the Midwest behind us. When we passed a sign for Highway 82 that I remembered from the map would get us to Paris, I wanted to tell him to at least get him to slip a smile. Instead, I pulled off at the next exit to get us a piece of pie.

Outside Plano, in the small city of McKinney, I drove until I found the right place to cheer him up. Certain we could do better than the Denny's we had passed, eventually, I found a dive that looked like it didn't let modern times dictate its style. Sitting at the Formica counter of the mid-century diner, I took in the details. The domed pie stands; the brown and tan speckled stone wall; a sign that read LEAVE YOUR SHOES ON AND YOUR POLITICS AT THE DOOR; and the waitress calling Pete doll baby.

Looking down into my hot chocolate and stirring the whipped cream around with the spoon, I had to smile because, with his freshly clean face, that was exactly what he looked like: a doll baby. One of the things on our trip I was getting a kick out of was seeing women of a certain age light up at his boyish face. They then lavished him with confectionary nicknames that made his eyelashes sparkle and dimples crease. Seeing him smile again—even if it *was* more blushing at the winking, gum-chewing waitress—was what I had hoped for. I kind of wanted to be the one to make him feel better...but I guess we'd always have Paris.

19

Pete

I had to get over what had happened. I mean, the officers ended up being nice, considering. But still, I shuddered in disgust and frustration, thinking of those who might not have gotten off so easily. As we cut across Texas, I noticed the countryside gradually changing from the flat farmlands of the Midwest to the arid landscape I associated with Texas. It didn't happen all at once, though. After crossing the Oklahoma state line, the land stayed mostly green. But by the time we hit Cisco, we got a glimpse of the sand-hued Southwest scenery that faded in and out with the small towns we drove through. Once we were on a cozy two-lane highway with country fields stretching out on both sides, we passed a sign that read, WELCOME TO NEW MEXICO; THE LAND OF ENCHANTMENT. I looked over at Carla because I knew she'd like that.

We decided to get a room in Las Cruces for no other reason than our backs and necks were fucking killing us. After getting a little lost, we eventually found a roadside motel that looked like the set of a Tarantino film and probably dated back to Carla's haircut. We pulled into the lot, with the line of motel room doors in front of us. I looked at her as she started to clap her hands in excitement at the retro vibe. There was something in the air I felt as soon as we entered New Mexico that I couldn't quite explain.

Maybe it was a response to seeing the desert for the first time or the warmer climate, but I felt a buzz throughout my entire body. Looking at Carla, I could tell something was different about her too.

In our room, while she soaked in a bath, I was supposed to be getting a new calling card but decided to blow it off, if only for a few minutes. Stretching out, my back appreciating the smooth surface of an actual bed, I listened to her through the door, sighing in her own relief. With my eyes closed, I heard the soft sounds of the water splashing around her body and pictured what she looked like at that very moment: the soap dripping down her arms, the way in which I imagined she washed her hair with it piled high as she combed all ten fingers through it, her eyes closed, back arched, heart pressed forward. When she came out, nothing in her appearance misled my visions. She had her hair wrapped in a towel, her expression relaxed, and she was wearing a fitted t-shirt that hugged the lines of her body. It all made sense, except for the pink sweatpants that looked like they belonged to a ten-year-old.

"What the fuck are those pants?" I laughed as I got off the bed and pulled my sweaty shirt over my head.

"I know." She looked down at herself. "I have this habit of not getting rid of old clothes, so I grabbed these sweatpants, probably from, like, the fifth grade, thinking they were another pair."

"You have another pair that looks like that?" I teased as I passed her with my smelly t-shirt in my hand.

"I do," she deadpanned, seeming unphased by my bare chest. "I have an entire closet of pink sweatpants, Pete. And what about you?" She picked up my bar soap I had at the sink. "You're weird too."

"What?" I put my hands out. "It's soap."

"You've never heard of body wash?"

"Do you know what a waste of money that stuff is? Plus, if it opens in your bag, you're fucked."

She picked up the brown soap from Marseille and examined it. "What the hell is noisette?" She then smirked at me, in which I knew she was fucking with me because her French pronunciation was better than that.

"No*ise*-ette," I repeated. "It's not Noise-ette. Like fucking Barbie's backup band."

"They were The Rockers." She placed her hand on her hip and tilted her head at *my* ignorance.

"Whatever. It's noisette. You know, *nwah-zhette*." I looked at her and shook my head.

"I know, I know. I'm just playing with you," she said in a sweet voice. "But what does it mean, noisette?"

"It means hazelnut."

She then started laughing wildly to herself, which I didn't really get. What was so funny about hazelnut? When she composed herself from the least funny thing I had ever heard, she opened the plastic bag containing our stage clothes where a stench of smokey bars and the brine of our sweat released into the air.

"Oh, that's vile!" She pulled her nose away and opened it toward me. I dumped my t-shirt in and began unbuttoning my jeans as she stood there...watching me. I had only unbuttoned the first two and looked up at her to see if I should keep going. With my eyes, I expressed that I would if she wanted me to. She looked at me and then back down to where my hands were. Then, as if zapped with a bolt of electricity, she appeared to snap out of it. "Anyway," she said, leaving the bathroom. "I'm going to go ask the front desk where the nearest laundromat is." And with a smile that slipped from the side of her mouth, she said, "Have a nice shower, Noisette."

Before doing laundry, we lingered over a late breakfast at a greasy spoon. From across the booth, I observed her as she read a local newspaper. Every so often, she'd look up to capture her surroundings; the air perfumed with butter the size of ice cream scoops that slid across the grill; the hiss of bacon cooking; and the sun kissing her shoulder. She glowed in the Southwest light that cut through the window. I wanted to tell her how beautiful she looked in this old café, an image I knew one day would make me feel old from how long ago it would feel. Looking at her, she already felt like a distant memory.

"What?" Her eyes looked up, twinkling as they met mine.

"Nothing."

"Okay." Her voice trailed off as she smiled to herself, looking back down at the paper. "You're weird."

"*You're* weird."

She let out a small laugh as she glanced up at me before reverting her eyes back down to the paper, still smiling.

"Hey, check it out," she said with her finger pointing to something. "Special Ed is also playing in town tonight."

"Oh." I said, trying to sound cool.

"In Mesilla, it says here," she said, mulling it over for a second. "I wonder if that's far." She then looked at me. "Now I remember. He *did* say they were coming down this way, and I don't know, I just didn't press further because what are the odds of it being the same night, you know?"

"Well, that was after how many rounds of 'Crimson and Clover'? Because that's enough to make anyone not think straight." I rolled my eyes.

"Oh, stop." Her eyes smiled at mine before dropping back down to the paper. "There's also a Pumpkin Festival going on, and if you're good." She grinned. "We'll go get your face painted."

"Tempting. But really," I said, scratching the back of my neck. "Did you want to go see them?"

"We'll see." She shrugged her shoulders as she ripped the announcement out of the paper and slipped it into her bag.

At the laundromat, I sat on a chair outside smoking, while Carla sat on a counter inside. She told me she liked laundromats, especially in the middle of the day when they were quiet. She said they comforted her; everything from the smell of the fabric softener, the linoleum floors, and the faded signs with illustrations of bubbles made her feel like she was going back to a better time of *Laverne and Shirley* reruns and ginger ale. Eyeing the expired *TV Guide* someone had left on the counter, I slid it over to her. "Here, go back to two weeks ago."

I looked out onto the parking lot, feeling the heat rise from the pavement. With the sun on my cheeks, I leaned back and let the nutrients absorb into my pasty skin. I closed my eyes and thought about Allison not knowing how to handle the inevitable. I knew I would have to do it in person because only a dickhead would break up with his girlfriend on the road. But I also didn't know how I was going to share a bed with Carla that night. And then there was the drama about Ed that I knew was only playing out in my head. I damned myself for letting any of this happen. Stupidly, I thought everything and everyone would stay exactly the same. But with each mile we traveled, I saw with more clarity what a childish hope that was. I opened my eyes when I heard a chair slide over. Next to me, she had her hair stacked high and held in place by a pencil, exposing the smooth nape of her long neck I used to admire in health class.

"I sometimes wished I smoked," she said, looking over at me as I looked for the shape of her eyes in her dark round sunglasses.

"No, you don't."

"It's just that smokers always look so calm and at peace when they're smoking."

"That's because we're assholes when we're not, so the contrast is just more obvious."

"Is that it?" She chuckled.

She let out a few deep sighs and exhales and began rolling her shoulders forward and back. Sitting next to her with only the sound of her joints cracking, it was then that I allowed myself to admit just how badly I was crushing on her. But it felt like so much more than that. I liked when she laughed, when she got impatient with me, when she sang to me. When I played her my song "Buttons," I think she figured out it was about her. And maybe, I thought, glancing at her from the corner of my eye as she stretched her arms over her head, it was why she agreed on the motel …

The sun continued to beat down, and I knew my skin was getting blotchy and red while hers started to look like olive oil. She got up from her chair to head back into the laundromat, and when she passed, the breeze carried her scent of mini-hotel soap and fake shampoo flowers.

"Come on." She swept her hand across the back of my neck. "Let's go fold some laundry."

Our show that night was at a barbecue restaurant that made me hungry the second we walked in. Carla's contact was the manager Danny, whom she was excited to meet. After he agreed to book our show, she told me they talked on the phone for about an hour. When they met, it was like they were old friends and greeted each other with a hug.

Carla introduced us, and the first thing I noticed about him was his Dodger's baseball hat. Seeing my quizzical expression, he said, "I'm from LA even though I've been in the Land of Entrapment for over twenty years." Carla and I looked at each other. "It's a nickname," he clarified. "The beauty entraps you, and no one ever leaves New Mexico without taking a part of it with them." He then looked off with mystic eyes as if recalling a memory before breaking out of it. "And if your van breaks down here, well, consider yourself a resident of New Mexico cuz you'll never leave."

That night, the stage was the smallest we had ever played on, so to avoid having her bump into the equipment or tap my cymbals with her guitar, we set up her mic at the best angle we could so she could face the room. But within this tight configuration, we could also look at each other.

That night as she sang to me, we communicated not only through the music but with our eyes as we absorbed each other. It was then I knew…we weren't just playing music anymore.

Carla

I was close! Hazelnut! Of course! I knew it wasn't my imagination that he smelled like *some kind* of sweet nut. I couldn't hold it together and was practically snorting in that tiny bathroom as he looked at me with his "what the fuck?" face. Then he started to undress. And I just stood there...wanting to know more. I didn't know what was up with me. Maybe it was just the crazies of the road finally getting to me or the glorious Southwest air against my skin. But I felt like someone else, someone screaming to be touched.

For the entire set, our eyes remained locked, making me feel more connected to him than ever. I couldn't tell if this newfound energy we had was physical or a creative wavelength we were fully peaking on as a band. Either way, it was something my body couldn't help but respond to as I pulsed in rhythm with him.

After our set, we quickly broke our stuff down and secured our gear in the van. When I returned from a trip to the bathroom, I found him near the service bar getting us water. Squeezing in between him and an occupied barstool that pressed into my back, I looked up at him.

"So," I said, my eyes trailing to the side. "That was an interesting set."

And with the faintest trace of a smile and a smokey stare, he looked down at me. "Interesting?" He raised an eyebrow. "Is that what we're calling it?"

"I don't know." I laughed nervously. "What would you call it?"

Standing inches apart, we then stared into each other, not moving. I felt us breathe together, the rising and falling of his shoulders in sync with the heaviness of my chest. Aware there was only an inch of space between us, I knew all it would take was one tiny step that would have us pressed up against each other. Then what? Overcome with curiosity, I accidentally let my hand brush against his. He then let his hand accidentally brush against mine. I looked away in hesitation and tucked my fingers into a soft fist. I then felt one of his fingers nudge mine, almost flirting with it to come back. Okay, my hand said and responded by loosening its grip to let our fingers slowly interlace. There, our musician's hands explored each other's calluses, as my heart felt like it was beating as loud as the kick drum being tested on stage. Our thumbs caressed and twisted around like they were like two tiny naked bodies quietly discovering each other.

"Look at me," he whispered in my ear.

And so I did. Deep in his regard with his hand in mine, I felt tiny stars shoot down to my stomach and in between my legs.

"I don't know what I'd call it," he then said. "But I kinda liked it."

"Me too." I lowered my eyes and smiled at how good I felt.

It was the first time my emotions had met this kind of physical contact, and I wanted to feel more of it with him at the motel room. I decided then that I wanted to share my body with him and to lose my second-guy virginity that night.

He then moved slightly closer and said, "Should we leave?"

Feeling the warmth of his words against my skin, I leaned in closer and told him I wanted to, as I let the tip of my nose touch his cheek. With my eyes heavy, I traced my nose up his jawline toward his ear as his hands smoothed around my waist, pulling me in close to him. Just as I was about to go for a small kiss on his cheek, a voice boomed through the moment like thunder and said, "You Pete?"

"Yeah?" he said in surprise of the impatient-looking bartender facing us.

"Telephone."

Pete

I had no idea I was going to like the way she touched me as much as I did. Oh, who was I kidding? Of course, I knew I'd like it. I had played our first kiss over in my head so many times; imagery that put me to sleep at night and got me through long shifts at work. Sometimes I envisioned it outdoors at Clark Gardens. Or after a practice, I imagined her asking to see my room where we'd end up making out on my bed with our shirts off. There were a few versions. However, none of them included a barbecue restaurant with us crammed between two barstools with some dude behind me who I think had just burped. It was happening, though, with her lips close to my neck and her breasts pressing against my chest. At that moment, nothing could have stopped me from kissing her . . . nothing except a phone call from my girlfriend.

"Make it quick, angel," the bartender said as she reluctantly handed me the cordless phone. Carla, who was still close to me with her fingers laced in mine, gave me eyes that told me to take the call.

"Thank you," I said to the bartender before raising the phone up to my ear dubiously. "Hello?"

"What's going on, Pete?" Allison huffed into the phone. "I haven't heard from you."

"Allison," I said, feeling disoriented.

Immediately Carla untangled her fingers and pulled away as much as she could in the small space.

"Hi...I know," I said into the phone. "I have to get another calling card."

I jiggled Carla's fingertips for her to look at me. She then gestured to the door, suggesting she should leave me to my phone call. But feeling like I had put her through enough with these calls, I mouthed for her to stay.

"I was going to call you," I told Allison, "with quarters at the payphone at the motel."

"Motel!" she shrieked. "What do you mean *motel*?"

"Allison," I said with some impatience. "We've been living like dirtbags sleeping on people's nasty floors or in a van. We just needed a decent night's sleep."

"A decent night's sleep?" she said with a bite. "How convenient."

I looked at Carla, who tightened her jaw in response, which disclosed she could hear Allison through the phone. She again motioned for the exit, in which I nodded, insisting she stay. The bartender, who had one eye on me, then gave me another look to hurry it up.

"Oh my God," Allison interpreted my silence. "You *were* planning on sleeping with that whore."

Carla flinched and shifted her body away from me as she pulled her gaze down to the floor.

"Stop! What's the matter with you?" I snapped at Allison while trying to maintain eye contact with Carla.

"Pete," she said, exasperated. "That's what she is: a low-class whore whose dad cleans my mom's shoes."

Carla then looked up at me with pupils enlarged like small planets. She looked like she was going to cry. With my eyes contrite, I tried to reach for her hand again, but she tucked it tightly behind her as she looked away in shame.

"Okay, if you're still not going to say anything," Allison continued. "I'll say that I can't believe I let this go on as long as I have. Face it. She's total trash," she barked. "At least you got *in* to a good school. Where the hell did she get in?" she scoffed. "She really was one of the stupider ones in our class. No AP to even speak of." She then exhaled. "I mean, you're the victim here. You've been manipulated, and being the good person that you are, you let it happen and with someone so simple, I guess is the right word."

Having had as much as she could take, Carla pushed past me as my back slammed into the guy behind me.

"Fuck this, Pete," she said and bolted to the door.

"Car!" I called out to the back of her head. "Please!"

As I started to move out of the small space, the bartender, who looked like she had no patience for what appeared to be teen drama, said with disinterest, "You'll be too far from the base." Her eyes peered at me with amusement as she pulled beer from the tap into a pint glass. "You'll lose the connection, so it looks like you're gonna have to choose."

"Um, no, Pete, you're not going anywhere," Allison said, which forced me to believe that all girls had sonic hearing skills.

"You're going to talk to me, you know, your *actual* girlfriend. I think *Car* can wait. God knows I waited all summer for my boyfriend to take even the slightest interest in me beyond blow jobs. So I think just this once you can choose me first."

Just as I was about to retaliate, I stopped myself not because this was getting to the point of fucking satire but because it was my fault. All of it. I had let it get to this point. It was then that I felt like a truly awful person as I hung my head down by how fucked I had let everything get. I thought I was being a good person by *not* breaking up with her when it turned out that staying together was the cruelest thing I could have done. She then began to scream into the phone, calling me an asshole, and I took it; I took it all, even if some of her complaints were unfair . . . notably the blow job comment.

"You're right," was all I could manage to say, which then incensed her even more.

"So you were purposefully being an asshole!"

"No," I said before backpedaling. "I mean, I just didn't want to hurt you."

"What! Hurt me *how* exactly?" she said, sounding appalled. "What are you saying, Pete?"

"I don't know, Allison." I closed my eyes.

"You think we should break up."

"Well..."

I then started to feel dizzy with sensory overload; the cigarette smoke of pretty much every person in the bar; the increased chatter; the second band warming up; and the bartender still giving me eyes that she wanted her phone back.

"Well, yeah," I said, finally giving in. "I mean, this isn't exactly working." We then sat on the phone for what felt like minutes as I ignored everything around me.

"Okay," she said with less hostility.

"I'm sorry," I exhaled, imagining her in Boston, probably sitting on her bed wearing her school hoodie she liked to wear at night. I took another breath and said, "It's just we've become two different people."

"No," she interjected. "You've become this whole other person with someone else while I've stayed exactly the same."

"You know that's not true. At least I hope you don't because how could you possibly think you've stayed the same person since high school?"

"I don't know, Pete," she said, sounding tired of the conversation.

And with that, we stopped talking and stayed on the phone to breathe together probably for the last time. I had already imagined this moment, something that pained me to admit. I figured it would have been this long dragged-out thing with tears, extraneous phone calls, and breakup sex. Instead, it was quiet with a sparse use of words to fill the negative space between us.

I leaned against the bar and mourned the end of our story that I would always hold close to me. More than anything, she was a dear friend even if we did ditch seventh period Humanities class to spend in bed while my parents were at work. But also, she was the person who unwittingly broke me out of a confusing time where I started to feel okay with being who I was...or rather, being what I was.

I felt sometimes like my heart was going to implode from how much affection I felt for her because I did care for her very much. I didn't know what I would have thought back then if I saw this ending of an otherwise sweet story reduced to a trite, long-distance apology. I almost offered to drive to Boston to end things properly, but there was no point since we were already sitting in the result. With my eyes lowered as the tears threatened to fall, I realized what I mourned most was my fading feelings. I resented myself for complicating everything. Why *couldn't* I have just stayed the same?

Because I couldn't.

Before we hung up, I told her to take care of herself. And I meant it.

Setting the cordless down and thanking the bartender, I then ran out to apologize to Carla. I wanted to reassure her that nothing Allison said was real. In the parking lot, though, I didn't find her, just the taillights of our van pulling out onto the main road as I inhaled dirt kicked up from our tires.

Carla

I'd had enough. Enough of it all. I felt stupid for opening up to Pete on stage and then for coming onto him like I did after. I waited for him outside, but after ten minutes or so, I had to ask myself what exactly was I waiting for? For him to return after another Allison tongue-lashing where he'd then act weird to me for the rest of the trip? No, thank you. Growing tired of being other people's scapegoat, in a huff, I grabbed the van keys out of my bag. I figured if I really was this whore I had been accused of my whole life, well, I might as well have some fun.

20

Pete

It didn't take a mastermind to know where she went. Even though I drove her to this point, I still resented her for leaving. For a few reasons. For one, it amazed me she couldn't give me ten minutes to end a four-year relationship. As I leaned against the stucco façade outside the bar, the jangle of the Rickenbacker from the alt-country band inside filtered out. I lit up a smoke and closed my eyes to replay the chaotic last twenty minutes.

"That was some set, man," said Danny's voice in my right ear, yanking me from my thoughts. I opened my eyes to turn to thank him as he pulled out a soft pack from his back pocket. With my lighter already in my hand, I reached out to light his cigarette. "Thanks," he murmured, cupping his hand to block an imaginary breeze. Once lit, he enjoyed his first puff and then looked at me and said, "You guys got a hot thing going on."

"Thanks." I stifled a laugh at how much mental energy went into a *hot thing*. "My girlfriend," I started to say before catching myself. "Rather, my ex-girlfriend back east doesn't seem to think so."

"Hold up." Danny looked to the side. "Carla's not your girl?"

I nodded that she wasn't as I took another drag, turning my cheek to exhale the smoke away from him.

"Fuck, man!" He looked out in disbelief. "Coulda fooled me."

"I guess," I said, trying to sound dismissive. "Anyway, I don't even know what's happening anymore."

"You okay?"

I turned to him, and feeling comfortable confiding in someone I had just met, I responded, "I don't know. I mean, everything was going fine, well, somewhat fine. And then we get here, and it's like everything just feels fucked."

"Since you got where?" His eyes narrowed slightly. "To New Mexico?"

"Yeah, I guess," I said. "But I don't know. It's probably in my head."

"Maybe," he said, seeming unconvinced. "Or maybe it's that New Mexico sees everything."

"What."

"Don't underestimate the clairvoyance of the vortexes," he said with an expression that hinted at his own experiences. "There are no coincidences."

"The vortexes?" I shot him a look, feeling like I was talking to Carla, who had compared herself to a unicorn the night before. "Get the fuck outta here. Come on."

"Or what?" He looked at me in all seriousness that vortexes were manifesting everything going on. "I'm telling you," he insisted. "It's real. The land is sitting on magnetic energy. How can you not feel it pulsing through your body?" He held both hands out as if absorbing actual auras. "How'd you guys get here? Which route?"

"380, I think."

"Well, there you go," he said as if it were so simple. "You drove through Roswell, home of the UFO vortex, and up north, you have Chimayo and Chaco Canyon energy sites."

"And?"

"Well, there, you have the sacred holy dirt known for its medicinal properties, both emotional and physical." He looked at me to see if I was keeping up. "I mean, it's a few hours away, but you don't think that energy travels, not to mention whatever *you've* been putting out?" He considered it as he nodded his head in complete belief. "I don't know; it makes sense to me."

"So is that why I've been confused and feeling like total crap?" I appeased him.

"Nah, man," he said while looking at me like I wasn't getting it. "You're healing, and in order to heal, you got to hurt a little, and that's when the truth comes out."

"The truth," I scoffed to myself.

"Look," he continued, "If there's some unresolved shit bubbling under the surface, you bet your ass it's gonna come out here. Didn't you learn anything at school?" He flicked my shoulder playfully.

"School?" I couldn't help but laugh. "Where I would've learned about avoiding UFO vortex sites when you're hiding the fact that you might have feelings for someone who *isn't* your girlfriend, who also happens to be in your band, all while wrestling with some *things* from your past?"

I smirked at how specific the lesson was as he looked at me as if it made total sense.

"Yeah, man," he said with wide eyes as if I was finally getting it.

"Well, fuck, maybe I did miss out on my education."

Carla

After stopping for directions, I pulled into the parking lot of another bar where I could hear Special Ed had already started their set. I walked into the packed house with people pressed against the bar, and out on the floor, fans danced and even sang along to the lyrics. I thought about how cool it was that they had actual fans. I slid onto the last empty barstool near the stage and signaled to the bartender. As she walked toward me down the long stretch of the bar, I couldn't help but take notice of her. She looked about my age with her taut skin rich as cocoa butter, but she had this incredible, thick gray hair she wore in a side braid that fell down her arm. Probably the most stunning girl I had ever seen, I became nervous and wanted to order something cooler than a beer.

"I'll have a shot of whiskey," I said as if I always ordered it.

"What kind?" She arched an eyebrow.

Shoot. I hadn't thought about that, I said to myself. Letting her catch my bluff that I wasn't this seasoned bar fly, I looked at her shyly and, with a small shrug, said, "One that doesn't hurt going down?"

We exchanged smiles as she set out two shot glasses. Expertly, she grabbed a bottle from behind her and poured one for me and one for her. We clinked our glasses, and together we threw them back, which felt like liquid drain cleaner burning down my throat. Instantly I felt its effect as my muscles loosened and my brain softened. I then thought of my mother and how her first few sips mellowed her out too. Wanting to keep feeling this way, I ordered another, along with a beer to wash it down with. The bartender then disappeared into the haze of thirsty patrons as I turned my attention back to the band.

After their fourth song, I recognized the order and knew the band was halfway through their set. Pete forbade us from repeating setlists. I guess it was his weird Phish education coming out, but he said he'd rather watch Tony air drum than have us repeat a show. I took a gulp of my beer and focused on Ed, who looked like he was showing signs of the road too. In a less contrived look, he traded out his yellow stripes for a comfortable white t-shirt with faded blue ringers around the sleeves. A shadow of stubble, the color of a Redwood tree trunk, marked his cheeks, reminding me of Pete's beard that was already starting to grow in.

With Ed's daydream blue Strat guitar around his neck, he flaunted his primal and catchy power chords. Then, as if responding to a magnetic force, he looked over to my corner of the bar; his green eyes appeared pleased to see me as we exchanged nods. My eyes then trailed down to his hands that had been up my shirt and then back up to his lips that had made me tickle in certain places. I looked away and felt a little bashful as I recalled exactly what we had been doing the last time we saw each other.

As the alcohol took more control of me, I felt like I suddenly understood my mom. When all feels like shit . . . drink! So maybe my mom *wasn't* a bitch...maybe she was a genius after all.

Loving the way that I was feeling, I swayed to the music, pulling longer sips while Ed sang his last song to me. They closed out to a powerhouse applause with their fans sweaty, standing shoulder-to-shoulder, and calling out song titles for their encore.

"Thanks a lot." Ed looked down at the crowd and absorbed their adoration like a professional. He then lit a cigarette, and as his drummer laid down a steady beat, Ed partook in a little stage banter. Regaling his fans with a story of the road, he held the room in his hand with all eyes on him. The crowd devoured these morsels as they lavished in his attention and even helped him out by calling out street names he forgot or shouting a "Woo!" when something excited them.

"Alright," he said, dropping his cigarette into a plastic cup that sat on his amp. "We have time for one more." He grinned at the crowd with radiance. "But we might need help with this one." He then looked at me. "Will Carla from The Disenchanted please come up and help us with this last song?"

Taken aback by the announcement, I squirmed as the crowd followed his line of eye contact to me. Suddenly I felt a little less buzzed with all the unfamiliar faces pressing into mine. These weren't *my* fans, I thought as I shot Ed a look as if he had lost his freaking mind.

"Please?" he begged flirtatiously before loud whispering into the mic. "Carla . . . Carla . . . Carla."

The crowd then joined in with claps as they chanted my name. People near me at the bar encouraged me by saying playful things like, "You can't leave a guy hangin' up there." Even the sexy bartender appeared intrigued. I looked back at Ed again, who I knew wouldn't let up, and rolled my eyes in agreement. After bottoming out my beer, I hopped down from my stool, which made me feel a little wobbly from the sudden movement. With the room erupting in cheers, I carefully stepped up onto the stage, hoping to deliver on the build-up. After a modest nod saying hello to the rest of the band, I made my way to Ed, and in his ear, I said, "But I don't know any of your songs by heart."

"Don't worry," he said as I felt his eyelash wink on my cheek. "I think you might know this one."

Certain it would be "Crimson and Clover," immediately I regretted coming up and imagined Pete walking in at this moment; I'd never hear the end of it. But instead of strumming the downhearted and sour-sounding B chord of the 1960s song, he hit a bright A minor and opened with lyrics about strawberries, cherries, and angels kissing in the spring. Not bad, I thought, as I looked at him with a devilish grin. Only inches away from each other's faces, I responded by singing about walking into town on silver spurs. With Ed taking Nancy Sinatra's part and me doing Lee Hazlewood's, together into the same microphone, we cooed a duet of "Summer Wine."

As one of my favorite songs poured out of me like sugar into black coffee, we sang with our lips centimeters apart, with only a mic in between us. It was then that I looked at him, and with my eyes, I made it clear that he could have me that night.

Pete

I hung out at the bar, waiting for her until I was the last man standing. Literally, the last man standing as I watched Danny help a few guys stumble into cabs. Leaning against the empty bar surrounded by turned-over barstools, I listened to the sounds of clinking pint glasses and the rattle of silverware coming out of the dishwasher. When the house lights came up, I resolved she wouldn't be coming back for me and accepted Danny's offer to drive me back to the motel.

After grabbing a spare key at the front desk, I walked into the room that smelled like our laundry mixed in with dirty motel carpet. Next to the bed was the large shopping bag containing our clean clothes. Doing laundry earlier that day already felt like a memory that lived in my head like a dusty postcard tossed off in a drawer.

I sat down on the edge of the bed, unsure of what to do. Too wired to sleep, too irritated to masturbate, and too tired to shower, I set my glasses down on the nightstand. Giving my eyes a rest, I let my focus obscure as the browns and oranges of the room's décor fused like watercolors. The room felt too still, though, too quiet, with only the hum of my own confusion pulsing in my head. I couldn't believe she was with him, and I felt like I couldn't take it because I was so...fucking...jealous.

I sat up breathing heavily as I gripped my chest and then grabbed my glasses to allow myself to see clearly again. But it didn't help because nothing was clear. Nothing was clear because I had to finally admit to myself that I was not just jealous because he had her...but also because she had him.

I threw myself back down on the bed. Squeezing the bridge of my nose to release the tension, I allowed myself to think about Ed...think about him because I was kind of into him too.

There.

I let the thought sit in my head as I tried to intellectualize it. But there was no way I could because it was just how I felt. It had been a while since I had felt like this. Six years, to be exact. I figured time had faded these feelings as a fleeting memory of a spirited summer spent in France...*experimenting*, as they say.

When I came back for my sophomore year after that summer, I didn't know what to think anymore. While, sure, I was attracted to guys on TV or whatever, I didn't have crushes on guys I actually knew. Like, I didn't suddenly have hidden feelings for fucking Tony. For one, he held his fork like you'd hold a potato masher, with all five fingers wrapped around it.

The rest of the school year was pure misery because I didn't know what was wrong with me because I still liked girls. But what really did it for me was hearing the guys on the soccer team refer to some of the kids at school as fags or cocksuckers. It didn't seem fair that they were being targeted, accused even, for what I had spent my entire summer doing with my friend.

And then there was him... my friend.

We wrote each other letters after that summer; long ones, with my heart pressing into my chest every time I saw the envelope on the kitchen counter with its mail stamp from France. That was until one day his correspondence stopped. He had decided to take himself away from me, and I never heard from him ever again. At that point, I had had enough, and I quit the soccer team, joined track only because I could run with my headphones on, and became a stoner to forget it all.

Then in eleventh grade, when Carla sat in front of me, I *did* want to go out with her, which made me feel like things were going back to normal? Whatever the fuck that meant. But she intimidated me that by the time senior year rolled around, I was emotionally exhausted. So when Allison expressed interest by flirting with me in AP English by pretending to like Beat poetry, I didn't resist because I was tired of fighting with myself. She was nice and smart, and I'd say I fell in love with the experience of being both physically and emotionally close to someone. With her, it felt easy, but also, it was my way of taking revenge on my first love to prove to him that our summer didn't mean anything to me either. I always wondered if it ever got back to him.

So I was accepting how I felt and who I was. Big fucking deal. That still didn't do anything to change the fact that the two people I wanted were fucking each other. I knew what a brat I was being since I *did* selfishly want them both. But I couldn't help it. I then pressed the pillow over my head to drown out my thoughts to make them go away. When nothing worked, and I couldn't take myself anymore, I left the room.

In a glass phone booth out in the dusty parking lot, the dark New Mexico sky watched over me like a prayer as I lit a cigarette. I leaned into the receiver until I heard the other end pick up.

"Hey, Dale?" I said. "You up?"

Carla

We finished the song to a roaring room. Borrowing some of the band's fan adoration, I took a small bow. Ed clapped for me and encouraged the crowd to keep going. The few times The Disenchanted had such an impassioned response, I never let myself hang around too long to enjoy it. That night, however, seeing Ed look at me like I was some kind of goddess, I allowed myself to be loved...and like Simone de Beauvoir...to be necessary.

I carefully stepped off the stage as I could feel my coordination begin to wane. With Ed behind me, we threaded through the crowd with his fans wanting a piece of him. Had I not been two whiskeys and a pint of beer in, on an empty stomach, I probably would have shown more tact and asked if he wanted to talk with them. Instead, I grabbed his hand and led him out to the parking lot.

"Hey," he said once we were at The Disenchanted van. "Did you want to put some of your CDs out on our merch table?"

When I didn't respond, he pulled me toward him and kissed me. Tasting his beer-stained tongue tangled with mine, we devoured each other with sloppy, wide-mouthed kisses.

"Hold on," I said, out of breath while holding his face in my hands. "Do you have to help the guys load out?"

"It's fine," he said on my lips. "I practically did it this afternoon. They owe me."

"Okay," I said, tilting my head to the side.

As I let him suck on my neck, he pressed me hard up against the van, making me sigh louder than I would have wanted to in a public place. Over his shoulder, I could see some of the people from the bar politely trying not to look at the second act of our performance. Feeling a little uncomfortable, I hid my face in his neck and in his ear whispered, "Let's go somewhere."

Pete

"Uh oh," Dale's raspy voice resounded through the phone. "I know an emergency on tour when I hear one… *ça va ma poule?*"

"I sound that bad, huh?" I held back from laughing that after all these years, he still called me a hen.

"Bad?" he said, letting out a deep chuckle. "I'd say you sound *dans la merde*." He laughed again, which then turned into a guttural cough he cleared with his throat. "What's the matter? The road gettin' to you, ma boy."

"I think it's a little more complicated than that," I said in defeat as I took a drag of my cigarette.

277

"Well, of course, it is," he said in the tone he used when he thought I was being a complete dumbass. "No one goes on the road if they ain't runnin' from somethin'." As if picking up on my surprise, he added, "You can't fool me. I'm Dale. So, let me guess, it's all catchin' up to you?"

"Sorta."

"Which is it? The girl I told you wasn't for you, the one who might be…" I heard him take a drag from his own cigarette. "Or somethin' else entirely?"

"A little of it all?"

"I figured," he said as I could hear him lean forward to ash his cigarette. "I've been waiting for this phone call for a few years now."

"I just thought—"

"Stop thinkin'," he cut me off. "You have all the answers you need in your heart because once you start thinkin' with that head of yours, that's when you get all kinds of confused."

Listening to him, I set my gaze on the names carved into the metal counter I was leaning on, my knee knocking against the upside-down phone book hanging under it.

"Like when we were doing 'A Night in Tunisia,'" he continued. "I saw you trying to rationalize the shit out of it, but Pete, you can't rationalize rhythm. You just have to feel it. Just like you can't rationalize love." He took a pause before saying, "Or who you are."

I nodded into the phone as if he could see me and closed my eyes to absorb his words.

"But listen to me," he said in a more serious tone, "you have to be honest with yourself."

"I know," I said, "and, really, I'm trying to. *Finally*. But it's just that I'm feeling so much, and I don't know where to direct it. I'm all fucked in the head."

"Well, that's the problem with fellas like us." He let out a small laugh. "We love everyone, and it took me a long time to realize it, especially back in my day when none of this was out in the open, but it's a gift."

"It really doesn't feel like one," I murmured. "I'm confused *all the time*."

"You'll come around to it," he said reassuringly. "But tell me, does your little Shangri-La know all about you?"

I had to laugh because Dale mostly kept in touch with my dad and knew this was my father's description of Carla, which wasn't *at all* inaccurate.

"She doesn't know," I responded. "And I don't even know how she'll take it. She comes from an Italian Catholic family, and who knows what kind of shit she's been fed her whole life. She might think I'm disgusting."

"I wouldn't be so sure," he said with a bit of certainty. "And if she does, then you know what kind of person she is."

"Yeah," I whispered as I tried to imagine her reaction. "The thing is, I didn't ask for any of this drama." I cranked my head back. "What the fuck. This was supposed to be just a band, not all this other shit."

"Son," he said before letting out one of his famous Dale guffaws when he found something humorously hopeless. "You of all people should know, especially with all those damn rock books you read, that it's never just a band."

Carla

Seeing Ed in the driver's seat of our van was a little weird. Unsure exactly where we were going, we drove down the streets of Las Cruces at night until he pulled into a parking lot. As sexy as it had been with me pressed up against the van, something about parking at Walmart had a way of taking the heat out of the moment. There was nothing smooth about the transition, like setting up the bed, unrolling the egg crate pad, and getting the pillows and blankets out without hitting our heads on the low ceiling. With our faces glowing in the neon sign of savings, Ed and I exchanged a few glances, followed by a nervous chuckle at the logistics involved in having spontaneous sex on tour. Once we made the bed, locked ourselves in, and downed some water, he lowered me down to recapture the passion from before. I pulled his t-shirt that smelled of cigarettes and stage sweat over his head and ran my hands up his chest, feeling his soft coating of hair against his sticky skin. He then pulled up my shirt that probably smelled about the same as his and grabbed at the lace of the one pretty bra I had brought on tour. He then lowered the straps and pulled it down to kiss my chest as I imagined how salty my skin must have tasted.

"Oh my God," Ed whispered as he sucked on one of my nipples. "Do you know how sexy you are?"

Squirming in discomfort of the attention and unsure if I was required to respond at how sexy I thought I was, I pulled him up toward my face and covered my breasts with my hair. We helped each other out of our clothing until we were naked, and I could feel his erection rubbing against my leg. We touched and kissed and breathed as our limbs tangled and our bodies glided in rhythm with each other ready to complete the physical transaction.

"Do you have anything?" I asked.

"I should."

Lying naked on my back with my socks on, I waited as Ed rummaged through his pants, pulling his wallet out of the back pocket. As he looked through it, I reminded myself that it had been three years since I'd had sex, which made me nervous. I didn't know what kind of lover I was, if I preferred one position over another, and if I'd even have an orgasm.

"Okay," he said to the sound of the crinkling plastic in his hand. "We're good."

He then placed his lips back on mine with his body hovering over me as he maneuvered the condom with one hand. When he started to slip himself inside me, I gasped like I did the first time. My body tightened up, and my knees clenched in like they did at the gynecologist. Ed stopped kissing my neck and looked at me. "You've..." He then appeared to look for the right words. "I mean, you've had –"

"Yeah," I quickly responded, feeling embarrassed he could sense my lack of experience. "Of course." I tried to control the heavy breathing of my discomfort.

"It's just been a while, so" – I looked away – "I don't know, I guess, just be gentle."

"Of course." He moved my hair away from my cheek to kiss it. "Let's just do this for now."

As he eased me in with kisses, he inched little by little deeper inside me until we were fully having sex. The problem with my first time with Alex's cousin was he was stressed about coming too soon. So he just stayed inside of me practically motionless because any slight movement would have been too much stimulation. I sort of felt him, but with Ed, there was no question; I very much felt him moving in and out of my body. Like I said, Science Fiction. As he increased his tempo, which hurt and felt good at the same time, the van rocked back and forth with us.

Just as I had gotten Pete off my mind, his steel snare wires began to rattle in tempo with Ed and me. What would Pete have thought of the bouncing van? So many things, I thought as I imagined the commentary. As the van squeaked on with our gear vibrating against their wooden cubbies, I envisioned what the bopping van must have looked like from the outside. I couldn't help but feel incredibly cheesy. And if that wasn't enough, Ed started whispering my name in my ear. Biting my lip to suppress my amusement, I didn't know what to say back and was just hoping he wasn't expecting me to return the gesture because there was no way I was going to moan the name Ed.

He eventually finished by releasing sounds of gratification in my ear as he concluded the event with a few final pushes that sort of hurt. He stayed on top of me for a few seconds, as the sweat of our chests rubbing against each other made a suctioning sound that I would have laughed at had we known each other better. As he caught his breath with his forehead resting on my shoulder, I could feel him soften inside me, and carefully he pulled out.

After discarding the condom in a tissue, Ed met me back on the floor and pulled me closer to him. In his arms, I looked up at the van's ceiling, thinking about the last time I had looked up at it with Pete. I then wondered what he was doing; begging for

Allison's forgiveness at a payphone somewhere, I presumed. Annoyed at the thought, I curled up closer to Ed in protest of Pete and thought about what I had just done. I finally broke my second-person virginity; the grand second sexual experience Alex liked to go on about...and I still didn't get what the big deal was about.

21

Pete

I woke up to the sun hot against the side of my face. It cut down my right eye burning my retinae as I cursed myself for not having closed the curtain all the way. I scrunched my pillow up and repositioned myself away from the daylight robbing me of an extra hour of sleep. On the cooler side of the bed, I felt better, only a little heavy-headed from the three beers and pack of cigarettes I'd had for dinner. It wasn't until I regained consciousness that I recalled the details from the night before. *Right*, I thought as I slumped over onto my back, reaching my arm out for my glasses...I'm in the middle of an emotional crisis. Well, good morning, Las Cruces.

I looked at her side of the bed to find it as smooth as it was when we checked in. I stopped waiting for her at around three in the morning and forced myself to sleep. I stayed on the phone with Dale as long as my baggie of quarters would allow me. And before hanging up with him, he again advised me to be honest with myself. He then told me to stop making such a big deal about how Carla spent her night.

"Shangri-La," he chuckled, "was also entitled to a little tour booty."

This, of course, only provided more imagery that annoyed me all over again.

Thinking about it in the morning light, I resolved that maybe nothing happened between her and Ed. And then I asked myself if I even had the right to be pissed at anyone. My brain was sore from too many questions and not enough food, making it impossible to think reasonably. I didn't know how I was supposed to feel or what an appropriate response would be, but I had to come up with something...and fast because out front, I heard the rusty squeaks of our van pull into the parking spot.

Carla

The next morning, I woke up freezing because Ed had rolled onto his side, taking the blankets with him. As my eyes adjusted to my surroundings, I looked over at him and then surveyed the rest of the van. Knowing I had disrespected the band's space, I cringed at the evidence from our clothes crumpled inside out and the two condom wrappers scattered on the floor. Still wearing only socks, I sat up where my throbbing brain reminded me that I drank whiskey for the first time the night before. My breath tasted bad, my skin felt waxy, like it had a layer of grime coating it, and my head felt like a sack of sand trying to stay balanced on a popsicle stick. I reached for the water and guzzled it down with my throat receiving it in desperate, audible gulps. Ed then rolled over, and with barely opened eyes, grumbled, "Morning, sexy," and reached out to touch the small of my bare back.

"Morning." I looked back at him and held up the water.

He sat up and took it and began gulping it down equally as loud. As he drank, I turned to my cubby drawer only to find it empty because all my clothes were at the motel. Refusing to put my stinky shirt back on, I grabbed one of Pete's out of his drawer.

"Your van is so comfortable." Ed set the water down as he looked around in admiration of Laurent's work. "You guys travel in style."

"Pete's dad is a contractor."

"And it's so clean," Ed said, amazed.

"Well." I cracked a smile. "Pete can be a little obsessive."

"So, Pete, what's his deal?"

"What do I mean?" I glanced at Ed over my shoulder.

"I don't know." He appeared to search for the words. "Well, for starters, where is he?"

"Probably on the phone somewhere crying to his girlfriend," I said, which came out more bitter than I wanted it to.

"Girlfriend?" Ed looked surprised. "Really."

"Yeah?"

"Okay." He made a face like he couldn't believe Pete would have a girlfriend, which I didn't get at all. Why? Because he was on tour? Or because he was in a band with me? Whatever, I thought as I reached forward to grab my underwear at the bottom of the bed, where my bare butt was in Ed's full vision. I hoped I didn't have something gross like lint in the upper crack, which then had me grab my things with more haste. As I gracefully tried to dress, Ed sat up and pulled me down with him.

"What are you doing?" I said with a squirm, feeling awkward that my underwear was stuck at my mid-thigh.

"Why are you getting dressed?" he whispered as he ran his fingers across my hipbone. "I thought maybe we could hang out a little more and—" He didn't finish his sentence and instead began kissing the side of my face as I thought about my crotch exposed in the daylight.

"I would," I lied with a gentle nudge to discourage him, "but I have to get going."

Even though Pete and I didn't have to be back out for another few hours, I was anxious to see him. I had already made my point by spending the night with Ed that I felt dragging it out any more would have only made things worse. I snaked Ed's arms over my head and got up to grab his clothes for him.

"We have to head out. We're going to Flagstaff tonight," I lied again because it was further away than our scheduled four-hour drive to Tucson.

"Nice," he said, trying to sound unmoved by my rejection. "We're in ABQ tonight, then we head to Denver."

"Nice," I echoed him as I pulled my jeans up.

After tidying up and discarding proof of our wild evening, I dropped Ed off at the RV site where his van was. We exchanged phone numbers, even though we knew neither of us would be home for another few weeks. Looking at him, though, in the New Mexico sun, I smiled as I noticed his hair blazed a deeper shade of auburn in the light. He looked tired but also relaxed in his post-coital haze of not having to sleep next to his three bandmates for one night. We gave each other a few pecks, careful not to breathe each other in since neither of us had brushed our teeth. And with a soft look, I gestured with my chin for him to go. When he closed the door behind him, I listened to the echo of his footsteps as they disappeared into the gravel and dirt of the desert.

Pulling the car into reverse to back out of the lot, I could feel the sun hinting at the hot day ahead of us. As I drove down the New Mexico streets, I admired the mountain range framing the city. The window cracked open blew in a soft breeze that allowed strands of my hair to billow across my face and tickle my shoulders. I felt both free and a little dirty, smiling to myself at what I'd done last night.

It was the first time in my life I felt like a woman.

My newfound sense of freedom and maturity, though, fizzled as soon as I pulled into the motel parking lot. My heart pounded in anticipation as I had no idea what was waiting for me on the other side of the door. For one, was he even there? Unsure of the mood I would be walking into, before slipping the key in, I listened for any sounds. Hoping to hear a jovial phone call, which was already farfetched since there had been none of those during the entire tour, or maybe even the buzz of the TV to distract us from us. But there was nothing, just the dread of silence before an uncomfortable conversation.

I softly pressed open the door, and the first image I caught was of my own in the room's mirror. Wearing Pete's gray t-shirt, I saw my dark make-up sprinkled like ashes under my eyes and my hair ratty with bangs shooting up like feathers. I hung my head as I closed the door behind me since I wasn't ready to look into his eyes, which I could feel digging into me. After a few moments of shared heavy breathing that felt like a warning, I slowly looked over to him.

There he was, sitting up on the bed, his forearms rested on bent knees, there he was . . . unmoved and unamused.

Pete

When she walked into our room wearing my Brain Records t-shirt, I didn't know what to say. With my theory on how she spent her night proven, there wasn't much *to* say because I guess it was none of my business. But still. As I sat on the bed, she leaned against the door, and together we locked ourselves into silence.

"So," I finally said.

She lifted her chin and turned to me with eyes cloudy and distant.

"So," she said back.

We then looked at each other, waiting for the other to say something. But we continued alternating between looking at each other and looking away. The room hummed with stillness, only the sounds of motel guests with children and luggage passing the window to break the monotony.

"I don't know if it even matters anymore," I said, "but, um, it's over with Allison." I rolled my eyes to the side. "I don't know; do what you want with that."

She nodded her head lightly, as if digesting the information, and then looked at me with a warmer regard. "Are you okay?"

"Yeah," I said with a shrug. "Thanks, though."

"Of course," she said with some tenderness in her voice. "I'm sure it wasn't easy."

With a softened posture, she lowered her shoulders and became more relaxed. She came to the bed and said, "If you want to, I don't know." She bit her lip. "If you want to talk about it, we can."

"Maybe we should."

She leaned forward and lightly bobbed her head, encouraging me to speak.

"I don't know how much you could hear through the phone," I started to say, "but look, she was just upset."

I then explained that Allison felt threatened and backed into a corner. Thinking I was putting Carla at ease, instead, I noticed her expression tighten the more I spoke. With eyes that grew dark and narrow, she charged past me and said, "I'm going to take a shower."

Carla

I wanted to let him talk, especially about the breakup that I imagined must have been painful for him. I then planned to apologize for the part *I* played in the chaos of the last twelve hours. But I couldn't get Allison's words out of my head. Her calling me a manipulative, uneducated, low-class whore would be words I don't think I could ever forget. However, it was her snark about my family that angered me most because only I got to talk shit about my family. When Pete referred to her, though, I didn't hear a hint of disagreement but rather excuses on her behalf.

At that moment, I decided I needed a shower, and in the words of PJ Harvey, I was going to wash these men right out of my hair.

After scrubbing the alcohol, second-hand smoke, and sex off my body, I walked out of the bathroom in my own clothes, smelling fresh but feeling like total crap. I noticed Pete—who also looked a little rough—with his glassy eyes and moving slower than he usually did. As he pulled clean clothes out of the shopping bag, I watched as he buried himself in his thoughts with a disinterest that I was even in the room. He then brushed past me and shut the bathroom door.

I crawled on the bed to rest my eyes that stung from a lack of sleep. My body felt heavy as if one of those lead aprons you wear at the dentist for X-Rays was pressed against me. My thoughts then drifted lazily into the imagery of irrelevant people and places that didn't make sense, which meant I was entering a dream. When my eyes opened, seemingly two minutes later, I found Pete sitting at the round table near the bed. Showered with the smell of his woodsy deodorant and hazelnut soap tickling my senses, I watched him organize change on the table.

"Hey," he said with an icy coolness when he noticed I had woken up.

"Hey," I mimicked his detachment. "Have I been asleep long?"

"About forty minutes," he said with his eyes following his fingers as they sorted the pennies from the nickels. "I went to the front desk and arranged a late checkout since we're supposed to leave, like, now."

"Okay," was all I could manage to say.

After he couldn't force any more interest in the loose change, he looked up at me and said, "Is this your first hangover?"

I told him it was.

"Alright." He scratched the back of his neck. "Let's just." He released a long exhale. "Let's just get some fucking food."

I then pulled myself up from the bed as the sudden rush of blood blurred my vision with black spots. Feeling him examine my face that I imagined looked bloated and tired, he said, "Yeah, I think food will be good for both of us." He then thought for a second, and as my eyesight came into focus to find his eyes on me, he added, "And maybe *not* a fruit cup."

Pete

As I climbed into the van, it occurred to me that this was probably where she and Ed had made their horizontal acquaintance. Careful not to look for evidence because I honestly didn't want to know, I rolled down the window and pulled into reverse.

At a different diner than the day before, we sat face-to-face in irritation of the other's presence. Out of necessity, not intimacy, we decided to split dishes. We ordered things we had never had before, like a chorizo breakfast burrito that the menu boasted came covered in green tomatillo sauce, huevos rancheros, southwestern style potatoes, and coffee. Lots of coffee.

After we ordered, the minutes crawled by with us looking in different directions, protecting ourselves from each other. When the food came, we exaggerated our engagement with the waitress with warm smiles that we made sure fell back to disinterest once she left. After splitting everything and careful not to be too cordial to each other, we cured ourselves in silence. Reveling in flavors and textures unknown to me, I closed my eyes to savor the experience. The bite of the jalapeño that pinched my tastebuds offset the salty and smooth finish of the guacamole. It felt like a temporary relief as I nurtured my soul, starving for answers.

Our empty plates stained red and green looked up at us as a memory of breakfast and also as a reminder that we no longer had food as a diversion from each other. Forcing the eye contact we had been stumbling over all morning, I felt like I should have said something. Just as I was about to introduce a little conversation with maybe some shit about the weather, she cut my banal thoughts and said, "Do you still want to be in a band with me?"

Stunned she initiated the talk with a real question, I looked at her in slight awe. *Who was this person?* I allowed myself to sit in the question because I still felt conflicted by it all. Playing in a band with someone who understood me on such an intense, sonic level was all I ever wanted. But with her, it came at a price. When we started this whole thing, never did it occur to me it would come with so much uncertainty, with none of it having to do with the actual music; the self-doubt, the pained silences, our secrets . . .

After considering these points, I looked into her eyes that had returned to their ocean marine color. Observing the outline of her eyelashes and the way they curled out to the side, I almost fell back into her. And I couldn't. Not this time. I pulled my regard away and looked out the diner windows where I saw our van, reminding me just how she used our space the night before.

"Carla," I finally said. "I don't know."

Carla

Breakfast comprised of folded arms and aggressive silences intended to antagonize and cause pain. I guzzled down two glasses of ice water to make up for my depleted hydration, hoping to erase the effects from the night before. When our food came, as much as I wanted to fight consuming so much of it, it felt even better than the sex I'd had the night before. As I allowed myself to eat, I could feel the fat absorbing the alcohol that snaked through me like sin. After breakfast, I was hoping to move on from the fight, but stealing a glance at Pete, I wasn't so sure we could. Feeling farther from him than ever with his intensity heavy like heartburn, I began to feel nervous.

"Do you still want to be in a band with me?"

Looking at me with almost hostile eyes, I admit to being a bit taken aback. I didn't think ending the band was an actual option since I thought our music was stronger than this. He withdrew eye contact and proceeded to stare out the window as the question hovered above us. I leaned toward him, pressing my elbows into the table, hoping to accelerate an answer. But he just looked off, leaving me out of the conversation he was having with himself. It would have been easier if he just called me a bitch or explained exactly what he was so mad about—me leaving the bar? Being with Ed? All of the above?—so we could move on already. As my impatience simmered under the pressure, I waited for an answer with my eyes feeling like they wanted to scream. It was then, though, that I realized what it must have been like to be with me. Every time he wanted to talk things out, I ignored him. I ignored his need to connect. I ignored his feelings. I ignored *him*. It was then I could see what a terrible friend I had also been.

"Carla," he said with a blank expression as he looked out the window. "I don't know."

Calling me by my full name felt like a petty way to demonstrate the distance between us. As he admitted to not knowing if he wanted me in his life anymore, I felt my chest burn with grief. Like my aunts abandoning me without so much as a

Christmas card, Pete seemed just as composed as their silence in doing away with me. Sick of being dumped into the recycling bin for someone else to collect and reuse, I got up. With the wooden chair screeching against the diner's tile floor, which had him look briefly in my direction, I fumbled through my bag to pull my wallet out. After slamming some money on the table, I said, "Do what you want, Pete."

Outside I leaned against the van, the metal warm against my back, as I waited for him to come out. With my arms crossed, I felt indignant because how dare he toss all the blame my way. He wasn't exactly the sacrificial lamb here either, I thought in irritation of his self-righteousness. Maybe I wasn't as secure with my feelings as he was, but that didn't make me disposable. My upbringing didn't exactly encourage self-belief. In my family, it was either you were born with it, or you weren't. And if you weren't, then the best you could do was fake it, which to me felt like being a fraud, an impersonation, a parody of the person I wanted to be so no one could see the emotional scars left from my childhood. It was then that I decided that I hated Pete. I hated him for his perfect upbringing, his perfect life, and how his biggest problem was that he had to call his girlfriend on a payphone. Must be nice. I hated him so much, I thought to myself as my knuckles turned pale thinking about him calling me *Carla*. Why couldn't I be this self-assured person like him? Because I couldn't, and it didn't feel fair.

I had worked myself up and had to take a few deep breaths because I knew that none of this was his fault. I wasn't this damaged person because of him. Turning my gaze over, I noticed a payphone eyeing me from across the parking lot. As if daring me to make the call, the phone blinked at me with its silver buttons reflecting in the sun like a shiny new appliance. After crossing the parking lot, I fed the phone with three dollars' worth of quarters leftover from doing laundry. As I felt the impact of a tractor trailer charging down the two-lane road in front of me, blowing hot air and exhaust on my cheeks, I pressed my ear into the phone as it rang.

"Hello?" She already sounded irritated.

"Mom?"

"Let me guess," she scoffed, "you're pregnant."

"No," I said in soft shame as if she could tell I'd had sex the night before.

"Okay, then."

"I guess, um," I started to say as I tried to ignore her disinterest in hearing from me. "I don't know. I'm calling to let you know that I'm okay?"

"Carla." She pushed out a deep exhale I was meant to hear. "I know you're okay."

Through the phone, I could hear the jingle for the Mount Airy Lodge commercial, which informed me that it was already afternoon on the East Coast. This meant she was well into her daytime television, as well as her daytime drinking.

"Well, do you even care?" I said, unaffected.

"Excuse you," she said with venom in her voice, which hinted she was drinking something stronger than white wine. "I don't know what you want me to say. I told you that only a floozy would travel across the country in a van with someone else's boyfriend. I can't help but think of that poor girl up in Boston. Or tell me, have you taken care of that already, and she's well out of the picture?" Not waiting for a response, she continued, "And don't give me that crap that it's about the music because no one is that good a guitar player. I don't care what he tells you."

Her words hurt just as much as they did every other time that she tried to rob me of my dedication and talent. But this time, I made the decision not to believe her. I zoned her out for a second and looked at the mountains that hugged the landscape like the nurturing mother I would never have. I took comfort in them; these mountains that had seen other disputes on this very payphone, car accidents on these roads, the destruction of nature over time, yet they remained still, patient . . . eternal.

"Hello?" my mother barked in protest to my silent musing. "Carla, you called *me,* and my show is on."

"I *did* call you."

"Well, then what do you want?"

Maybe it was being in the desert, far from anything I had ever known. Or maybe it was the heat, my hangover, or that Pete also wanted nothing to do with me, but I decided to answer my mom's question.

"What do I want?" I responded. "I want you to think that I'm good enough." I let the words fall out of my mouth.

"What," she snarled.

"I want you to think that I am good enough." I said slower and clearer. "I mean, I barely got by at school because no one cared to even check my homework, but still, I didn't do drugs, I didn't worry anyone, I took Grandma to church every Sunday. So, tell me, what exactly have I done *so* wrong?"

"Please," she said in the scornful tone she used when she didn't have a quick enough response to a valid point. "I wouldn't even know where to start."

"Sure you do, and I deserve to know. What did I do that was so bad?" I felt myself gaining momentum in my anger. "Let's see," I snapped. "I read. What else? I listened to music on my headphones. I came home early and always did my chores." I could feel my heart pounding as I visualized snapshots of an unfulfilled childhood. "What else? I had a job!" I let my voice get louder. "I kept my mouth shut! Please tell me, what part of all of this was *such* a nuisance for you!"

When she didn't respond, only the sound of short breaths could be heard on her end, I demanded, "Well, tell me!" I waited for her to comment before continuing. "You can't! That's why you're not saying anything. You know it, and I know it! I did nothing wrong . . . *Angie.*"

"If," her voice thundered through the phone, which I could feel the thousands of miles away. "If I *ever* spoke to my mother that way!" She stopped to take what I could hear was a sip of her drink. "Who the *hell* do you think you are, little girl!"

"Who do I think I am?" I responded with a bitter tongue. "I'm someone who only wanted a little attention, maybe even some respect, or some acknowledgment from my own fucking family."

"Respect is earned, not given," she said predictably. "As for attention, you seem to be getting enough of it, shaking your ass for anyone willing to watch."

Refusing the baited comment, I continued, "All I ever wanted was to make myself as perfect as possible for you. I made sure to never get fat and taught myself how to eat just like you. I used to think everything from your drinking to your moods to *your* anorexia—which by the way, mom thanks for sharing—was my fault, but you know what, that's over." I started to lose my breath. "Because I realize now that none of it is my fault!"

"I don't have time for this."

"You never did, and I don't fucking care anymore because none of it is my fault!" I screamed as the tears tumbled down my cheeks. "It's not my fault! It's not . . . my . . . fucking . . . fault!"

When I caught my breath, I pressed my ear into the phone and realized she had hung up on me. I looked at it, the only thing I could take my anger out on, and began slamming it down on the metal hook as I screamed for the person I could have become. I screamed for the thousands of thoughts I was never allowed to express. I screamed for my wasted childhood. I smashed the receiver on and off the base as the tears poured down my face.

"Car!" I heard Pete's voice rushing toward me from across the parking lot. When he got to me, he gently pulled my shoulders away from the phone and took it out of my hand to put it back on the hook. "It's okay, it's okay," he said with worried eyes. "Come here."

With his arms extended, he wrapped me in them as I let myself cry. Wiping my nose on his t-shirt, I squeezed my eyes closed and buried my face in his chest as he softly swayed side to side. As ugly sounds snorted out of my nose, he ran his hands soothingly up and down my back, offering calm words and soft hushes. My crying began to subside with my breathing returning to its natural flow, but still, I held on tight with my hands gripping onto him. When I calmed down, I broke our seal by gently pulling back, and with swollen eyes, I looked up at him and said, "I'm sorry, Pete." I began to cry again as my throat hiccupped on the words. "I'm sorry about last night and about everything."

Looking at me, I noticed his eyes also swelled from emotion as he ran his thumb across my cheek to collect fallen tears.

Quietly he said, "I am too." He then leaned his forehead against mine and breathed, "I'm so sorry."

Our tired faces looked at each other as we breathed in the same air. I ran my fingertips down his cheek and my thumb across his wet eyelashes. He then pulled me back in close to him, and in his arms, we whispered apologies to each other. As we swayed in each other's natural cadence, I started to get dizzy and had to stop moving. I didn't know what was happening, but I started feeling heavy with the desert air starting to look wavy, like a flashback.

"Pete," I released myself from his sweet security.

"You okay?"

Reaching out for his arm for support, I felt my knees shake with instability. He said some words I couldn't process as I focused on the stabbing sensation in my digestive tract. "Pete," I mumbled, grabbing his arm tighter as my body keeled forward to control the pain. That was when it all came rushing out . . . rushing out of my mouth . . . and all over Pete.

22

Pete

Standing in the parking lot in the middle of New Mexico, covered in her puke, I could say it was one of the less predictable moments on tour. After helping her into the van, I ran to the back to strip off my clothes. Wearing only cutoff jeans, I looked like such a tool driving a van with no shirt on. But we made it back to the motel just in time for her to slam the bathroom door in my face, where I could hear her all come out, sounding like an alien childbirth. Having no choice but to stay an extra night, I left for reception to extend it, and there, I used the payphone to cancel our show in Tucson. I then headed to the laundromat to clean my clothes; otherwise, the van would stink forever, and then to the supermarket to get bananas, crackers, peppermint tea, and Gatorade; the blue flavor, she managed to request.

When I returned, I found her face down on the bed, motionless and miserable. Immediately I cracked open a window and set her up with enough liquids on the nightstand. On top of her duffle bag, I then placed a little gift I had picked up for her. Off the main road, I found a woman selling scarves and wraps out of her car. She had this turquoise tie-dyed one that immediately caught my eye. It was a color I had never seen on Carla before and thought maybe she'd hate it, but then again, maybe not since she'd look like a mermaid in it.

Since the bathroom was no longer available to me, I used the one at reception, where I became friendly with the clerk Dorothy, who asked how my "girl" was doing. I didn't have the energy to correct her. Out in the parking lot where I gave her my last cigarette, she recommended I pick up Menudo soup, hailing it as a cure-all. Sounds good, I told her and went back to the diner where we had been earlier and picked up a pint to-go. Back in the room, however, I had trouble selling the tripe soup to Carla, who groaned in agony. Then, with a finger pointed to the door like a sorcerer in one of her books, she banished me from the room. Before leaving, though, she sat up and, with groggy skepticism, said, "Menudo?" Appearing to consider it, her bangs damp and her cheeks glistening with sweat, she asked, "Like Ricky Martin's boy band?" With a cracked smile, I thought, we might just be okay.

I dragged a chair outside to eat the soup that reminded me that I, too, felt like total shit. Amid the hysteria, I had forgotten, as I let the spicy soup burn away my own hangover. I then grabbed the acoustic from the van and played around with some melodies as I watched the sky go from afternoon blue to streaks of bloodshot red, scraping across the pink sunset sky. It eventually descended into the early evening with a light flicker of stars turning on one by one like tiny nightlights.

When I went back inside, I found her asleep with the sheets kicked down to her feet. Her usually honeyed skin now had an almost phosphorescent glow, and her already thin arms looked listless and brittle. Noticing her shoulders reflecting a slight sheen, I grabbed a cardigan my grandmother had made me for Christmas one year and placed it over her shoulders to not "catch a chill," as my mom would say. Even though I wanted nothing more than to hold her in my arms, I knew what she needed was space to recover. With an extra blanket Dorothy had given me, I slept on the floor and stared at the blur of the ceiling, unable to fall asleep at eight-thirty at night.

Thinking back on the past year, I couldn't exactly write it off as being the worst one ever. As bad as it was, I had to describe it as a year of contrasts. There was the optimism and hope of turning twenty-one, which was then contrasted by the despair of September 11; the comfort of my long-term relationship conflicted with inconvenient desires; the joy of making music met with the questioning of its motivation; the excitement of discovering the world as an adult with opinions I felt mattered was now obscured by the "new normal" we were all embarking upon.

There were too many questions, but the one that sat heavily on my heart as I listened to her sleep was how long were we going to betray the truth from each other? The truth about our feelings...our secrets...our past.

Carla

The following morning, I woke up alone in bed with his red sweater draped over my shoulders. I pulled my arms through its thick sleeves and breathed in the woodsy-smelling mohair blend. Hearing him sleeping somewhere on the floor, I took my time adjusting to the new day. As I lay on my side, pulling the sweater tighter around me, the events of the day before began to drip in, with each mortifying detail outdoing the next. At one point in the evening, I thought I was going to hack up an actual organ since I was sure there was nothing else left inside to come out . . . from either end. I palmed my forehead in embarrassment just thinking about it. No wonder he chose to sleep on the floor because I wouldn't have wanted to be near me either. Segments of the phone call to my mom then came to light with certain parts repeating like the refrain of a bad song stuck in my head. Before I could try to figure out what to make of it all, I heard Pete waking up, the sound of his neck cracking, and him mumbling to himself in French as I imagined him pawing around for his glasses.

The morning then proceeded quietly with us sort of tiptoeing around each other. When he left to settle out at the front desk, I found the sarong sitting on top of my bag. In a deep ocean green, it had streaks of turquoise and sage with small flashes of bright pink, reminding me of the smooth iridescent labradorite stone I once picked up at a street fair. In my hands, I closed my eyes to feel the softest piece of cotton I think I had ever felt between my fingers. I then held it up to my nose, where it smelled of Nag Champa incense and a wooden cabin. I looked at the door and smiled.

When he returned, we had a Saltine and mint tea breakfast and were then back on the road. He drove the long stretch of New Mexico that became the long stretch of Arizona. Driving to the sound of our tires that made their way like trusted soldiers, we echoed the stillness of our landscape. With the window cracked for air, I felt it cool against my skin as it breathed through the sarong I let fall over my knee. Looking out the window, I observed the washed-out hues of the scenery. The sky, a faded blue like broken-in jeans, and the pale desert spotted with dry grassland that I imagined crunched under your feet.

Pete

On our quiet drive through the Southwest, I felt nostalgic for the landscape I would be saying goodbye to, the prehistoric rock formations and the miles of arid land that impressed my East Coast frame of reference. I couldn't believe we were already heading to our last show and that I had work in less than a week where this would all seem like a dream. I glanced over at her in the passenger's seat. Wearing the wrap that she called a sarong, or whatever, I noticed how she let the fabric fall off her leg. With her foot propped on the window roller, the soft fabric skimmed her bare inner thigh, and only a small knot tied on the side kept it on her body. She wore it with a boxy t-shirt that must have dated back to the tiny pink sweatpants because it exposed her stomach when she stretched her arms over her head. I could tell she wasn't wearing anything underneath it all…which left a little too much to my imagination.

Carla

The cactuses in Arizona turned into the palm trees of California, which truly felt magical since I had never seen either before. The farmlands with their wide-turning turbines became the suburbs, which then became the city. The country highway eventually expanded into vast multi-lanes, and just like that, we were in Southern California.

We pulled into Solana Beach in San Diego, where we were playing that night. Before heading to the club, as if pulled by instinct, we walked down to the beach. Just off the main road, we found a small cove closed in by towering bluffs reflecting a golden hue. The ocean glided across the sand, and out in the distance were actual surfers, making it a picture-perfect first image of California.

I couldn't help but hear "Malibu" by Hole because this was what I had always imagined the song to look like.

Pete

Cruising by the WELCOME TO CALIFORNIA sign felt monumental. I guess when we were organizing the trip, I hadn't considered the emotional pay-off I'd feel from driving from one coast to another. But it was like there we were; we had leaped over three time zones. When we walked down to Fletcher's Cove, it made it official that we were as far as the van would take us. I noticed that even in the warm climate and California's promise of an endless summer, the sun still took on a reddish autumn glow that reflected like wildflower honey on Carla's skin. Thinking back on all we had seen, our country with its good-hearted people, the billboards, Baptist churches, casinos, endless opportunities to purchase fireworks . . . we were now at the end of the continent. Looking out onto the Pacific Ocean, I reveled in the fact that Japan was on the other side and imagined who was looking out from that coastline.

Carla

Barefoot on the beach, I held the hem of my sarong in one hand and my flip-flops in another. As we walked along the coast, I felt the cool Pacific wash up to my ankles; the salt stinging my shaved legs, and the foam tickling my feet. We got to the end of the inlet, where we found a dry spot. Next to each other, we sat, his arms hanging over his knees, feet buried in the sand, and me propped on my elbows with my legs stretched out in front of me.

I broke the silence. "We drove to California."

"We did." He grimaced while looking out onto the horizon. "Kind of cool, no?"

"Definitely cool."

"By the way." I turned to look at him. "Thanks for taking care of me."

"No problem."

Admiring our scenery, I watched the sun inch its way lower as the russet color deepened and highlighted the sand like an iodine tincture.

"So." He looked at me and then down, seeming unsure. "Do you want to talk about what happened with your mom?"

As I thought about it, I listened to the waves, letting them transport me back to summers at Rocky Point. I absorbed the sound of their crashes as they reached the shore; I smelled the brine of the wind that made my hair feel thick and tangly; and just for a second, I pretended the childhood version of my mother was there with me. The mom who made my dad smile, the mom who gardened in crochet bikinis and work boots while singing out loud to the Doobie Brothers...the mom who thought I was an okay kid.

"I'm not sure there's much *to* talk about." I released a gentle sigh. "I mean, I don't think I'll be welcomed back unless I do some major groveling, which I just don't see happening."

"Welcomed back?" He sounded surprised. "Over a fight?"

"Pete." I held back from grinning as I turned onto my side to face him. "I called my mom by her first name."

"Okay." He appeared to somewhat process what I was saying, but I could tell he didn't get it. "I mean, it's not cool, but it's not, like, the worst thing, right?"

Allowing myself now to fully smile at how cute his naiveté could sometimes be, I told him, "You still don't get Italian families, do you?"

"I guess not," he said with sad eyes as he lowered himself down. Facing me with his ear resting on his stretched-out arm, he traced his fingers in the sand. Flicking his eyes up to meet mine, he said, "I wish there was something I could do."

"There's not much *to* do," I said, drawing my own circles in the sand.

"I just don't like seeing people I care about hurt like this."

"People?" I deepened my stare.

"You know what I mean."

"Do I?"

"Yeah," he asserted. "You do. At least you should." He looked off to think before coming back. "*My* question is, what am I to you?"

"Pete," I said dismissively.

"What?" He tossed his hand out. "I think, at this point, we can exchange actual words, right?"

"Pete, you know what you mean to me."

"I really don't," he said evenly.

"Okay, you're someone," I started to say, but the words were unwilling to come out. "You're," I continued unconvincingly, "someone important to me." To avoid his face expecting answers, I looked down in front of me and observed the tiny grains of sand, noticing they weren't all the same color. Sensing his dissatisfaction, I said quietly, "I'm sorry, Pete. I can't articulate myself like you."

We then lay there facing each other on our sides. I felt the sand mold to the shape of my body and the waves approaching with each passing moment as we rested in each other's regard. Gently, I reached out to pull his glasses off to see his eyes match the golden bluffs behind him. He then placed his hand on mine, and in soft resignation, he said, "You don't have to articulate yourself." He nodded as if agreeing to something and weaved his fingers through mine. "It's fine."

Pete

Sprawled out on the sand with her, it felt like there was no better time to talk. Where to start though. Everything from our last show to what almost happened between us to my breakup to her mom certainly gave us an assortment of uncomfortable topics to dive into. However, I didn't want to talk about Ed—I wasn't quite ready for that talk— just as I imagined she didn't want to talk about food poisoning. I figured I'd start with the most painful and was surprised by her breezy acceptance that she may not see her parents for a while, which then sprouted more questions I knew not to ask just yet. When she apologized for her inarticulate nature, I couldn't be mad at her because I knew it wasn't her fault. But there was so much I wanted to say, and despite everything, so much I still wanted to do with her. And I know...I know it wasn't the right moment, but I *did* want to kiss her right there and feel her lips that were so close to mine. As her soft, sad eyes looked at me, I reached for her hand. Feeling her skin again, its smooth texture contrasting the rough sand caught in between our fingers, it was certainly an improvement from our barbecue moment at the bar...but still, we *were* on the beach at sunset, which was a little too cheesy love song for my taste. Maybe, in the end, that's just what we were, an old-fashioned love song...but with a post-apocalyptic, bisexual twist.

Carla

I didn't want to leave the beach and could have stayed until nightfall. I wanted to watch the stars come out with him by my side. With his hand still on mine, he caressed it with soft strokes as we looked up at the sky. I gave him his glasses back, and together we waited until we saw one star come out and then a second; both of them winking at us through the sorbet-hued sky. I could feel him smiling with me because these were our stars. One blinked softer than the other, and they both appeared aware of each other, aware of us.

Officially late, we arrived at the bar with my hair matted with sand and his glasses crooked. Looking like we had just returned from actually having sex on the beach or something, the bar manager didn't seem to completely buy that we got stuck in California traffic. Since we didn't have time to do a full set-up, he agreed to an acoustic set. On stage, we sat side-by-side on wooden stools, and together we sang folk covers, along with stripped-down versions of our own songs. I let him sing to me and read into every lyric of the cover songs he chose because I knew I was supposed to. *We don't have to talk at all…*

After the show, Pete suggested we celebrate our last night of tour by going out to dinner, which felt like he was testing me. I couldn't eat a thing since I told him I still felt sick. But to assuage what I read as an accusation, I forced down a lemon sorbet while he had veggie tacos that we ate on the boardwalk.

In the van that night, we lay in silence. I could feel him thinking as his chest rose and fell in resonance with his long, even breaths. I couldn't get comfortable and kept changing sides to sleep on. On my back, there was too much space above me; on my side away from him felt distant with our questions practically throbbing against my back; and on my side toward him felt evasive yet the most comfortable.

Sensing my restlessness, he stretched his arm out to invite me in. I accepted the offer and settled into the nook between his chest and under his arm. Feeling the remedy of our embrace, we melted into each other's arms like a lazy afternoon. With my leg draped over him and his legs warming my feet up, I took in deep breaths of him as he combed his fingers through my hair, catching a knot here and there. I wanted to give him a kiss goodnight but knew I wouldn't have wanted to stop there. I wanted to kiss his neck…kiss his heart beating under my cheek… I wanted to kiss his lips…and then continue to kiss him. *Everywhere.*

The next morning, I woke up to the suggestion of daylight peering through the curtains of the van. Tinted in early morning shades of pale pink, it reminded me of the taffeta lining of my childhood jewelry box, the one with the ballerina spinning in front of the diamond-shaped mirror. Feeling him awake, I looked up in his direction and asked, "Did you get any sleep?"

"Some."

"Okay." I didn't know what more to say as I lay still tangled in his arms.

"Car," he said, where I could feel his chin angle down toward me. "What do you want to do?"

When I didn't immediately respond, he continued, "I mean, you said yesterday you couldn't go back home." He took a deep breath. "So, where exactly am I taking you?"

He gave me time to think since going back home didn't make sense anymore. Silently, I reviewed my options. He could have dropped me off in Illinois to stay with Alex. Or he could have left me anywhere along the route. Could I see myself starting over in, say, New Mexico? Or what about Missouri? I enjoyed our time in Joplin and imagined myself in a cute apartment downtown and working at a café. My options from San Diego to New York felt exciting with the promise of a new beginning, but it also felt sad because what about Pete? Was this how we would say goodbye to each other? Would it be "The Last Goodbye" where my understanding of the song would be the correct one? It all felt so final as I fought back tears, envisioning him leaving me somewhere on the side of the road with my guitar. I didn't know what to tell him, so instead, I looked up and said, "Pete?"

"Yeah?"

"Can we go to Hollywood?"

Pete

I didn't get much sleep that night in the van, with the issues seeming to mount by the mile. Let's see…there was us and what we were going to do; there was her family and where she was going to go; the band and its future; her inability to communicate and my impatience; my secret and then, of course, hers...which was her eating. As I held her that night in the van, she felt tired and frail, like she would disintegrate into dust, this sad soul in my arms. Part of me wanted to run away from it all and teach English in Paris. I knew I could stay with Guy and just live openly without having to explain myself. We'd probably end up competing for the same dudes, though.

When she told me she wanted to go to Hollywood, I thought she was kidding since it wasn't on our route. But of course, she wasn't. As we headed two hours north out of our way, we stopped in San Juan Capistrano for gas. After filling up, I went to pay as she cleaned the windshield with the squeegee that made it dirtier, as black water ran down the glass like the font on a classic horror movie poster. As I was about to pull open the door of the mini-mart, I heard the French language. Hearing my second mother tongue spoken, I realized I was a little homesick and found myself propelled toward the Gallic sounds. Their accents, I could hear, were composed with even inflections hinting at a refined Parisian upbringing.

In front of a Volkswagen Beetle the color of grenadine were two girls having trouble with the convertible top. Looking at each other in wonder, one girl in the passenger's seat pressed buttons while the other leaned over the carriage top that appeared stuck. She looked at her friend, mystified, who kept pressing the buttons as the winding sounds of the mechanics implied internal movement.

"*Avez-vous besoin d'aide?*" I offered her help.

Hearing French, they screeched in excitement, hinting they too hadn't run into our kind on these open American roads. They looked at each other in desperate amazement and simultaneously asked, "*T'es français?*"

Oui, I confirmed I was French and then asked what brought them to California. They were on *Toussaint*, autumn break, from their ritzy Parisian business school and had ventured on a road trip from San Diego to San Francisco. I then asked if I could look at the car, recalling the time I borrowed my cousin Amy's Beetle and the roof got stuck. Remembering the windows had a reset function, I got into the driver's seat, and it all came back. I pressed the power window buttons for a few seconds and then restarted the car. I manipulated the maneuver a few times, trying it in different ways until it finally worked. The girls then asked me what I did in case it happened again, and I told them I honestly didn't know.

"Okay," I said, turning to the girl sitting next to me. I noticed her waist-length thick brown hair parted down the middle like a '70s folk singer and her eyes the color of mink looking at me. She wore a denim miniskirt, and with her legs crossed in my direction, she rubbed one up and down the other. "*Bah,*" I mumbled, unsure what to say. "*Bonne route?*" I raised an eyebrow as I reached for the door handle.

"*Mais, attends.*" She stopped me as she pushed her hair off her shoulder.

"*Oui?*" I said, unintentionally looking at her long legs before meeting her eyes again.

Along with having trouble with the roof, she explained, they were also having trouble getting to the beach because they couldn't understand the gas station attendant who spoke too fast. Maybe I'd have better luck, she said, and asked me if I spoke English. I did, I told her. And for some reason, her face lit up when

I explained my half-American origins. I then told her I was in a band, which met the same results.

After getting their directions to the beach, I was about to head back to the van when they told me they wished there was something they could do to thank me. I told them it was nothing, but the girl with the long hair gave off something more than wanting to offer me a few smokes for my time. She repeated she would *love* to thank me somehow and then invited the band to go to the beach with them. The band, I thought with a laugh. I was pretty sure she assumed our van contained other guys like me or at least one for her friend. Certain these girls didn't want to go to the beach with Carla, and *knowing* Carla would not want to go to the beach with two cute French girls, which would have been the equivalent of pressing the nuclear button on us, I politely declined the offer.

"*Dommage,*" she said while holding her gaze.

"Okay…"

Resting in her suggestive stare, I agreed it *was* too bad and told her maybe another time. We looked at each other a little longer than deemed neighborly until I had to break away thinking, I can't fucking do this right now.

Carla

I got jealous, as in completely out of my mind jealous. It was something I had never experienced before, and it freaked me out. Seeing him talk to the girls, I suddenly felt ugly, uninteresting, and stupid while my stomach burned in rage. But how could I be mad? Girls were always going to like Pete, and I didn't think I was strong enough for the competition ahead of me.

As I watched him, he seemed relaxed as he flirted back with his dimples practically winking from across the parking lot. There was a fluidity to his movements I had never seen with Allison, or with me, for that matter. With us, his shoulders were tight and on guard, ready to protect himself from whatever emotional landmine was about to go off. Never did I think I'd share something in common with Allison, I thought as I sneered at the irony. With my arms hanging over the steering wheel, I observed the girls knowing I could never offer Pete that airiness. I couldn't giggle like that or unnecessarily brush a swath of hair over my shoulder. After years of him being a loyal boyfriend, Pete *was* single now, and I wondered where that left me. If the band stayed together, would I become the eye-rolling bandmate or the jealous girlfriend? I thought about it as I watched him approach the van. This beautiful boy in my life who I knew would only end up hurting me.

"Just some girls who needed help," he said dismissively as he pulled himself up into the van.

"I see." I pretended not to have witnessed the entire exchange.

We drove north on the 5, a highway, I thought in amazement, that cut up the entire west coast and ended in Canada. As we got closer, passing exit signs for Disneyland, I thought about what was most important to me. Without giving it a second thought, I knew my answer was the band. I had never felt more at peace with who I was than when crafting songs with him. Everything about the process made me feel good about myself: the quietude of writing lyrics in my notebook, the anticipation of sharing my words with him, and the experimentation of molding our words into songs we were proud of. It was what made me feel worthy.

In the distance, tall glass buildings pierced out of the landscape like a cluster of smoky quartz. Haloed by a greyish, black fog, I blinked in recognition of the famous LA smog I had always heard about and was now shamefully contributing to with our old van. As we got closer to the city, the choices of highways available to us became overwhelming. In choreography with each other, the highway ramps packed with cars swept down, overpasses wove above our heads, and highways fused into one another. Without the map in front of me or having any reference, the highway numbers held no significance ... 110, 405, 10, 101...The Hollywood Freeway? We looked at each other and nodded that that sounded good. With Pete signaling his hand out the window for drivers below us to make way, we made it across five lanes and merged onto the 101.

Even though it was my first time in Los Angeles, a lifetime of consuming pop culture had prepared me for it as I recognized the highway signs: Silver Lake, Melrose, Santa Monica Boulevard, Ventura; it all rang familiar. I felt Pete also absorbing the scenery as he stared out the window at the sagging palm trees, hazy skies, and rundown apartment buildings.

Where do we go from here? I wondered to myself as we sat in weekday morning traffic. I didn't know what to do other than try to find myself...with or without the band. I had spent my entire life hiding behind fear that I had no idea who I was without it. I glanced at him, wondering what he planned to do. Go back to New York and get another girlfriend? Or stay with me wherever I ended up? With or without each other, though, I knew we had left an impact on each other and wondered if, in the end, we would survive it.

Pete

What exactly were we doing? As she drove, our deep thoughts weighed the van down like the past, as the air quality diminished into what I imagined the air filtration system in the corridors of hell. I looked out the window as a new American city greeted us; something my New York sensibilities would always find quaint, like a provincial rendering of the real thing. No wonder everyone hates New Yorkers. Being the last moments of our trip, I struck myself with the realization that we had ended up with less than we started with: she didn't have her family to go back to; I didn't have a girlfriend anymore, and I had lost my mind somewhere outside of Sapulpa, Oklahoma.

We got off at the Sunset Boulevard exit exchanging "When in Rome" looks. She then pulled the van into the parking lot of one of the many strip malls we had passed in our short time off the highway. Stretching my arms over my head, I watched the Hollywood neighborhood unfold like a Bukowski novel: there was a man sleeping in front of a closed-down storefront, and next to him, a shopping cart heartbreakingly packed with what I could only imagine was his life possessions. A dirty donut shop with stained windows discharged fryer exhaust that I couldn't decide smelled good or totally disgusting. A woman in a wheelchair walked forward, her bare feet touching the dirty pavement while drinking a Venti Frappuccino, reminding me I had work in a few days. My eyes flicked over in Carla's direction for a reaction, but it seemed like nothing registered as she stared blankly in front of her.

"Pete."

"Yeah?"

She indulged in another long pause as her eyes looked out, appearing to search for words. Finally, she let out a small exhale and said, "I still really want to do this," she then motioned her head back toward the gear.

"Okay."

"I mean, do *you* still want to do the band?" She looked at me seemingly for the first time that day; her eyes glazed over with worry from the decisions we needed to make. *Would* I be driving back to the East Coast alone as she started a new life somewhere? Or would we continue doing what we loved most while still misunderstanding each other...ourselves?

"I do." I looked at her with an expression that told her to forget about what I had said in New Mexico. "But I do think there are things we need to discuss first." I took a deep breath. "Stipulations, if you will."

"Stipulations?" She looked offended.

"Well, really, just one."

"Okay." She now looked suspicious.

"Food, Carla," I asserted while being careful with my words because it was probably the hardest request I had ever made of someone, "you're going to start eating it."

After the words came out, I thought she'd protest or even storm out of the van, which I really hoped she wouldn't do because the man with the shopping cart had woken up and was now taking a shit. But she didn't. Instead, she squeezed her eyes shut, looking like she was trying to seal in her tears.

"It's okay," I whispered as I placed my hand on hers. "We all have our shit, believe me."

She looked at me like she didn't believe me because she was still accusing me of having everything figured out. I wanted to tell her about me and about some of *my* heartbreaking experiences, but I just wasn't ready.

"Look," I continued to keep the focus on her. "You don't need to minimize yourself with me. In fact, please be the exact opposite. I want to hear you. I *want* to see you. I want you to tell me to fuck off when I'm being an impatient prick." This elicited her to laugh as she hooked her pinky around mine as she stared at the dashboard in front of her. "Let me be your family now." My pinky tugged hers, imploring her to look at me. "Please."

Squeezing my hand, she finally looked at me but with a shameful expression like I had exposed her big secret. As she let soft tears trickle down her cheeks, I said, "It's okay. We're going to fix this, okay?"

Appearing to process my words, her eyes scanned left and right as if she was talking herself into trusting me. Then with a slight nod, she looked up, the whites of her eyes a dusty pink, and said, "Okay, Pete." And together, we sat in the stuffy van holding hands in silence until she repeated, "I just really want to do this."

"Okay." I pushed out a smile, and using the last bit of energy the road had sucked out of me, I said, "So let's do this then."

"And everything is out in the open now, right?" she said with hopeful eyes. "I mean, we'll figure things out between us, the band, and whatever, but no more secrets?"

With my gaze fixed on her, I squeezed her hand and said, "No more secrets."

fin.

Mixtape Vibes

Scan below to check out what Carla and Pete were majorly rocking out to on the road!

Lyrics deliciously meant to be read into!

Stay in touch!

To stay updated on future book launches, advanced reader copy programs, more playlists, gossip, French touches, and all sorts of other fun goodies, join Lisa Czarina Michaud's mailing list!

<u>www.lisamichaudauthor.com</u>

It'll be fun.

I also hang around these places @lisacmichaud

Acknowledgments

I'd like to first thank my husband Aurélien, for this book would not have existed without you. I am grateful for your reading and rereading and rereading of this story, for our intense conversations about fictional characters, and for being you. And for Georges and his bocconcini cheeks.

My mother Andrea, for being the greatest mother a weird girl could ask for. And for my late father George for introducing me to your world of progressive rock, jazz and for our late-night talks on the Upper West Side; you fiddling with your practice pad while we talked ad nauseam about the gravity of music from Miles to Metallica.

Terri and the late Dean Chaplin for being my Los Angeles parents, just as nutty as my real parents. Thank you for the late-night phone calls, the visits, and for being there as I wandered aimlessly into adulthood. I'll see you both in the second book.

My stepmother Rosalinde for introducing me to Saturday morning Motown, recovery, and for your radiance. I couldn't imagine my dad spending his last years with anyone else.

Grandma, Grandpa, and Aunt Marta, and the rest of the Balducci family for food, family, and tradition to balance out the twitchy rock n' roll side of my brain.

My two grandmothers Nina Balducci and Stella Aguilar-Levitt. A girl couldn't have asked for two tougher and trailblazing grandmothers than you. I really am made up of both of you and think of you every day. Please don't fight up there.

Merci à mes beaux-parents Pierre et Brigitte pour votre aide énorme avec notre petit bonhomme. Sans vous je n'aurais pas pu terminer ce projet. Merci mille fois ! Je vous aime.

My musical genius brothers Andy and Joe for just *getting* how music works.

Brett Sills for being such a good friend to me these past decades (yep, decades), and for reading my work all these years.

It took a village to create Carla and Alex, and that village was my girls. From the 100 Corridor to the Cooler to Harper Avenue to 221 South 3rd Street.... much lurve to Katie Banks, Michelle Effron, Marygrace Brennan, Yoko Kikuchi, Robin Goldberg, Claire Beaudreault, Christine Latham, and Kristina Effron.

To the coolest guys I know who keep me sharp with insightful discussions on music and pop culture and who helped me on this project: Andrew Mega, Dimitri Vial, Shachar Hershkovitz, and Jeff McMillan. And to Ryan Spahn and Paul Foster Johnson.

My third-grade teacher and first mentor Miss Michaud. It still amazes me.

Derek Doepker for the Tuesday night mentor calls and for always being so available. The indie publishing world needs more of you!

My editor Monica Baker for asking the hard questions and for the care you put into this story.

Merci Gabriel Omnes pour ta vision et ta gentillesse. Les photos sont magnifiques.

My very first reader Marie "Duchess" Labbe and for that very first comment I received from you in my chambre de bonne. It was at that moment that I suspected I may have a story to tell. Thank you for your support all these years.

Blog readers who became friends: Cara, Mary-Kay, Daisy, Sara-Louise, Jo, Kristen, Lindsey, Jenna, Dana, Nick, Damon, Mica, and the rest of the readers who had the patience and beauty of Saint Thérèse de Lisieux, reading me daily as I strengthened my writing muscles and who have been cheering me on the whole way.

FIAF New York, The Evergreen State College and the 2nd floor at 72 Spring Street where this whole "French thing" started.

Jeremy and Sandra of La Poterne in Moret-sur-Loing, and the rest of the team, Ange, Luca and Flo for keeping me caffeinated with early morning cafés allongés while writing at *"ma table fétiche."*

The East Williston Library for summer editing and always having a table for me to sit at.

To the kindness of the many Alsatians who have answered my wide-eyed questions, whether in cafes in Strasbourg or along the wine route from Gertwiller to Ammerschwihr to Orschwihr. I hope I did right by you. Extra special thanks to Patrice Dupuis and Pascal Fluck. Villsmols merci!

Every band, musician, rock biographer who have poured their souls into their work for the benefit of us music nerds who listen to every note, read every juicy little morsel from the liner notes to the books. This is what makes up our DNA. Never stop creating. Never stop documenting.

About the Author

Born and raised in New York, Lisa Czarina Michaud comes from a family of food and music. When she wasn't slicing bread at her family's Italian market in Greenwich Village, she was spending part of her paycheck at downtown record shops.

In 2009, Lisa followed in the footsteps of her jazz singer grandmother Stella Levitt (née Aguilar) and moved to Paris, where she began writing about life in France.

Lisa currently resides in the French countryside with her husband, son, and cat Le Tigre who opposes to when Lisa wears leopard print.